KATHLEEN MCGURL lives near the sea in Bournemouth, UK, with her husband and elderly tabby cat. She has two sons who are now grown up and have left home. She began her writing career creating short stories, and sold dozens to women's magazines in the UK and Australia. Then she got side-tracked onto family history research – which led eventually to writing novels with genealogy themes. She has always been fascinated by the past, and the ways in which the past can influence the present, and enjoys exploring these links in her novels.

When not writing or working at her full-time job in IT, she likes to go out running. She also adores mountains and is never happier than when striding across the Lake District fells, following a route from a Wainwright guidebook.

You can find out more at her website: http://kathleenmcgurl.com/, or follow her on Twitter: @KathMcGurl.

Also by Kathleen McGurl

Readers Love *The Pearl Locket*

'I simply didn't want to leave this book down'

'A delicious delightful story'

'One of the best books I've ever read'

'A lovely story'

'Brilliant from start to finish'

'A real page turner, and a thoroughly enjoyable read'

The Pearl Locket

KATHLEEN MCGURL

ONE PLACE. MANY STORIES

HQ
An imprint of HarperCollins*Publishers* Ltd
1 London Bridge Street
London SE1 9GF

First published in Great Britain by
HQ, an imprint of HarperCollins*Publishers* Ltd 2020

Copyright © Kathleen McGurl

Kathleen McGurl asserts the moral right to be
identified as the author of this work.
A catalogue record for this book is
available from the British Library.

ISBN: 9780008389208

MIX
Paper from
responsible sources
FSC® C007454

This book is produced from independently certified FSC™ paper
to ensure responsible forest management.

For more information visit: www.harpercollins.co.uk/green

Printed and bound in Great Britain by
CPI Group (UK) Ltd, Croydon, CR0 4YY

Chapter One

July–August 2014

'So, this is it,' Ali said, gazing up at the house. 'It's smaller than I remember. But I was just a child when I was last here.' She had only vague memories of being here before—muddled images of an imposing, double-fronted art-deco-style house, with bay windows, a large garden and, best of all, the beach just a couple of minutes' walk away. It had been her spinster great-aunt's house, and the childless Betty had left it to Ali in her will.

'Smaller?' said her husband, Pete. 'It's huge! Well, compared with everywhere else we've ever lived.'

Ali nodded. She couldn't argue with that. But the size didn't matter, as she was going to put the house on the market immediately. They had no intention of living in it. 'I suppose we should have a look round inside, now that we're here.'

'Well, that *was* the point of the visit,' Pete said, smiling. He took Ali's hand and led her to the front door. She was grateful for the gesture of support. It was strange being here. Although the house now belonged to her, it didn't feel like it did. She'd never owned a house before; they'd always rented. She felt like an intruder. The front door was stiff—Betty had spent the last couple of years of her life in a nursing home, and apparently very few people had entered the house in that time. A pile of junk mail lay on the doormat. Ali gathered it up and placed it on a dusty sideboard in the hallway. She glanced around.

'What a state. I guess we'll have to clear everything out before we can sell it. What'll we do with all the furniture? I suppose we might want to keep a few pieces but not much.' She opened a drawer in the sideboard. It was full of pens, coins, elastic bands, buttons, old receipts and other odds and ends. 'And we'll have to sort all the contents out as well. Gran might want to keep a few things. It's going to be a huge job.'

Pete had peeked into a room on the left—the sitting room as far as Ali recalled—and was now crossing to the room on the right, the dining room. He turned back to Ali with shining eyes. 'Fantastic rooms, those two. Great proportions. They'd look amazing if they were done up. Come and see the kitchen.' He pulled her to the back of the house where they entered a large but very dated kitchen. Probably last fitted out some time back in the sixties, Ali thought, wrinkling her nose at the musty, unlived-in smell. 'Imagine it, Ali, with a run of units along that wall, an island there, an American-style fridge-freezer there, granite worktops and Shaker-style cupboard doors. This house could really be something special.'

It could; she could see that. Someone else with money and the time and energy for an awful lot of DIY would have a lot of fun with this house. She just wanted her hands on the money they'd get from selling it. With Pete's redundancy money fast running out and their landlord about to put up the rent, they could certainly do with it. She was already working full time, and as yet Pete had had no luck finding another job since Harrison's had laid him off.

'Let's go upstairs,' Pete said, again reaching for her hand. She followed him up. The stairs turned on a half landing, a grand newel post supporting the oak-panelled banisters. There was a cold draught as they turned the corner. Ali shivered. 'There's a crack in that window,' Pete said, nodding at the bowed and leaded window on the half landing.

Upstairs were four double bedrooms, a box room and a bathroom. As a child Ali had never been up here. She'd only ever paid a few duty visits to her great-aunt, with her father, so many years ago.

As they gazed out of the front bedroom window, from where you could just about get a glimpse of the sea, Pete turned to Ali. 'What if,' he said, with a glint in his eye, 'we didn't sell up? What if we cleared it out, then moved in?'

'Pete, it's in a horrible state! And we need the money from the sale. You know we do.'

'We could use the rest of my redundancy money to do it up. And if we didn't have to pay rent, we could easily live off your salary for a while. Think about it, Ali! If this place was modernised and redecorated, it'd be worth twice as much. Then we could sell it, if we still needed the money, and buy somewhere smaller. But with luck I'd get a job then, and we could just stay here.'

Ali opened and closed her mouth a few times. So many thoughts were racing around her head she didn't know which one to articulate first. 'But, Pete, the risk! What if the property market goes downhill and we can't sell it? What if we run out of money before we've finished doing it? What if you get offered a job but it's away from here and we need to move to another town?'

Pete smiled at her and shook his head. 'Don't just look at the negatives. There are loads of positives. The kids would love this house. Ryan could kick a football around in that garden. And look how close we are to the beach—Kelly would adore that! But at least you didn't say no. Does that mean you'll consider it?'

Ali sat down on the bed. It had a pink candlewick bedspread neatly placed across it. A puff of dust rose up around her and she flapped it away. 'The safe option is to sell. Some property developer would probably snap it up quickly, at the right price.

And then we could buy a smaller, cheaper house, perhaps a little further from the sea. We'd be rent- and mortgage free, and wouldn't have a big mess of a house to do up. And we'd have a big pot of money in the bank to add to what's left of your redundancy. Then you could concentrate on finding another job.'

'You're right.' Pete sat down beside her and put an arm around her shoulder. Ali was surprised he was giving in so quickly. Usually once he had an idea in his head he'd keep at it, trying endless different angles, until she either gave in and agreed or threatened to cut up his prize Munster rugby shirt signed by the entire team of 2008 if he mentioned it even one more time. 'That would indeed be the safe option. And the boring option. Ali, you only live once! This would be a fabulous house to live in, even if it's only for a year or two while we do it up. And we could make a fortune on it. If we sell it as it is, we'd barely have enough to buy another place big enough for the four of us. There'd certainly be none left over. But if we do it up and *then* sell it, we could buy a smaller place and have stacks of money spare for holidays or cars or a new handbag for you or whatever you'd want. Or' – he looked sideways at her – 'to help finance the kids through university.'

Ali smiled wryly. He always knew which buttons to press. The thought that they might not be able to help first Kelly and then Ryan with their university living expenses had always tormented her, especially since Pete had been made redundant. They'd never had enough to be able to put some by for that purpose, but she was determined that the kids would go to university if they wanted to. Even if she had to ask her parents, who'd retired to Spain, for financial help. Great-aunt Betty's will had meant they'd be financially secure, buying a house and living off Ali's salary until Pete found a job. But now, this plan meant that in a year or two there could be a lot more money on top. Did they dare take the risk? Another thought struck her. 'But, Pete, who'd do the work? This house would need so much doing and we'd be living in a building site for months.'

'I'd do it. Except for the electrics—I'd get a professional in for that. But I'm quite handy, you know. And we could go room by room, so some of it is liveable while we do up other rooms. I'd do some of it, the really disruptive stuff like the kitchen, before we move in. We've got to give a month's notice to the landlord anyway. And as probate's complete and this house is yours already, there's no reason I can't start tomorrow. If you agree, of course. It's your house . . .'

He was giving her that puppy-dog look, the one that always made her melt. Ali still had misgivings about the project but there was some sense in what he said, and maybe it would work out. 'I suppose—it's not as if the decision is irreversible—we could give it a go. We could always put it on the market later if things changed or the work was too hard for you.'

Pete flung his arms around her and kissed her. 'I love you, Mrs Bradshaw! The work won't be too hard for me; I'm a man not a mouse! Right then, I'll get started today. First things first, I'll need to hire a skip. Can you go through and mark all the things you want to keep? Wow, the kids are going to be so excited when they hear we're moving in!'

* * *

'I can't believe how unlucky we are with the weather today,' shouted Ali to Pete, over the noise of the lashing rain, raging wind and swearing removal men. She pushed a strand of wet hair out of her eyes and stood aside to let two men past her into the house, carrying sodden boxes. Of all the days to get a huge summer storm, why did it have to happen on their moving day? It was just a month after they'd visited the house for the first time.

Things had started well that morning. The van had arrived on time and everything was loaded into it within four hours. The keys had been handed back to the landlord. Both the family and the removal men had gone for lunch then met outside number nine at three p.m. to unload. But as soon as the van had pulled up outside it had begun to rain, and now it was coming down in sheets.

'Bugger!' The sound of smashing glass and swearing sent Ali running out to the back of the van. One of the removal men was standing amid a pile of broken wine bottles, with a wet bottom-less cardboard box in his hands.

'Er, sorry, love, the box got wet and the bottom just gave way. Saved one. Look.' The man held out one bottle, which had stayed in the box. Ali took it and sighed. There goes our wine cellar, she thought. At least there was one left intact to celebrate their move later this evening.

'Don't worry; it wasn't your fault. I'll find a broom and clear this lot up.' She went inside in search of the cleaning equipment. Maybe it was still on the van, but she thought she'd seen someone come in with an armful of mops and buckets earlier.

Inside, Pete was shifting boxes around in the newly fitted kitchen to make way for those yet to be unloaded from the van. 'Who'd have thought we had this much stuff?' he said. 'The rented house was half the size of this one, but I'm wondering where on earth we're going to put everything.'

'It'll be OK when we unpack. Seen the broom?'

'Downstairs loo.'

'What's it doing in there?'

'Removal bloke thought it was an under-stairs cupboard and just dumped it and a pile of other stuff in there. We'll sort it later, I thought.'

Ali shrugged and went to collect the broom. Passing the bottom of the stairs she came across seventeen-year-old Kelly, who was sitting on the third step, phone in hand, composing a text.

'Kelly, love, you'll be in the way there. Can't you go up and start organising your bedroom?'

'Yeah, Mum. Will do. Just updating Matt on progress. Is it cool if he comes round tomorrow? He said he'd help sort out my new room.'

Ali nodded. She liked her daughter's boyfriend. He was a pleasant, steady lad and a good influence on Kelly. 'Of course he can come. But you'll have to do some of the sorting out tonight, or you'll be sleeping among piles of boxes.'

Two men pushed past carrying a chest of drawers destined for thirteen-year-old Ryan's room. Ali grimaced as she saw how the rain had caused the veneer to lift off around the front edge. Well, it was only a cheap thing. They'd probably have to buy some better furniture more in keeping with the house. She turned back to Kelly. 'Come on. Out of the way. Go up and make a start.'

Kelly stood up and slipped her phone into her jeans pocket. 'OK. It's such a nightmare up there, though. I don't know where to start.'

'You and me both, love,' Ali said. It was exciting moving into a house they owned, but daunting as well. And she still had occasional misgivings about whether it had been the right thing to do. She shooed the thoughts out of her mind and went back outside into the rain with the broom.

* * *

Eventually, after hours of chaos, the removal men left, and the family were sitting in the living room on a jumble of sofas, chairs and boxes, eating take-away pizza. Ali had managed to find the box containing the wine glasses, and was opening the only unbroken bottle of wine.

'Can I have some, Mum?' Kelly asked.

'Why not? We're celebrating,' Ali said, smiling, as she poured out three glasses.

Ryan made a face. 'Ugh, wine's disgusting.'

'None for you, anyway,' said Pete. 'You stick to your lemonade.'

'Well, cheers, family,' said Ali, raising her glass. 'Here's to our new home. I hope we're going to be really happy here. It's twice the size of our old house, close to the beach, nearer Ryan's school, nearer the station for Kelly to get to college, and renovating it will give your dad something to do until he finds a new job. Everyone's a winner!'

'Cheers!' said Pete, clinking his glass against the others. 'Which room shall I decorate next?'

'Sitting room,' said Ali. 'So we have somewhere nice to bring guests into. I can't bear this worn out, stained carpet.'

'Mine,' said Ryan. 'I love how big my room is, but I hate that flowery wallpaper.'

'Well my wallpaper is already peeling off, around the sink in the corner,' said Kelly. 'Also I'll be moving out in another year and a half when I go to uni. So it makes sense to do mine first so I get a chance to enjoy it.'

Pete laughed. 'Looks like I'm going to be a busy boy, doesn't it? Well, you can all chip in and help me get it all done.'

Ali smiled. She wouldn't be chipping in to help. She was the breadwinner in the family at the moment, and the chief cook. It would be exciting as Pete worked his way through the house, renovating each room. He'd done a great job on the kitchen, though it wasn't completely finished yet. He'd also managed to get an electrician to do most of the rewiring before they moved in, but they needed a new central heating system and a new bathroom as well as all the general decorating. They'd done the figures and it looked as though the remains of the redundancy money would just about cover the work. It'd be tight, but if they budgeted carefully, and if Pete got a new job quickly after the work on the house was done, they'd manage.

After everyone had finished their pizzas and the boxes had been put out in the recycling bin, Kelly and Ryan went upstairs to sort out their rooms or—more likely, Ali thought—text their mates. She and Pete stayed in the living room, finishing the bottle of wine. Pete was on the sofa in the middle of the room, and Ali went to join him, curling up beside him. Outside the rain was still lashing down.

'Once we're sorted, we'll have to get that chimney swept so we can have a real fire in the winter,' Pete said.

'Mmm, that'd be nice,' Ali replied. She could picture the room, decorated, with new curtains and a blazing fire in the grate. It was a big room but well proportioned and she was sure she could make it look cosy. 'The kids seem happy with the move. I'm glad about that. You never quite know how they'll react.'

'What's not to like, here? It's not as though we've taken them away from their friends or schools or anything. And with the beach just down the end of the road, they'll have a fabulous time all summer. You'll be forever sweeping up sand and washing beach towels, I bet.'

Ali laughed. 'They can sweep up their own sand. Anyway, tomorrow shall we call on our new neighbours and introduce ourselves?'

'Good idea.' Pete kissed the top of her head. 'And when do you want to bring your gran round? It'll be quite a surprise for her that we've moved here, after you'd told her we were going to sell it.'

'Next weekend, I think, once we've got everything straightened out. I think she'll be delighted we've moved in and are bringing the house back to life again. It's been empty so long. This is where she grew up, of course.'

'She must have such happy memories of living here,' Pete said. 'Shame Margaret didn't get on with Betty in her later years.'

'I'm not sure she ever got on very well with her,' Ali replied.

Chapter Two

January 1944

There was no jam for tea. No cake, either. Just plain bread and margarine, and one rich tea biscuit each. Joan craved something sweet, anything sweet. She poured herself a cup of tea, dipped her teaspoon in the sugar bowl and tried to heap it up as much as possible without being noticed.

'Put that sugar back at once! No more than a quarter teaspoon per cup of tea. You know the family rules.' Father glared at her from the other end of the table. Joan shook the spoon so that most of the sugar fell back into the bowl, and meekly stirred in the remaining quarter. She tasted her tea and grimaced. Her sister Mags, who was sitting next to her, winked in sympathy, and whispered, 'You're sweet enough already.' They were sitting in the dining room, the second-best lace tablecloth spread over the table. War or no war, Father insisted on sticking to traditions and doing things 'properly', as he put it. They were firmly in the middle class, and he refused to let standards slip. Joan thought it all a complete waste of time and effort. Why couldn't they just eat their tea at the kitchen table? So much less fuss and work!

'Mother, when do you think rationing will end?' she asked.

Her mother smiled weakly and looked at Father. Just like Mother. She wouldn't dare answer a question like that herself. She would always defer to the head of the household. That was why Joan had directed the question to her mother—just to stir things up a bit.

'Not until this war's over. We all have to put up with it until then, so stop making such a fuss. You're not a baby any more.' Father gave her a stern look, and tapped the side of his cup with his teaspoon. Joan sighed as her mother immediately leapt into action, pouring her husband a second cup of tea. Why was she such a doormat? If Joan ever married she liked to think she and her husband would be on a much more equal footing than her parents were.

'Would you like more bread and margarine, Father?' asked her other sister Elizabeth, pushing the serving plate towards his end of the table.

'Thank you, Betty,' he said. Stuck-up Elizabeth, sucking up to Father as always, thought Joan. Another doormat. Well, it was now or never. She knew what the answer would be, but she had to ask anyway. Nothing ventured, nothing gained, as Mags would say.

'Father, may I ask a question?'

'Not if it's anything more about rationing, child.'

'No, it's something else. The thing is, there is a dance on at the Pavilion tomorrow evening, to celebrate the New Year, and I would rather like to go.'

Father put down his teacup and stared at her over the top of his horn-rimmed spectacles. Joan forced herself to keep her eyes on his. If she looked away, she'd lose her nerve.

'You? But you're far too young to be attending dances. You're only sixteen.'

'I had my birthday yesterday. I'm seventeen, Father.'

'Don't contradict me! You're too young. I forbid you to go.'

'But, Father, Elizabeth and Margaret went to their first dances when they were seventeen.'

'Are you arguing with me? I've said no, and that's that.'

'Mother, Mags is going and she said she'd look after me. Please,

11

may I?' What was the point? Her mother just shook her head gently and looked again at Father. Of course she would never go against anything he said.

'Mother agrees with me. You are not to go. And, Margaret, you will be home by ten o'clock. There's an end to it.' He picked up his newspaper and flicked it open, signifying that the topic was closed.

'Please may I leave the table?' Joan asked. Not waiting for an answer, she pushed her chair back and began gathering up plates and cups for washing up. Mags quickly joined her, and the two girls took the dirty crockery through to the kitchen.

'It's so unfair. *Why* can't I go? He's always stricter with me than he ever was with you or Betty.' Joan turned the tap on full blast, spraying water everywhere.

'Watch out, you're making me wet!' yelped Mags, as she jumped out of the way, brushing droplets off her skirt and blouse. Joan turned off the tap and clattered some plates into the sink. 'And now you're going to chip those plates. Let me do it. You're too cross.'

Joan stood aside and let Mags take her place. Mags was right; she was cross.

'Elizabeth's not going, is she?' she asked.

'No. She's going to the cinema to see some worthy French subtitled film. So I'm going to the dance on my own. But Mary and Noreen will be there, and some of the other girls from the WVS, so I won't be alone.'

Joan picked a plate from the draining board and began wiping it roughly with a tea towel. She liked Mary and Noreen. It would be such fun attending a proper, grown-up dance with them and Mags.

'I wish I could go. I feel like Cinderella, having to stay home while my sisters go out and enjoy themselves.'

Mags flicked soapsuds at her. 'Are you calling me an ugly sister, Joanie?'

'No.' Joan giggled. 'Betty's the ugly one.'

'Just think,' said Mags. 'If there was any way you could come to the dance, you might just meet your own Prince Charming.'

Both girls giggled uncontrollably at this, until Mother appeared at the kitchen door and told them to shush. They were annoying Father.

* * *

Washing up completed, they went upstairs to Joan's bedroom. It was only four-thirty but already dark, and time to close the blackout curtains. Although their coastal town hadn't suffered many air raids, unlike London, it had still had its fair share. Besides, Joan knew Father would be angry if they didn't draw the blackout blinds before putting on any lights. And she'd annoyed him enough already for one day.

'Mags,' she said, as they flopped down onto Joan's bed, 'do you think I could sneak out and go to the dance? Without the parents finding out?'

'How on earth could you do that? Father would expect you to be downstairs after supper, to listen to the news on the wireless.'

'What if he thought I was out but somewhere else? Maybe, I don't know, volunteering at the WVS? The soup kitchen's open tomorrow night isn't it? I could say I'm working there . . .'

'Ooh, Joanie, there's an idea! But what if he checked up on you?'

'He wouldn't check. Well, at most he might ask Noreen or Mary. Do you think they would cover for me?' Lie for me, Joan thought. It was probably a bit much to ask, but she knew the other girls sympathised with her and Mags over their draconian father.

'I'm sure they would. You know, I think that's a plan! I'll see Noreen this evening anyway—I'm doing a shift at the soup kitchen from six till eight. I'll get her to put your name down on the rota. You were about to start volunteering anyway, weren't you? He agreed to you doing it after Christmas, and we're already into the New Year. Won't he be suspicious though—first you ask if you can go to the dance, then when he says no, you announce you're starting at the WVS?'

'I'll mention the WVS tomorrow at teatime. He'll have forgotten I asked about the dance by then. You know he never takes any real interest in what you or I do. Not like Elizabeth. He'll be asking her about every detail of the film she's going to.' Joan clapped her hands with excitement. 'Now then, what shall I wear?'

'Well, you can't pretend you're going to the WVS if you're in a party frock,' Mags pointed out. 'Unless you put your coat on over it, and don't let him see what you've got on underneath. And no lipstick, until you've left the house. Tell you what, I'll ask Noreen if we can meet up at her house and you could get ready there.'

'Perfect! And shall I wear my blue frock? It's my newest.'

'You look lovely in that one. I'll help you do your hair at Noreen's,' said Mags.

Joan hugged her. 'You're definitely not an ugly sister. More like a Fairy Godmother, saying, "Joanie, you *shall* go to the ball!" '

'But I wouldn't recommend wearing glass slippers. It's a long walk home.'

Both girls dissolved into giggles at this, and continued laughing until Elizabeth came into the room.

'What's so funny? Father's really cross at you both again. He says if you can't stop your silly giggling, you'll have no supper. And it's rabbit stew with dumplings tonight. I made it.'

'All right, we'll stop laughing. No fun allowed in this house. We should have remembered,' said Mags. Joan stifled more giggles.

'What was so funny anyway?' asked Elizabeth again. 'You two always leave me out of things. It's not fair.'

'It's only silly little girl jokes,' Joan said. 'You're too grown-up to find them funny. Mags has almost grown out of them, too.'

'Hmm, well. I'll leave you to it, then. But don't annoy Father any further. That would be my grown-up advice.' Elizabeth turned on her heel and left the room.

'I hate rabbit stew,' said Mags.

Joan had to stuff a pillow in her mouth to stop herself guffawing aloud at that comment. She felt so happy. She was going to the dance, and no one could stop her!

* * *

Everything went according to plan. At teatime on the day of the dance, Joan announced Noreen had put her on the WVS soup kitchen rota, and that she would be starting that evening. Father just grunted in reply from behind his newspaper. Mother opened her mouth as if to make some comment, but after a glance at Father presumably thought better of it. Elizabeth appeared not to have heard, and chattered happily about the film she was going to see with her friend from work.

After supper, Mags and Joan washed up quickly then ran upstairs to get ready. They left the house separately, and reconvened at the corner of the street before going together to Noreen's, and then on to the Pavilion. Joan was buzzing with excitement. Every time they saw someone else heading the same way she couldn't help herself asking the older girls whether they knew the person, whether they were going to the dance as well.

It was a long cold walk along the seafront to the Pavilion and Joan giggled to herself as she found herself being thankful she hadn't worn glass slippers. At last they arrived and went quickly inside out of the biting wind. Joan gazed around in awe as she handed her coat to the cloakroom attendant. There may be a war on, but the Pavilion was glittering. The Christmas decorations were still up, as it was not yet Twelfth Night. Tinsel and baubles hung from the ceiling, and boughs of holly garlanded the hall above head height. Joan followed Mags to the bar and bought herself a lemonade. Young men in various uniforms stood in groups, trying to catch the eye of any girl who passed.

Mags and Noreen found their friend Mary, who immediately

began to regale them with a long, funny story about her last WVS shift. Joan listened at first, but soon found her attention wandering. The band had started up—a ten-piece swing band playing Glenn Miller's hits. She couldn't help but jiggle around to the music; she was most definitely 'in the mood'. There was a group of Canadian airmen standing across the room, their loud voices and raucous laughter at times almost drowning out the music. All of them were tall and handsome. One, especially, was very good-looking—with sandy hair, broad shoulders and a mischievous look in his eyes. Joan wondered whether she would manage to catch the eye of any of them. She supposed not. After all she was probably too young, and not pretty enough for them. But just imagine, if one of them asked her to dance, how exciting that would be!

As couples began to take to the dance floor, Joan noticed a shy-looking young man in civilian clothing watching her. He had dark, floppy hair and wore a pair of spectacles that had one broken arm, held together by tape. His jacket looked worn but clean. He raised his glass in her direction, but Joan gave him a small, non-committal smile. He was no Prince Charming, though he had a kind and gentle look about his eyes.

'Hey, beautiful, why are you standing on your own?'

Joan turned to find the sandy-haired Canadian airman beside her. This was more like it! She felt her tummy flip over as she smiled encouragingly at him. 'I was just waiting for the right person to come and sweep me off my feet,' she replied.

'And here I am,' the airman said, winking at her. He took her glass out of her hand and put it on a nearby table, then scooped her into his arms and whirled her onto the dance floor. Joan laughed and gasped, trying desperately to keep up with his lightning-fast dance steps. She couldn't believe this was happening—she was dancing with the best-looking man in the room!

'What's your name?' he asked her.

'Joan. What's yours?'

'Ah, Joan, Joan, you'll make me moan,' he said, grinning. 'I'm Freddie, and always at the ready.'

She giggled, and he pulled her in tighter. She saw Mags, Noreen and Mary dancing with a group of soldiers. Mags caught her eye and raised an eyebrow. She looked as though she disapproved of Joan's dance partner. Well, it wasn't up to her, was it? Joan was enjoying herself. Freddie was handsome and funny, and seemed to really like her. She was determined to make the most of her evening out.

The music ended, and Freddie let her go. 'I'll get you some refreshments,' he said. 'Don't go away.'

A moment later he was back with an iced drink for her. She sipped it gratefully. 'What is this?'

'G and T,' he said. 'Mostly T though, so don't worry. I'm not trying to get you drunk.'

Joan had never had an alcoholic drink before. It was quite pleasant, she thought. She gulped it down.

'Nice, eh? Here, have mine as well.' Freddie handed her his own glass.

'Let's dance some more,' Joan said. 'It's such fun!'

'I've a better idea,' he said. 'We'll dance again later but for now let's find somewhere quiet where we can sit and get to know each other better. Finish that drink quickly. I know where we can go.' He took her hand and pulled her towards the cloakrooms. Joan giggled as she knocked back her drink and followed him. He pushed open a door that led into a narrow corridor with other doors leading off.

'Where are we?' she asked.

'Backstage of the theatre. There's nothing playing tonight. Come on, in here.' He opened a door and pulled her into a dressing room, flicking on the light switch. 'That's better. We can properly get to know each other now. Come here, beautiful.'

Joan looked around her at the tatty room, with its smells of greasepaint and powder. There was a worn sofa against one wall,

17

opposite a dressing table. Freddie sat on the sofa and pulled her gently down beside him. He put an arm around her shoulders, and with his other hand, stroked her cheek.

'There, now. This is cosy, isn't it?' he said. He leaned towards her and kissed her gently.

She was being kissed! Her first time, and by such a handsome fellow! But what would Mags say? Was she being too forward? She tentatively kissed him back, and he must have taken this as encouragement because his kiss became more urgent, and his hand slid down from her face, over her neck and shoulder, and onto her breast. Suddenly he thrust her roughly back on the sofa and lay on top of her, kissing her harshly.

No, this wasn't what she wanted! She turned her head away and tried to push him off, but he was too heavy and strong.

'Stop it, Freddie, oh please stop it. Can't we go back and dance now?'

'Aw, sweetheart, I only want a kiss. That's not too much to ask, is it? My leave finishes tomorrow then I'm back to the war. You wouldn't deny a poor airman his last bit of fun, would you? Not when he's putting his life on the line for you?' He kissed her again, his mouth hard against hers, his tongue forcing its way into her mouth.

'Stop it! I shall scream!'

'Aw, no you won't. Just relax; enjoy it,' he said. 'I'm not going to hurt you.'

But he was hurting her. He was lying on top of her, his elbow digging into her ribs and his stubble scratching her cheeks as he continued to kiss her.

'Get off her, you thug! Get off! Off!' It was the boy with the broken glasses, his hair flopping over his eyes as he burst through the door, hauled Freddie off her, and landed a punch on his nose.

'Ow, you little shit. What did you do that for? Me and my girl were just getting comfortable.' Freddie clutched at his bleeding nose and spat on the floor.

'She didn't look very comfortable to me. Get out, and leave her alone.'

'Oh yeah? Who's going to make me?'

'I am. Now get out before I hit you again!' The boy squared up to Freddie. He was a little taller, but not as well built. Nevertheless, there must have been something in his eyes that made Freddie think the better of taking him on, for he spat again and took a step towards the door.

'She's nothing but a tease. Maybe you'll get more out of her, mate,' he said, as he slammed the door behind him.

'Are you all right?' said the boy, extending a hand to pull Joan up from the sofa.

She nodded, stood and straightened her clothing. 'Thank you. I shouldn't have come with him.'

'I saw him pull you out of the dance hall and thought you might be in trouble. Are you sure you're all right? Can I get your friend for you?'

Mags. How would she tell her how stupid she'd been? She wouldn't. Not unless she had to. If Mags hadn't seen her leave with Freddie maybe she could get away with not saying anything.

'She's my sister. But it's all right. You've been very kind. I'll freshen up now and then go back to the dance hall. I hope that airman has gone home.'

The boy nodded. 'I hope so, too. But I'll keep an eye out, just in case.' He held the door open for her and followed her back along the corridor towards the cloakrooms. Joan ducked into the ladies' room, and when she came out, he was no longer around. She felt a pang of guilt—he'd rescued her but she hadn't even asked him his name.

Chapter Three

August 2014

The day after moving day, a Saturday, dawned fresh and clear, cool for the time of year but sunny, with the promise of warmth later on once the sun was higher. Thank goodness for that, thought Ali. They could get on with sorting out the house, emptying boxes and filling cupboards. Though if it got too hot she knew she would just want to take a picnic rug and a book down to the beach for the afternoon. Well, maybe if they made good progress she could do that—start as she meant to go on, now that she lived so close to the sea. Might as well make the most of it while they lived here, however long that would be.

She was busy in the kitchen, unpacking endless boxes of kitchen utensils and deciding which of the many shiny new cupboards they should go in. Pete certainly hadn't skimped on cupboard space when refitting it. He'd done a great job. Now, he was trying to get the TV and hard-disk recorder to work and the kids were upstairs organising their respective rooms. The radio was on, playing cheerful Saturday morning music, the sun was shining in through the window ánd, all in all, life was pretty good.

Kelly came downstairs. 'Hi, Mum. My room's sorted, as much

as I can do right now. Did you know the wallpaper's peeling off, behind that god-awful blue sink in the corner? There's a bit of a smell of damp in there as well.'

'The house was tested for damp, Kelly, when we had the survey done. There's no damp in your room.' Pete had come into the kitchen and heard her comments. He pushed his way past piles of boxes and grabbed the kettle. 'I need more tea. Anyone else?'

'Yes, please,' Ali said.

'Even if it's not damp, will you do my room soon, please?' said Kelly. 'I want something really cool and classy. I had to put up with that Barbie wallpaper in the old house for far too long.'

'Ha, well you chose it,' laughed Ali.

'Yeah, when I was, like, six. I grew up, Mum, or hadn't you noticed?' Kelly gave her a playful thump on the arm. She was right, Ali thought, she had grown up. So quickly. At seventeen she was almost a woman. What had happened to their little girl?

'As soon as Matt gets here is it cool if we go out for a bit?'

'Yes, it's, er, cool. It'll do you good. Go down to the beach or something. Make the most of the day.' Ali gave her daughter a quick hug. She was glad they had a good relationship. Many of Kelly's friends seemed to barely ever speak to their parents.

The doorbell rang. Ali glanced at her watch. It was too early for Matt to arrive, surely? Kelly went to answer it.

'Hi, are your parents in?' Ali heard a male voice in the hallway. Not Matt. She brushed cardboard-dust off her T-shirt and went out to see who it was. Standing on the doorstep was a man in his forties, tanned, wearing a white T-shirt and a pair of loose denim shorts. 'Hello,' he said. 'Sorry to interrupt your unpacking. I'm Jason Bergmann, your new neighbour from number seven.' He held out his hand.

Ali shook it. 'Lovely to meet you, Jason. I'm Ali Bradshaw; this is my daughter, Kelly. Do come in. It's a mess but we can offer you a cup of tea or coffee.' She stood aside to let him pass.

'I was just calling to welcome you to the street. And if you're free this evening, come round about eight for a glass of wine in my garden? You'll be sick of unpacking by then, I'd say.'

He had a nice smile. Ali warmed to him instantly. 'Thanks, that would be lovely.'

'What would be lovely?' said Pete, coming out of the kitchen with his mug of tea. 'Oh, hello.' He shook Jason's hand.

'Jason Bergmann. From next door. Bottle of wine round at mine this evening? To celebrate your move.'

'Sounds good to me,' Pete said. 'I'm Pete. We also have a son, Ryan, around somewhere. He's thirteen.'

'Kelly and Ryan are most welcome, too. I'll leave you to your unpacking, and see you later, then.'

'Seems like a nice chap,' Pete said, after Ali had closed the door. 'It'll be good to get to know a neighbour so quickly.'

* * *

Kelly went back upstairs. The new neighbour seemed nice, but she wasn't sure she wanted to go round to his drinks party this evening. Sounded a bit dull. She was barely in her bedroom when the doorbell rang again. This time it must be Matt! She raced down the stairs, almost tripping on a loose corner of carpet on the half landing, and got to the door just as her mother was opening it. It was Matt. She launched herself into his arms before he was even over the threshold.

'Steady on! What a welcome. Hi, Ali. Settling in OK?'

'Hi, Matt. Yes, thanks. Lots of unpacking to do, but we'll get there. Tea?'

'No, Mum. We'll be going out in a few minutes,' Kelly said.

'Er, no thanks then, Ali. Kells, can I at least have a tour before we go out? I can't wait to see the house. It's huge!'

'OK, a quick one, though. I'm desperate to get down to the beach.' Kelly took him by the hand and dragged him on a whistle-stop tour of the downstairs. 'Living room. Dining room, though I think it's going to be more of a library cum playroom cum office, whatever. Kitchen. Dad's already done that up. Big enough to have a table and eat in. There's a coal shed out there. Mum wants it converted to a utility room. Downstairs loo under the stairs.'

She pulled him upstairs. 'Ryan's room, Mum and Dad's room. Bathroom, spare room. My room.'

'It's big!' Matt stepped inside and spun around.

'Ryan's is bigger.'

'This is way nicer than your old room. I like it!'

'What? Seriously? With this hideous wallpaper?'

'Better than Barbie. And look at the size, the space and hey, the view!' He crossed to the window and gazed out at the garden.

'A view of the coal-shed roof.'

'And that oak tree at the end of the garden. Love it!'

Kelly grinned. His enthusiasm was infectious. She put her arms around him from behind and nuzzled her face into his back. 'Dad's going to decorate it soon. I'm going to have cream walls and aubergine curtains, with some hot-pink accessories. It'll be gorgeous.'

'Like its inhabitant, then.' He twisted around to face her, and put his arms around her waist.

'Charmer.' She reached up and kissed him, full on the mouth.

'Hey, slow down. Your mum and dad are in the house! Thought you wanted to go to the beach?'

'I do. Let me grab my bikini and stuff and we'll go.' She let go of him and started rummaging in the drawers she'd so recently filled, looking for her beach gear.

'You've got a sink in your room.'

'You're *so* observant.'

'Useful.'

'Horrible. I want Dad to take it out. Look at the peeling wall-paper around it!' Kelly grabbed a loose corner of paper above the skirting board and pulled. The paper came away in a huge long strip to halfway up the wall.

Matt gasped. 'God, you'll get in trouble for that!'

'No, I won't. It's all got to come off soon anyway.' She tore another strip upwards, screwed up the paper and stuffed it in her bin.

'Hey, there's something written on the wall, here.' Matt moved closer to get a better look. 'A love heart—how sweet! What's it say? Joanne, no wait, *Joan loves Jack*. Aw! Joan and Jack. Wonder who they were? Give us a pencil, Kells. I'll add our names—Kelly 4 Matt, hey? What do you think, babe?'

Kelly felt a shiver go down her spine. Joan, Jack. Who were they, indeed? One of them presumably lived in this bedroom before her, and had written this on the wall. Mum had said that her great-aunt Betty had lived here alone for fifty years, so it had to be before then, unless it was a visitor. But a visitor wouldn't write on the wall. It had to be someone who'd lived here. Joan, whoever she was, was probably dead by now. A picture flashed into her mind of a young girl, her own age but from a time way back, with blonde hair caught at the side in a Kirby grip. That was the problem with old houses. They were full of the ghosts of past occupants.

'Kelly? Are you OK?' Matt's voice broke into her thoughts.

'Fine. Let's get out of here. I need some fresh air.' She grabbed her beach bag and ran down the stairs.

'You've got the window wide open. How much air do you need?' Matt called after her.

But Kelly felt she just needed to escape from the house for a while. 'See you, Mum. We'll be back for tea.' She dragged Matt after her.

'Er, bye, Ali. See you later.' He waved as Kelly dragged him out of the front door, down the garden path.

She banged the garden gate closed behind them and took a deep breath. Better already.

'What's the matter, Kells? You seem really wound up.'

'I am. *Joan loves Jack*. That really creeped me out, you know.'

24

'Why? It's only a couple of names.'

Kelly shook her head and began walking down the road towards the clifftop and beach. 'I don't know, Matt. I just thought, what if they were, like, our age when they wrote that, and maybe that was like fifty or sixty or seventy years ago, before Mum's great-aunt had the house. They'd be ancient now. Or dead. And it's just weird to think of kids like us, being in love and everything, and then getting old and dying.'

'Babe, it happens to us all, you know? Everyone gets old and dies sometime. Unless they die young.'

'Dying young would be better than fading away.'

'Bet you won't say that when you're fifty.' Matt playfully punched her arm.

'Fifty's already old.'

'You should try to find out who that Joan and Jack were,' Matt said. 'Like, if one of them lived in the house, maybe your great-gran would know. Maybe one of them was some relative of yours. You might not feel so creeped out about them if you knew who they were. My mum's into the whole genealogy thing, you know. She spends hours online, trying to fill in gaps in the family tree. It's kind of interesting, in a way.'

Kelly considered this. Maybe it would be a good idea to do a bit of research and find out who they were. Joan was such an old-fashioned name. It had to be someone from long ago. But who?

* * *

A week later, Ali and Pete had unpacked everything and flattened the hundreds of boxes, which were now stacked in the garage waiting for the removal company to come and collect them. They'd arranged the furniture and hung curtains, and the house looked respectable enough to entertain visitors. It was beginning to feel like home, though Ali could still not believe they actually owned the house outright, after their years of renting. They'd met several neighbours as well as spending a pleasant evening with Jason from next door, the day after moving in. He seemed to be a thoroughly pleasant chap. In some ways he reminded Ali a little of her father.

She had invited her grandmother to tea that afternoon and was busy making preparations. Kelly was sitting at the kitchen table drinking a cup of tea and texting.

'Kelly, will you help me make a cake for your great-gran?' Ali asked. 'You know what a sweet tooth she has. Dad's collecting her this afternoon. She'd love a home-made cake.'

'Aw, Mum. I hate baking. I've got loads of homework to do as well. We've started a module in history about life for ordinary people during the Second World War. I've got a stack of reading to do for it.'

'Oh. All right then, I'll do it. You should go and get on with your homework now. Get it out of the way before she comes, so you can spend some time with her. Remember it's going to be a lovely big surprise for her, that we're in this house where she grew up.'

Kelly looked up from her phone and frowned. 'I don't get why you didn't tell her we were moving.'

Ali began collecting together the ingredients for a Victoria sponge cake. 'Well, I did tell her we were moving house, just didn't say we were moving here. She knows we inherited it from Betty, but I'd let on that we were planning to sell it. I thought it'd be a lovely surprise for her to find that we've actually moved in, and are bringing the house back to life. I can't wait to see her face when she arrives.'

'Hmm, well. I'll go and do my homework now, then,' said Kelly. She picked up her phone and tea mug, scraped back her chair and left the room.

At ten to three Pete was dispatched to collect Margaret Eliot from her nursing home. Gran was 89, and as Ali's parents lived in Spain it had fallen to Ali to make arrangements for her when she'd become unable to cope in her own home any longer. She'd also had to sort out a place for Great-aunt Betty, who'd spent the last couple of years of her life in a different nursing home. Ali had always felt it was sad that the two sisters didn't get on, but Gran had never said much about why that was. Anyway, it was too late now.

Ali bustled round, putting plates, cups and saucers ready on a tray, filling the kettle, and sprinkling icing sugar over the top of the Victoria sponge. It had come out well. She wasn't much of a baker herself, but it was worth making the effort for Gran, who would certainly appreciate it.

She went into the living room, the window of which looked out onto the street, to await Gran's arrival. A couple of minutes later, Pete's car pulled into the driveway. Ali rushed out to the front door, calling up the stairs to Kelly and Ryan as she went.

Outside, Pete was wrestling with Gran's Zimmer frame, trying to pull it out of the boot, while Gran remained sitting in the passenger seat. He was swearing quietly. 'Darn thing went in all right. Why won't it come out?'

Ali went round to open Margaret's door.

'Gran! I've been so looking forward to bringing you here. What do you think of our new house? Of course, you know it well. I'll hardly need to give you a guided tour!'

Margaret's face was stony. 'Hello, Alison. I think you've got a bit of explaining to do. Why didn't you tell me you were moving into this house?'

'I thought it would be a lovely surprise for you,' Ali said. Oh no. Don't say Gran was upset by it. Had she got it all wrong?

'Well it's certainly a surprise, but not a lovely one. I'm here now. May as well come inside, I suppose. Never thought I would have to set foot inside this cursed place again.'

Pete, standing by with the walking frame, raised his eyebrows at Ali. She gave a small shrug in response. 'Come on then, Gran. Let me help you out of the car.'

Inside, Kelly and Ryan came running down the stairs. Each of them hugged Margaret tightly, and Ali was relieved to see her grandmother smile at them. Whatever had put her in a bad mood, she still seemed delighted to see the children.

Kelly took the old lady's arm and led her into the sitting room. Gran sat down in an armchair and looked about the room. 'It's strange. This room feels so familiar but so different. It must be ten years or more since I was here last. Yes, it was back in 2002, after my poor Roy died. Betty came to his funeral and then a week later invited me for tea. Just a duty invitation, it was. She didn't really want to see me, but I suppose she thought she ought to. And I didn't really want to come, but felt I should. Alison, I thought you were going to sell this house?'

'We were, but we thought if we modernised it first it'd be worth more. And it seemed sensible to live in it while we did the work, rather than pay rent,' Pete said.

Margaret nodded thoughtfully. Ali was glad at least that their reasoning seemed to make sense to her.

'Great-gran, which room did you have when you lived here?' Kelly asked.

'Well now, it was the one on the left, next to the bathroom,' Margaret replied.

'That's mine, now,' Ryan said, triumphantly. 'I got the big one.'

'I'm in the smaller one at the back, over the kitchen,' Kelly said. 'Whose was that? Was it Betty's?'

'No,' Gran said sharply. 'It wasn't Betty's. She had the one at the front of the house. The back one was . . . just a storage room.'

'Who was . . .' began Kelly, at the same time that Ali said, 'Tea, Gran? I've been baking. I know how much you like a home-made cake, and though I say it myself, I think I've done well.' She brought in the tray with the Victoria sponge, and smiled as Gran's eyes lit up.

'Alison, that looks magnificent. I shall have to visit more often. Though I can't help but wish you'd sold this house as you said you were going to. You could have bought a lovely modern one with all the money. This house looks so dated. I don't believe Betty did a thing to it for years.'

'It is certainly in need of some TLC,' Ali replied, pouring a cup of tea. 'But that'll be half the fun. We can really make it our own. We've already done the kitchen. I'll show you when you've finished your tea. And with Pete off work, he has plenty of time to do it.'

'They're going to work my fingers to the bone, Mrs E,' Pete said, rolling his eyes. 'They've already told me I need to do the sitting room, Ryan's room and Kelly's room all before next weekend.'

'You'd best get on with it, then, Peter. Maybe there'll be a better feeling in this house once it's been brought up to date. Perhaps it'll then feel like a home.'

'It feels like a home now,' said Ali. 'To us, anyway. I thought it would to you, as well, as you grew up here.'

Gran took a bite of the cake Ali had passed her, and chewed it thoughtfully before answering. 'I'm sorry, Alison. I hate this house. I always have done, ever since . . . ever since I left. I didn't have a very happy childhood. My father was a tyrant; I think I told you that before. I couldn't wait to leave home. I'd have gone into digs if I could, but then I met my lovely Roy and he took me away from here. I was so happy to move out. Things happened here. Things you don't know about and I don't want to talk about.'

'Ooh er,' said Ryan. 'Is the house haunted or something?' Ali glared at him, and glanced at Gran. Thankfully she seemed not to have heard.

'Why did Betty never move out?' Ali asked, steering the conversation onto a safer track.

'She never married. And when our parents died, as the eldest she inherited the house and stayed on. She was still in her twenties then. She'd always been Father's favourite in any case. Whatever he said, she would agree with. That's one reason I didn't get on with her. She was too much like him.'

Ali nodded. Gran had told her before about her bully of a

father. She watched as the old lady ate the rest of her cake. Gran was looking tired and frail today. Ali hoped it hadn't all been too much for her—the trip out, the shock of finding out where they'd moved to, and the emotional upheaval of visiting this house. She cursed herself inwardly. She should never have kept it secret. She should have discussed their move with Gran before, rather than springing it on her like this. 'I'm sorry, Gran, for not telling you we were moving here. I should have done. If you're not comfortable here, next time we'll take you out to a café somewhere, or we'll visit you at The Beeches.'

Gran smiled weakly. 'Don't you worry, Alison, dear. I'm just a little tired today. Another slice of that lovely cake might help perk me up a little. And it is lovely to see you all. I'll get used to the idea of you living here, I'm sure. It's time I moved on and forgot about it all. It was all so long ago, after all.'

'Forgot what, Great-gran?' asked Kelly.

'Just—the way things were back then. The war. Everything that happened. Ah, thank you, Alison.' She tucked into her second slice of cake, as Pete began chatting about his plans to knock down the coal shed at the back of the house and rebuild it as a utility room.

'What do you think your gran meant, about things that happened here?' asked Pete, as they sat together watching TV later that evening.

Ali shrugged. 'I don't know. I feel so bad about the whole thing, springing that surprise on her like that. I should have thought it through a bit more.'

'You weren't to know. She'd never said before that she hated this house, had she? Not even after Betty died and you told her you'd inherited it.'

'No. But I think I said that we'd just sell it straight away. Now I can't help but wonder what happened here that made her hate the house so much.'

'You'll have to ask her. Maybe she'll talk about it when she's away from here.'

'I'd be afraid of upsetting her. She looked quite unwell by the time we took her back to The Beeches. I'm worried about her, Pete.'

He hugged her. 'She's a tough old bird, your gran. She was just a bit tired, that's all. And probably it's just the memories of her bullying father that makes her hate the house. I doubt there's anything more sinister than that.'

Ali leaned her head on his shoulder. He was probably right. But she was concerned about Gran. She hadn't been on good form at all today.

Chapter Four

January 1944

Joan made her way back into the dance hall to look for Mags and the others.

'There you are. We wondered where you'd got to,' Mags said, clasping Joan's hands. 'I was scared you'd got caught up in that fight.'

'What fight? I was in the ladies' room. Oh, Mags, I've done something very silly.' Joan felt her eyes well up with tears.

But Mags had turned her attention away. 'Oh look, there's that Canadian airman. They've pulled him off the boy. Looks like he came off worse anyway—that'll be quite a shiner he's got there. He started it. Did you see? He just went for that poor boy with glasses, totally unprovoked, from what I could see. Joanie, did you see any of the fight?'

'No, not at all. Mags, I think I'd like to go home now,' said Joan, trying to hide behind her sister so that Freddie would not see her. He certainly did look a bit of a mess. She hoped the other boy was all right.

Mags pulled a face. 'Aw, Joan, I'm not ready to go yet. Things are just beginning to get lively. What's happened? You seemed to be enjoying yourself earlier. Weren't you dancing—oh, you were dancing with that Canadian who was in the fight!'

'You stay, Mags. I'm going home.'

'On your own?'

'I'll be all right. Don't worry. See you later.' Joan kissed her sister on the cheek and hurried away before Mags's sense of sisterly duty got the better of her. She retrieved her coat from the cloakroom and gratefully stepped outside into the fresh night air. She breathed deeply, two shuddering breaths, and rubbed her eyes with the back of her hand. Next time she'd know better.

'Are you all right?'

Joan turned to see who had spoken, and gasped. It was the boy with broken glasses. They were even more broken now—he was holding them in his hand. He had a split, bloodied lip and his shirt collar was torn. Despite all this, his eyes were full of concern for her, and she felt touched by his care.

'I am, yes. But you look in a bad way. I heard you were in a fight with that horrible chap. What happened?'

'I thought I'd seen him off, but he grabbed me as I went back into the dance hall, and managed to land a punch on me.' He took a handkerchief out of his pocket and dabbed at his lip.

'That looks sore. I'm so sorry.'

'What for? It wasn't you who threw the punch. Besides, I got a good right hook in and I think he came off worse.'

Joan bit her lip. To think this boy had taken a beating and all because he had tried to protect her. And she still didn't know his name!

'But it was all because of me, wasn't it? I'm sorry, I haven't even introduced myself. I'm Joan.'

The boy smiled. Despite his swollen lip his face lit up when he smiled, his cheeks dimpled and his eyes shone. He held out a hand. 'I'm Jack. Jack McBride. I suppose circumstances weren't really right for us to be properly introduced in there.'

33

She shook his hand. It felt warm and strong. 'Hello, Jack McBride. I'm pleased to meet you. And thank you for defending me.'

He made a formal bow. 'At your service, my lady.'

She smiled. 'Wish I was a lady. With a horse and carriage waiting here to take me home.'

'I'm no horse, and I have no carriage, but if you are going home now, I will walk you. With your permission, of course. I shall understand if you've had enough of young men's attentions for one evening. Though I can assure you, I am *nothing* like that thug in there.'

Joan had little experience of boys, but she could already tell there were at least two types, and that Jack and Freddie were polar opposites. She also knew which type she preferred, by far. She felt safe with Jack.

'I should very much like you to walk me home. But I must warn you, it is quite a long way. I live on the east side of town, near the beach.'

'That's no problem at all. I'm going that way myself. Is your sister coming?'

'She's staying for a while longer.'

'All right. Shall we walk along the promenade?'

'In the dark?'

'Nonsense, it's not dark. Look, there's a full moon tonight.' He gestured upwards, and Joan noticed the moon for the first time. The streetlamps that usually lit the promenade had been turned off due to blackout restrictions, but the moon was providing more than enough silvery light to show them the way.

'All right then, why not?'

Jack crooked his elbow and Joan slipped her hand through, as he led her down to the pier entrance then along the promenade. The pier was closed, of course. Its middle section had been removed at the start of the war to prevent it being used by invading forces. Thankfully the beach had not been mined, although there were anti-tank obstacles poking out of the sand throughout its length.

It felt so natural to be walking along with Jack, holding on to his arm like this. Natural, grown-up and very pleasant. She put all thoughts of the repulsive Freddie out of her head. Thank goodness not all boys were like that. She'd found a good one in Jack. Or rather, he'd found, and rescued, her. She smiled up at him as they walked, hoping he liked her as much as she was beginning to like him.

'Look. Do you see the moonlight reflecting off the sea?' Jack pointed across the bay.

'It looks like a silver path, leading over the horizon. I wonder where you would end up if you could follow it.'

'France, I should think. Or maybe somewhere magical, where you would never be found.' Jack led her to a bench under a Victorian wrought-iron shelter on the edge of the prom and they sat down, gazing out over the silken sea. The tide was high, and the anti-invasion defences were only just visible.

'It's so beautiful. Maybe in the land at the end of the moonlight road there is no war.'

Jack nodded. 'Mmm. Everyone lives in peace there. No bombs, no guns, no one dying or being hurt.'

'If only it could be like that here. I can scarcely remember how things were before the war. It seems as though it's been going on for ever.' She moved a little closer to him for the warmth.

'It'll be a while longer yet,' he said. 'But maybe this year the tide will turn.'

'Why have you not joined up? Do you mind me asking?'

'I don't mind at all. I've only just turned eighteen, that's why. I'll probably be joining up quite soon now. I'm not a conchie, if that's what you thought.'

'No, I didn't think that, although I wouldn't mind if you were. Nobody should be forced to fight. Everyone's entitled to their own opinion, aren't they?'

He turned to look at her, and nodded seriously. 'Yes. I wish everyone thought like you. The world would be a happier place if only people would live and let live. But I do want to do my bit. Maybe there's some little thing I'll do as a soldier that will be the start of a chain of events, and the end of that chain will be that Britain wins the war sooner and thousands of lives are saved. Or maybe I'll save the life of someone who goes on to be important to the whole human race. We can't know what's ahead of us, or where our actions will take us. All we can do is follow where our hearts lead, and act upon our beliefs.'

He had turned to look at the shimmering sea again. She watched him, as a small muscle in his jaw clenched and relaxed. He seemed lost in his own thoughts, not feeling the intensity of her gaze upon him. She considered his words. How right he was! Follow your heart. Act upon your beliefs. Stay true to yourself, even in this time of war. She let her eyes follow his across the water, towards the dark distant horizon, and then up to the night sky, to where the moon hung, huge and full. That was where the moonlight trail led. Off this planet, away from its wars, and across the universe to a peaceful, untroubled world. She wished she could step onto the sea and follow it.

'Where will your heart lead you, Joan?' His voice broke into her thoughts. She leaned back on the bench, and his arm slipped around her shoulders. She nestled into his warmth.

'To tell the truth, Jack, I don't know. I'm only seventeen. My life is ahead of me. The only thing I'm certain of is that you are right—we must all follow wherever our hearts lead. When my heart calls to me I shall follow. I promise you that.'

He smiled at her. For a moment she thought he was going to try to kiss her, and she wondered how that would feel. Not like Freddie's rough, urgent slobberings, she guessed. Jack would be gentle and considerate. But he turned his face away, and she felt an unexpected shiver of disappointment.

'You're cold. Here, take my coat.' He shrugged off his thin tweed jacket and tucked it around her shoulders. She pulled it close around her neck. The collar smelt of wool and spice, as though his aftershave had rubbed off on it.

'Thank you. You are very kind.'

'It's my pleasure.'

They sat in silence for a few minutes more. Joan was still considering what he had said about doing his part in the war. Could it really be that a small action from one person could change the whole course of the war? She supposed it was like dominoes—as a child she had spent hours standing her set in a row up on their ends, then gently flicking the first one and watching as the whole series tumbled down. Maybe what Jack meant was that he might be the first domino. Some action of his in the future could be like the toppling of that first domino, and could lead ultimately to the toppling of Hitler. It was the most compelling reason she'd heard yet for why a man would want to join up.

'I wonder if perhaps I should take you home, now?'

Joan wished she could sit there on the bench gazing at the moonlit sea, with Jack's arm around her shoulders, for ever. But no doubt he was cold without his coat, and it must be getting late. She nodded, and stood up, handing him back his jacket. 'I shan't need that while I'm walking, but thank you so much.'

He slipped it on, and she held out her hand to him. After a moment's hesitation he took it. His hand was surprisingly warm despite the chilly evening. They walked in step along the prom, under the cliffs, and finally up a zigzag path that led to the clifftop. 'This is my road,' Joan said, as they turned away from the sea.

'I'd better say goodbye to you here,' said Jack, stopping on the corner. 'In case your parents are looking out of the window. I don't want you to get in trouble for walking home with a boy.' He let go of her hand and stuffed his hands in his pockets.

'Goodbye, then, and thank you, again, for saving me from that horrible thug.' On a whim she put her hands on his shoulders, reached up and kissed his cheek, before turning and running along the street and back to her house. At the garden gate she looked back. He was still standing there on the corner, shoulders hunched, watching her. He lifted a hand to wave. She waved back, and darted into the house by the back door into the kitchen.

Mother was sitting at the kitchen table. She wagged a finger at Joan. 'There you are! Margaret was back ten minutes ago. I know you were at the dance with her and not at the WVS, so you needn't try to pretend you weren't. Thankfully, your father went out to his bridge club and isn't home yet, or you'd be in real trouble, my girl. You're very lucky.'

'We walked back separately. I came along the prom as it is such a beautiful evening. I stopped to look at the moonlight on the sea.' Best to be as truthful as possible, Joan reasoned, but no need to say she'd walked home with a young man. Mother would only suspect the worst. With a shudder Joan realised that Mother would suspect Jack of being like Freddie, trying to take advantage of innocent young girls.

'Are you all right? You look frozen half to death. I don't know, wandering along the prom on your own at this time of night. Anything could have happened to you! There are bad people out there, Joan, bad men who will hurt girls like you.'

'I'm all right, Mother. I'll go to bed now, I think.' Joan left the kitchen and ran up the stairs, before she found herself blurting out that she knew all about the bad men Mother was talking about. With Jack she had felt safe and secure, but back home the horrors of the earlier part of the evening were catching up with her, and she felt like sobbing. She took a deep breath before entering her bedroom. She didn't want to explain any of it to Mags, either. It was strange. Until this evening she'd always told Mags everything of importance that happened to her, and a lot of things that weren't important as well. But the events with Freddie and then Jack had changed her. She felt as though she'd crossed some kind of line between girlhood and womanhood. Or at least taken the first steps towards crossing it. And it felt like a journey she would need to make on her own, without her sister.

Chapter Five

September 2014

'Ali, give us a hand with this,' called Pete from the hallway. Ali put down her magazine—it had been too much to hope that she might get a few minutes' quiet reading time with a cup of tea—and went to see what he was up to. He was half inside the under-stairs cupboard, in which a downstairs loo had been installed at some point in the house's history. They had agreed to rip out this cloakroom and replace it with one in a planned, back extension, beside a new utility room, which would replace the old coal shed.

'What do you need doing?' she asked. He'd made good progress since she last checked, and the old toilet was now in the driveway awaiting a trip to the tip.

'I'm trying to pull off this old wooden cladding,' he said. 'It's just so tight working in this confined space. If you can stand there and pull at the boards as I wrench them off, then stack them out in the hallway, that'll halve the time it takes.'

'Sure. Will do.' Ali positioned herself, and they began work. He was right. It was a quick job with the two of them working, now that Pete didn't have to keep squeezing in and out of the tiny space.

Soon they had all the cladding off and neatly stacked in the hallway. More for the tip, thought Ali, although maybe it could be used as firewood in the winter, after they'd had the chimneys swept.

'Interesting,' said Pete, who was examining the newly uncovered wall.

'What is?' Ali poked her head inside the cupboard.

'That cladding covered up a door.' Pete picked up his crowbar and began forcing it into a crack.

'A door? Leading where?'

'Let's find out. I'd imagine it leads to an under-floor space.'

'A cellar?' Wow. So perhaps this already enormous house had a cellar as well? Ali felt a little rush of excitement. More to explore!

There was a huge crack as the door splintered open. Pete put down the crowbar, kicked his toolbox aside and took hold of the door with both hands to pull it open further. Ali looked inside. Beyond the door were steep steps leading downwards— it *was* a cellar!

'Bloody hell! As if we needed any more space!' exclaimed Pete. 'Fetch the inspection torch, will you? It's hanging up in the garage.'

Ali ran to get the torch, and plugged it in a nearby socket in the hallway. Carefully, Pete made his way down the crumbling concrete steps. Ali followed, her hand on his shoulder to steady herself.

The inspection torch was bright, and lit the space well. 'Mind your head,' said Pete, bending double to dodge the joists from the floor above. 'It's not full height, sadly. I'd hoped we could put a games room or home cinema down here.'

Ali laughed. 'Typical boy stuff. I had in mind a storage area for Christmas decorations and camping gear. Probably easier to get it from here than going up in the loft.' The loft wasn't boarded. If they could use the cellar instead it'd save a big job.

'Sounds like a good idea. As long as it's not damp down here. And we'll need to do some clearing up.'

Ali looked around. He was right. There were several disintegrating cardboard boxes, a pile of empty glass bottles, evidence of mice infestation, a roll of mildewed old carpet and numerous other abandoned items. Nothing they couldn't sort out with a bit of hard work though.

'What's in that box?' She pointed to a wooden crate that stood centred on a piece of old carpet.

Pete knelt beside it, and pulled away the piece of cloth that was draped over the top. 'Papers, photos, a few books. All a bit the worse for wear.'

'Can we take that box up? I'd love to have a rummage through. Maybe it's something my great-grandparents put down here and forgot about. Or Gran's schoolbooks or something.'

'I think you're right,' said Pete, pulling out a framed photo from the top of the box. 'Isn't that your grandmother? I'm sure I've seen a photo similar to this one in your album of old family pictures.' He passed it to her and angled the light so she could see.

The photo was a black-and-white snap of three young girls. Two were laughing, and one looked more serious. They were all wearing school uniform blouses and pinafore dresses, and the photographer's mark at the bottom gave the date as 1938. Ali recognised her grandmother at once. She had another photo, of just her grandmother in school uniform, presumably taken on the same date by the same photographer, in her album. One of the other girls was probably Great-aunt Betty. The serious, elder girl, she thought. So who was the other one? She looked younger than Margaret or Betty. She was giggling, and there was a mischievous look in her eye.

Some masonry dust fell on Ali's head, and she coughed. 'Let's go back up. I think we'll need to wear masks when we clean out this place. Bring up that box, will you please?'

Pete nodded, and handed her the torch. He lifted the box and carried it up, followed by Ali. She was glad to be out of that dusty, musty place. It was a bit creepy down there, knowing no one could have touched those items for decades. Maybe they would just throw away the rubbish and board it back up again. It wasn't as if they needed the space anyway.

'Spread some newspaper on the kitchen table,' Pete said, 'and I'll put the box on there.'

Ali did as he suggested. How wonderful if there were old family documents in the box! She'd always felt she should ask Gran to tell her more of her childhood memories. Once Gran had gone there would be no one left from that generation who could remember the war years and before. Maybe this box would be a good starting point.

There was a thundering of feet on the stairs, and Kelly and Ryan burst into the kitchen.

'Mum, Kelly won't lend me her laptop. I need it for homework.'

'He's been really annoying me, Mum. I'm trying to do my own homework and he just stands by my door telling me I have to lend him it. He should buy his own. Took me years to save up for this, didn't it?'

They were like toddlers, Ali thought. Soon they would have to get a computer for Ryan. They'd resisted it so far, as he was only thirteen and they wanted to be able to control how much time he spent online. But increasingly it seemed he needed to do his homework on a computer. 'You can use mine for today, Ryan. Let Kelly get on with her own work.'

'Cheers, Mum. What's that old box?' Ryan peered into it.

'We found a door to a cellar in the under-stairs cupboard. That box was down there,' Pete explained.

'Cool! Can I go down and have a look?'

'Sure. Come on.' Pete left the kitchen followed by an excited Ryan.

'I knew this house would have a cellar. I just knew it,' said Kelly.

'Seems you were right. Want to help me sort through this stuff?'

'Yeah! More exciting than homework.' Kelly sat down and began pulling things out of the box. There were some old school exercise books, a moth-eaten teddy with a loose arm and one eye missing, a handful of hair ribbons, a small bundle of letters rolled and tied with a piece of string, and another framed photo. This one was of a young man in army uniform.

'I wonder who he was?' said Ali.

'Jack, I expect.'

Ali glanced at her daughter.

'Who's Jack?'

Kelly shook her head as if to bring herself back to the present. 'You know, on my bedroom wall it says *Joan loves Jack*. I bet this is Jack.'

'And who was Joan, I wonder?'

Kelly picked up the photo of the three girls and considered it. She pointed to the youngest. 'That'll be Joan, I reckon. That's Great-gran, isn't it? And your great-aunt Betty was older, so that must be her. The youngest one must be Joan.'

'But who was she? My great-grandparents only had two daughters. Elizabeth—that's Betty, and Margaret—that is, my gran. There wasn't a third daughter. I think this third girl in the photo must be a friend of theirs. A close friend—that will be why they had their photo taken together. Or maybe a cousin. I must take it and show Gran, the next time I visit. I'll ask her about it.'

Kelly was staring at the photo of the young man. Ali watched as she ran her fingers over the image, tracing the outline of his face. 'Can I keep this, Mum?' she asked.

'Of course. I'll want to borrow it to ask Gran about him, but if you want to keep it in your room till then that's fine by me.'

'Thanks.' Kelly picked up the old teddy and stroked its head, fondly. 'This old thing looks well loved. He deserves to be cleaned up and looked after in his old age, rather than left to rot in a cellar, poor darling. I wonder if this belonged to Joan?'

Ali continued pulling items out of the box. Right at the bottom was a small leather box, its surface covered in a fine layer of mould. Inside was a gold locket on a chain. The front was inlaid with mother-of-pearl in an intricate design of flowers and leaves.

43

'Look at this, Kelly. I wonder why it was put in this box along with all the other stuff.'

Kelly gasped as she saw the locket. 'It's gorgeous. Really pretty. May I try it on?' Without waiting for an answer she took it from Ali and fastened it around her neck. 'I'd like to keep this, too.'

'Well, I suppose so, though again I'd like to ask Gran if she knows who it belonged to.'

'Joan, I expect,' said Kelly, as she went upstairs with the teddy and photo.

Ali watched her leave, then looked again at the photo of the three girls. The little one must be a cousin. She'd never heard Gran mention any cousins but that wasn't surprising. You tend to lose touch with more distant relatives as you get older. Not that she knew. Ali had no cousins, neither had her father. They were both only children. Her mother had a brother but he'd never married. It must be nice to have siblings and cousins.

The three girls looked so happy. At least, the youngest one and Gran did—Betty looked as though she was disapproving of whatever the other two were giggling at. Gran always did say Betty had been the serious one, who took after her father. It was sad to think that just a year or so after this photo was taken, Britain was plunged into war. It had changed everything. All three girls would have spent the rest of their childhood and teenage years in a war-torn country. They'd have had to grow up fast. It was so sad. The current generation of teenagers was so much more lucky, Ali thought. They had so many more opportunities, and freedom to do whatever they wanted. It was a shame they didn't always realise it.

Kelly came downstairs again an hour or so later, while Ali was peeling potatoes for the Sunday roast. She was still wearing the locket, and had tonged her hair into waves, held at the sides with Kirby grips.

'I like your hair,' Ali said. 'Very retro.'

'Thanks. I was kind of copying Amelia Fay.'

'Who?'

'The singer. She does forties and fifties stuff, only updated. She's cool.'

'Ah, OK. Get me a roasting tin out of that cupboard, could you?'

Kelly handed her the tin. 'I was thinking, Mum, we should definitely ask Great-gran about those photos, and find out who the third girl really is. I mean, I'm sure it's the Joan who wrote her name on my bedroom wall, but I guess only Great-gran would know for certain. But more than that—I'd like to research the whole family tree. Ask her about her parents and grandparents. She'd probably remember her grandparents, and wow, just think about it—they'd be my great-great-great-grandparents. That's way back! So, like, can we go and see her, and ask her stuff?'

It was an interesting idea. Ali had often wondered about researching the family tree. So many people did it these days, and there was lots of information online, but nothing beat starting with your own elderly relatives and capturing their memories before they were gone for good. 'I think that's a lovely idea, Kelly. But your great-gran's not been too well lately. She's had a chest infection, which has laid her low. We'll need to wait a bit, until she's stronger, before we go bothering her too much. I won't be able to help you with it—I've not enough time as it is, what with having to work full time since your dad was made redundant.' She tipped the peeled potatoes into the tray, drizzled olive oil over them and popped them into the oven. 'There. Right then, what other veg shall we have?'

'Dunno.' Kelly shrugged. 'Hey, I know. Now we've got a decent-sized garden, can we grow our own? We could put a vegetable plot down the end, and plant carrots and beans and stuff. I bet Great-gran's family had a veg plot during the war. All that dig for victory stuff.'

'That'll be one more thing to ask her, then. Perhaps you should start a list.' Ali began peeling and chopping some carrots. 'But remember, she didn't get on with Betty or her father much, so she might not want to answer all your questions.'

'Can try though, can't wē, when she's better?' Kelly grinned, stealing a chunk of raw carrot before waltzing out of the room, singing a jazzed-up version of 'White Cliffs of Dover'. Presumably an Amelia Fay song, Ali thought.

Chapter Six

January 1944

'You wash; I'll dry,' said Joan. She tugged a tea towel off the drying rack hanging over the kitchen table and stood ready to deal with the breakfast dishes. Elizabeth began running water into the sink. 'Are you helping at the WVS today as well, Betty? Mags and I are.'

'No, my next shift isn't until Monday,' answered Elizabeth. 'I'm not sure I'd want to be there when you two giggling schoolgirls are around. Pass me those dirty plates.'

'We're hardly schoolgirls. Mags has been working for two years now. Even I've left school. Besides we work really hard at the WVS. You ask Mrs Atkins. She'll tell you.' Joan rubbed at a plate and stacked it with the others in a cupboard.

'You've left school, but you're not yet earning. That makes you no better than a schoolgirl, in my opinion.'

It was just like Elizabeth to try to put her down. Joan pouted. 'It's not my fault I haven't got a job. I wanted to go and be a land girl last harvest time but Father wouldn't let me. Even now he won't let me go out to look for work. He says I'm too young.'

'You should have stayed at school as he wanted, and learned

to type.' Elizabeth sniffed as she placed a teacup on the draining board. 'Then you might have got a proper job.'

'Who wants a proper job?' said Father. 'I'm in need of my second cup of tea. Is there any more in the pot?'

'Sorry, Father, no. I emptied it, just now.' How was Joan to know he hadn't had his second cup? He usually poured it before leaving the breakfast table at the weekend, and took it through to his study to drink while he read the paper.

'You threw it away? Aren't you aware there's a war on, and tea is rationed along with everything else, girl?'

'Yes, Father; sorry, Father. I thought you'd already—'

'Well, I hadn't, and you didn't think to come and check. Now what about answering my question? Who's wanting a proper job? Elizabeth, my dear, I assume it isn't you, for you already hold a splendid position at the bank.'

'No, Father,' Elizabeth replied. 'We were talking about Joan and that time she said it was her dream to join the land army.'

Father glared at Joan. 'No daughter of mine is going to work in the fields. There are far better jobs to be had than that. Besides, dreaming is a waste of time, as I've told you before.'

Joan tried to stop herself from answering back but it was no good. She'd always been the defiant one, and it had always got her into trouble, but sometimes she just couldn't help herself. 'But, Father, what job could be more important than raising crops and gathering in the harvest? England has to feed herself. The men are all at war so the women and girls must step in to help on the land.'

'Let the *working class* girls work on the land. You are not of that class, and I won't have you doing that sort of work. Look at Elizabeth—she does a useful job at the bank, which is befitting of a girl of her station. Elizabeth, ask at the bank if they can find a position for your sister. Not as a counter clerk—I won't have her dealing with the public. But perhaps there's something she could do in the back offices.'

48

'I will. I'll ask on Monday.'

'Thank you. I suppose I shall have to do without that second cup of tea.' Father dropped his cup in the washing-up water and left the room.

Joan carried on drying up in silence. She could think of nothing more dull than working in a stuffy bank, with stuck-up Betty breathing down her neck. Well, maybe something else would come up. But it would be nice to have a proper full-time job, rather than just staying at home to help Mother with the housework. And if she was earning money, she'd be able to go to more dances, like the one last week. She had put the incident with Freddie out of her mind. She would never let herself get into that situation again. The rest of the evening had been fun. For a moment she found herself wondering what that boy, Jack, who'd walked her home, was doing now.

Half an hour later, Joan and Mags arrived at the church hall, which was currently home to the WVS. Mags was put to work in the kitchen making huge pots of soup to sustain the air-raid wardens who would be on shift that evening and Joan was asked to sort some bags of donated children's clothes. She followed the ample girth of Mrs Atkins through to a small room off the main hall, where several piles of clothes stood waiting.

'Sort them by age and sex,' said Mrs Atkins. 'Then we can send them out to the county villages that took in evacuees. They'll be needing more warm items now the weather's turned so cold.' She turned to go. 'Oh, and anything that's dirty, put it in a pile over there and I'll take it home to wash before we send it away.'

'All right. Thanks, Mrs Atkins. I'll get this done quickly.' Joan spread out the first pile on a trestle table and began sorting through. It was easy work, though she hadn't much idea of children's sizes or what clothes would fit each age group. She wondered about the evacuee children. There were none in the town itself but the outlying farms and villages, away from the danger of bombs, had all taken some children who'd been sent down from London. It must be awful to be sent away from your family like that, especially for the little ones. Although she had to admit, she wouldn't have much minded being sent away from her father. He was just so bossy and controlling. It was all right for Betty, his favourite, but life with him was hard for herself and Mags. He never let her do anything or go anywhere.

She was holding up a girl's smock and deciding whether to put it in the five-to-six pile or the seven-to-eight pile, when she heard Mrs Atkins's strident tones in the main hall.

'Miss Perkins is busy at the moment. I'm afraid she can't come out right now. Besides, you haven't even given your name. I'm hardly going to let her come out to meet a young man who won't even give his name.'

Joan strained her ears to hear more. Which Miss Perkins did the young man want? Her or Mags?

'I'm so sorry, ma'am. My name is Jack McBride. I met Miss Perkins last week and I just wanted to see her again to check she was all right. She'd had an upset, you see. I remember she told me she was going to begin working here, so I was hoping . . .' Joan suppressed a gasp. He'd come looking for her! She put down the child's dress, dusted off her skirt and patted her hair.

'That's better, young man. A little politeness will get you far. Joan, dear? Could you come through?' Mrs Atkins pushed the door open and nodded to Joan. 'There's a young man here to see you. You may have a five-minute break.'

Joan thanked Mrs Atkins and hoped she didn't notice the blush she could feel rising up her neck. For that matter she hoped Jack couldn't see it either.

'I didn't dare call at your house,' he said, as they crossed the large hall towards the entrance. 'In fact, I wasn't sure which number it was, anyway.' He held a battered tweed cap in his hands.

'Father would have turned you away so it's just as well.' She smiled gently at him. He had a sweet, kind-looking face, now she saw him in daylight.

'The truth is, I wanted to see you again, to ask you . . . well, to ask you whether perhaps you might like, well . . . What I mean to say is, I'd like to take you out for tea. Today, perhaps, when you finish here?'

Joan had nothing to fear from her own blushes compared to Jack's. His face was cranberry red and his hands were shaking as they twisted his cap round and around. 'Yes, Jack. I would like that very much. I finish today at four o'clock. Will you meet me outside?'

She smiled to see delight and relief wash over his face. 'Four o'clock, yes. I'll be waiting outside. Wonderful! Thank you, Joan.' He grinned, and waved at her as he skipped down the steps and out of the hall. Joan went back to her task, passing Mrs Atkins who unexpectedly winked at her. She looked at her watch. Three hours to go until four o'clock.

She soon had all the children's clothes sorted, re-bagged and labelled. Mrs Atkins came to check. 'Excellent job, young Joan. Now then, we've got the playgroup to run this afternoon and I wondered if you wouldn't mind helping with that until four o'clock.'

'Of course, I'd love to,' Joan said. She went into the main hall where the usual playgroup leaders were just getting ready for the children. There were boxes of donated toys to take out of cupboards, and chairs to arrange in a circle. The children were supposed to stay inside the circle. Joan had seen it in action before and had thought it looked like a fun job.

She had barely finished arranging the chairs when the first children arrived. A flustered-looking woman pushed a small boy and a smaller girl into the circle. 'I need about forty minutes,' she said to Joan. 'Depending on whether I can get hold of any sugar. It's her birthday tomorrow' – she nodded at the little girl – 'and I must make some sort of a cake. You'll be all right now, children? This nice lady is going to play with you.' With that the woman hurried out of the hall.

As soon as she'd gone the girl began crying. Her brother ignored her and sat down to play with a wooden train. Joan knelt beside the crying child.

'What's your name?'

'Her name's Patricia' said the boy, not looking up from his game.

'What a pretty name, Patricia! How about we dry those tears and see if we can find a dolly to dress?' Joan pulled out her handkerchief and gently dabbed at the child's face. To her surprise it worked; little Patricia's sobs quickly subsided. She took her hand and led her over to a box she knew contained a couple of grubby old dolls. One was a rag doll, sewn into her dress, but the other had a removable outfit. Joan sat on the floor with Patricia and helped her undress and redress the doll.

'You don't need to actually *play* with them—just let them play on their own. You can sit up here and just watch.' The woman running the playgroup was a thin-faced woman named Valerie whom Joan judged to be around thirty. She was sitting on one of the chairs in the circle, with a magazine in her hand.

'It's all right. I don't mind,' said Joan. She looked up and caught Mrs Atkins's eye. The older woman smiled and nodded encouragingly.

Three more mothers arrived with children. One child was crying, not wanting to be left, so Joan picked up the sniffling boy. 'Mummy won't be long, and while she's away, you and I can play with a brum-brum car. How about that?'

'Oh, I am grateful to you,' said the boy's mother. 'You've no idea how useful it is to have somewhere to leave them for a little while. The queues can be so long and little ones just get fed up. It's all very well if you've older children to stay at home with the little ones, but when you haven't it's a problem. You do seem to have a knack with them. Look, Georgie's stopped crying already. I'll be back in an hour. Bye-bye, Georgie! Mummy will see if there are any biscuits at the baker's for you.'

Joan settled down to play cars with the boy. Patricia's brother and another little lad joined in, and soon they'd made a garage from one of the boxes, and had an assortment of vehicles parked within it. Valerie peered over the top of her magazine and sniffed with disapproval from time to time.

Halfway through the afternoon it was time for the children to have a drink of squash each. Mrs Atkins brought out the tray and Joan helped each child to a drink.

'You're really rather good with the children,' said Mrs Atkins. 'And I'd better whisper it, you're more natural with them than poor Valerie there. How do you like doing that job?'

'I'm really enjoying myself, actually. Once they got over their mothers leaving, they settled down quickly. I like playing with them. I'm sure I've a few old toys at home, and some colouring books I could bring in as well.' Joan bent to take an empty beaker from Patricia and put it back on the tray.

'Play with dolly?' asked Patricia.

'Yes, of course. You fetch dolly while I finish chatting with Mrs Atkins.' The little girl ran off happily to find the doll.

'Well, Joan, if you would like it, I think there's a permanent job for you running the playgroup. I'd like to open it every weekday morning from ten till twelve, and again in the afternoons from two till four. Could you take it on, do you think?' Mrs Atkins dropped her voice again. 'There are other jobs that might be more suited to Valerie's talents.'

'Oh, I'd love to!' Joan grinned at Mrs Atkins, delighted by the prospect.

'Wonderful. So can you start from tomorrow?'

'Of course. I'll be here by half past nine to set things up. Now I must go and play with little Patricia, as I promised.' She turned to the little girl who was tugging at her skirt. Mrs Atkins nodded and left her to it.

The rest of the afternoon passed quickly. Joan wondered whether after the war was over, she might be able to get some kind of paid job looking after children. Perhaps she could even train as a primary school teacher? Would Father accept that as suitable employment for one of his daughters? Probably not, unless it was a private school for children from rich families. He wouldn't want her mixing with children from the working classes, would he? She put the thoughts out of her mind and concentrated on the children and their games. One by one each child was collected and Joan was gratified to discover that some of them didn't want to leave her. Mrs Atkins informed each mother of the new opening hours for the playgroup as they left, while Valerie scowled and packed up early.

* * *

Jack was waiting outside for her at four o'clock, as he had promised. She smiled shyly as she came down the entrance steps and took his arm.

'Did you have a good afternoon?' he asked.

'Oh yes! I have a new job, running the playgroup. From tomorrow morning I'll be in charge of it. I have all sorts of ideas—rather than just play with the same toys every time I think the children could draw, or make things, or play party games.'

He laughed. 'That hardly sounds like work!'

'I know; it's fun. Some of the children need comforting when they arrive but it's nice to give them cuddles as well.'

'It sounds like the perfect job for you. Now then, I thought we'd pop into Lyons for a cup of tea and a slice of cake. My treat. How does that sound?'

'Perfect! Today is getting better and better. I love cake. I like making them too. Mags says my lemon drizzle is the best she's ever tasted.' Joan smiled happily as they walked arm in arm to the Lyons corner house. Jack found a table by the window, and placed their order.

'This is lovely,' said Joan. 'I used to come here with Mother and my sisters when we went out shopping, before the war.'

'My aunt used to bring me, as a special treat, if it was my birthday or I'd had a good report from school.'

'Your aunt?'

'Yes, I live with her—in fact, she brought me up. My mother died when I was a baby, and my father went to America to seek his fortune. My mother's sister took me in, as she had lost her husband in the Great War and had no children of her own.'

What a sad story, thought Joan. Imagine growing up with no parents or siblings. 'Do you ever hear from your father?'

'We had Christmas cards each year before the war started. They would usually arrive in about February. I think he would only remember to send one when Christmas actually arrived, by which time it was too late to send it across the Atlantic in time. He was living in New York, the last we heard.'

'Perhaps when this war is over you might want to go and find him?' Although to Joan it didn't sound as though Jack's father cared very much about his son.

Jack shook his head. 'When this war's over I'd rather look forwards than backwards. I mean, I'd hope to find a girl and start a family of my own, then. I never had that kind of family life as a child. I hope to be able to experience it as a man.'

'I'm sure you will.' On a whim, Joan reached out across the table and touched his hand. He looked down at her fingers on his hand for a moment, then raised his eyes to hers, and entwined his fingers with hers.

The moment felt charged, as though electricity was running through her. She opened her mouth to speak but no words came. The truth in his eyes told her he cared for her, that for that moment at least *she* was the girl he had hoped to find.

'Your tea, and the cakes. We're out of the ginger so I swapped it for the Victoria sponge.' They released hands quickly as a waitress plonked her tray down on the table between them, and set about unloading it.

'The Victoria sponge is perfect, thank you,' Jack told the waitress.

Joan looked down at her lap, feeling herself blush once more. There had been something about Jack's look, and the touch of his hand, that thrilled her. Before today she wouldn't have considered him to be her type. He'd been nice to her after the terrible events with Freddie but she'd thought that was all she felt for him—a kind boy who'd helped her out of trouble and walked her home. But now—now she felt differently. His floppy fringe was endearing. His eyes behind his repaired glasses were dark and full of soul. His hand was warm and strong.

'So you are going to work every day at the WVS now, running the playgroup?'

She was pulled back to the present by his words. A safe topic. 'Yes, as long as my father doesn't object. He can be, well, a bit difficult at times.'

'You've finished school?'

'Last summer. Since then I've just helped Mother in the home, apart from a few sessions at the WVS. What do you do?'

'I've just left college. I had applied to study engineering but now I'm going to put that on hold for the duration. I'm going to join up.'

Joan remembered that he'd talked about wanting to play his part in the war, while they'd sat on the bench on the prom, looking out at the silvery moon reflecting off the sea. It was all right for boys in wartime. There was a definite and obvious role for them. Not so easy for girls. At least now with the playgroup job she felt she could be doing something useful. It might not be directly helping the war effort but even so, it was worth doing.

'When will you join up?'

'This week. Aunt Marion doesn't want me to but I'm eighteen now and I've made my decision.'

Joan felt a pang of sorrow. This week! So soon. Just as she was beginning to really like him.

* * *

All too soon the tea was drunk, the cake eaten, and dusk was falling outside. Reluctantly, Joan pushed back her chair and got to her feet. 'I've had a lovely time, Jack, but my family will be expecting me home. I must help Mother prepare supper.'

'Of course. Perhaps we can do this again?' Jack helped her with her coat.

'But you are joining up—won't you be sent away?'

'I suppose so. But I'll be home on leave now and again, and if you would like it, perhaps every time I come home I'll call on you?'

She smiled. 'I would like that very much, Jack.'

She slipped her arm through his and they left the tea shop together.

'I'll walk you home,' Jack said.

She leaned in close to him. She would have a few minutes more of his company as they walked, and perhaps he might not be sent away immediately and they'd have another chance to meet during the week.

'Joan? What do you think you are doing?'

She spun around in horror. 'Father! I was just walking home. I've been out to tea—ah, Father, this is Jack McBride. Jack, my father, Mr Perkins.'

'Pleased to meet you, sir.' Jack stretched out his hand but Father ignored it, and stared at Joan.

'Joan, you had hold of this fellow's arm as you were walking along. Explain yourself.'

'We were just walking home. Jack bought me tea and cake . . .'

'Well, his services are no longer required. You can come with me, now. I have the motor car just around the corner.' Father took her arm and pulled her away.

'But, Father, there's no harm in it. Jack's a good sort. Please may I walk with him?'

'No, you may not. A daughter of mine, and one barely out of school, holding hands with a boy in public! And a boy from the working classes, to boot.'

'Sir, I meant no harm. I wanted to ensure your daughter reached home safely. May I please call on her tomorrow?'

'No. You may not. Come on, Joan. I want to know where and how you met this young man. You will tell me everything when we are in the car.'

Joan had no choice. She cast an agonised glance over her shoulder at Jack, who shrugged helplessly. Mouthing 'WVS tomorrow' at him, she stumbled along after her father who still had a firm grip on her arm.

Chapter Seven

October 2014

The doorbell rang. It was the postman, with a package for Kelly. Ali accepted it, and then called her daughter. Kelly took the stairs two at a time.

'Oh my God, I've been desperate for this one to come!' she squealed, as she took the package, ran through to the kitchen and tore it open.

'What is it, love?' Ali asked, following her.

'Something I bought off eBay,' she said, pulling a pale blue item out of the package. She held it up against her.

Ali forced herself to smile. 'Very pretty,' she said. 'Isn't it a bit old-fashioned, though?' It was a dress made of blue cotton with tiny sprigged flowers. There was a rounded Peter Pan collar in white, buttons up the front, and a narrow belt made from the same fabric as the collar.

'It's gorgeous,' Kelly said. 'Forties stuff is really cool. I'm off to try it on. I can wear Joan's locket with it.' She stuffed the packaging into the recycling bin and ran upstairs with the dress.

Ali sat down with her morning cup of coffee to wait for the fashion show. Kelly had only recently opened an account on eBay. She'd sold her old Barbie dolls and some Disney DVDs, and was spending the proceeds, along with money from a babysitting job, on clothes or cheap jewellery. Kelly's friend Leanne was coming later. The girls were heading out for a Saturday shopping trip. It would be interesting to see what Leanne thought of the dress.

'Ta-dah!' Kelly entered the kitchen and gave a twirl. Ali gasped. The dress fitted Kelly perfectly, and showed off her lovely figure. She was wearing the pearl locket, and she'd also tonged her hair into waves again. All in all she looked as though she'd stepped out of the pages of *Woman's Weekly* circa 1942.

Pete came into the kitchen in search of coffee. He stopped and stared at Kelly. 'Great outfit. You going to a fancy-dress party or something?'

'No! This look is cool—like Amelia Fay. Pretty, isn't it? I think I'll wear it this afternoon, out with Leanne.'

'Well, I know nothing of fashion but if that's what you young things are wearing these days then yes, I suppose it is pretty,' Pete said. He poured himself a coffee from the jug, raised his eyebrows at Ali and left the room.

Kelly looked at Ali. 'You do like it, don't you, Mum? It was quite dear, but I really like this forties stuff and I loved this the moment I saw it.'

'It does look nice on you, love,' Ali said. 'Good for you to have your own sense of style. I like that. How much was it?'

'Thirty shillings.' Kelly ran her hands over her skirt, smoothing wrinkles.

'Shillings? What do you mean?'

'Thirty pounds. Sorry, what did I say?'

'You said thirty shillings.'

'Did I? What am I like?' Kelly shook her head. 'Living in the past. Send Leanne upstairs when she comes, will you?'

* * *

60

Kelly was lying on her bed reading *Rebecca*, one of the books she had to read as part of her A level English Literature course, when Leanne arrived. She heard her come up the stairs and stood, ready to greet her. Leanne burst through the door in her usual exuberant manner.

'Hey, Kells. How's it going? Wow, what are you wearing?' Leanne flopped down onto the bed, staring at Kelly's dress.

'Do you like it?' said Kelly, twirling around. Leanne was wearing skinny-leg hipster jeans and a cropped T-shirt. A stud sparkled in her belly button.

'Er, do you want the truth?' said Leanne, wrinkling her forehead.

'Go on.' Suddenly Kelly felt less sure about the dress. Was it really *her*? And the hair, why had she curled it like that?

'You look like you're auditioning for a part in *Foyle's War*,' Leanne said. 'Kind of works, but, why?'

'I don't know,' said Kelly, pulling the grips out of her hair. 'Suppose I've been listening to too much Amelia Fay music lately.' Wearing the dress and pinning her hair into curls suddenly made no sense to her. But it wasn't the influence of Amelia Fay music—it was more likely she'd been thinking too much about Joan and Jack, especially after having read some of the letters. They were dated 1944, and written from Jack to Joan after he'd gone away to fight in the war. She'd found herself fascinated by their story, and was longing to find out more about them, as soon as she had the chance to talk to Great-gran. She wrenched open the buttons on the dress, and let it slip to the floor, then kicked it under the bed, out of sight.

'Here,' said Leanne, passing her a denim mini-skirt that had been draped over the back of a chair. 'Wear this, and your *Girls R Us* T-shirt.'

'Thanks.' Kelly put the clothes on, brushed out her hair and applied some mascara. 'Better?'

'Much,' said Leanne. 'Ready to go? I want some new boots for the autumn. Ones I can wear with jeans. And they've got some fabulous jackets in Top Shop which I might ask Mum to get me for my birthday. What will you be looking for?'

'Don't know. I haven't got much money.'

'Thought you had loads from babysitting?'

'Spent it on that dress,' Kelly said, sighing.

'You dolt. Send it back and say it doesn't fit.'

'I might. Come on, then, let's go.' Kelly grabbed her bag and rushed out of the room and down the stairs.

'How's the lovely Matt?' asked Leanne later, as they browsed the rails of new season tops in River Island.

'He's good,' Kelly replied.

'What does he think of your new house?'

'He likes it, I think.'

'You don't though, do you?'

Kelly turned and stared at Leanne. 'Sort of. It's good being near the beach. But sometimes I get a weird feeling when I'm at home. I can't explain it, but there's something there.'

'Ooh er, like a . . . a *presence*, you mean?'

'Yes, something like that. I can feel it. Like in *Rebecca*—you know how the second Mrs de Winter can somehow still feel Rebecca's presence lingering in the house. Do you get what I mean?' Kelly spoke urgently.

'You think it's haunted?' Leanne's eyes were wide.

'Yeah, well no . . . I mean, maybe. I don't, you know, believe in ghosts or anything, but there's definitely something strange going on.'

'Ooh!' Leanne hummed spooky music. 'Who's the ghost? Some headless horseman?'

Kelly shook her head, and told Leanne about the writing on her wall, and the discoveries in the cellar.

'Cool! No wonder you've started wearing forties clothes—that's Joan's ghost trying to influence you!'

'Ugh, don't say that—makes it sound like I'm going mad or

something.' Kelly turned and walked out of the shop, jostling past the Saturday crowds. Leanne's comment felt far too close to the truth for comfort.

Leanne caught her up. 'It was only a joke, Kells.'

Kelly spun round to face her friend. 'Well, it wasn't funny. Sometimes that house really spooks me. There's this cold draught on the stairs. Gives me prickles down the back of my neck sometimes. Like when you know someone's crept up behind you but you haven't turned to look yet.'

'Don't turn to look while you're on the stairs. You might fall down. Maybe that's what the ghost wants? Do you think it's an evil ghost?'

'It's not a blinking ghost, Leanne. A presence, maybe. Not an actual ghost. They don't exist. You die; that's the end.' She started walking away from the shops, into the park, heading towards the pier.

'So what's a presence if not a ghost? Doesn't matter what you call it, does it? I think it's kind of cool. Living in a haunted house, being the only one who can feel the presence of someone from the past. You should try to communicate with it—especially if it is this Joan. You could be like some kind of medium.' She put on a deep, wavering voice. 'Is there anybody there? Answer me two knocks for yes, three for no.'

Kelly shook her head violently. 'No! I don't want to communicate with it. I wish I couldn't feel it. I thought you'd be a bit more sympathetic. Leanne, you're supposed to be my best friend, but all you can do is take the piss. Well, you can just piss off, now. I've had enough of it.'

'Calm down! I'm only trying to lighten the tone.' Leanne held out her hands and shrugged.

'Yeah, well, don't,' said Kelly. 'I'm going home.'

'But we haven't bought anything yet!'

'I'm not in the mood. See you around, Leanne.' Kelly headed off towards the bus stop. Was her house haunted? She felt she was mad even considering it, but ever since they'd found the box of stuff in the cellar, she had definitely felt something there. And *something* was making her want to dress in forties clothes. Or was it just her imagination? What with the stuff they'd found in the cellar, reading *Rebecca*, and her history A level project about life during the war, perhaps she was just spending too much time thinking about the past. But it felt like more than that. More of a compulsion. She *had* to find out more about Joan and Jack. If she was to live comfortably in the house she had to know who they were and what happened to them. Lay them to rest.

There was only one way to find out. She needed to talk to Great-gran. She set off for home. Hopefully her mum would agree to take her to Great-gran's the next day. Perhaps she could bake a lemon drizzle cake for her. She'd wear her forties dress, to help jog the old lady's memory. And she'd take the photo of the three girls.

* * *

Gran was delighted with the cake when Ali arrived with Kelly at her care home, in the middle of the afternoon the following day. 'Splendid! Did you make it, Kelly, dear? Gosh, what a pretty frock you're wearing. I used to have something like that, a long, long time ago.'

'Thank you, I love this style,' said Kelly, as she leaned over to give her a kiss. Margaret was sitting in the residents' communal lounge, beside a patio door that looked out over the garden. Although it was late in the year there was still much colour. A large cotoneaster festooned with red berries brightened up the scene. They had the lounge to themselves today. It was a good care home, and Ali was pleased with her choice. Gran was happy there, and that was the most important thing.

'Really? I would have thought it too old-fashioned for young things like you. Must be fifty years ago or more that I had it. Longer. Probably just after the war, or maybe even earlier. I didn't get many new clothes during the war of course; none of us did, although sometimes you could pick up a second-hand dress or cardigan at one of the WVS sales. Betty used to make her own things of course, but I never did. I was no good at sewing. Shall we ask for some tea, and I'll cut this cake? It is teatime, isn't it?'

'Just about,' said Ali, grinning at Gran's fondness for sweet things. She never could wait to get her dentures sunk into cakes or cookies. 'I'll make the tea.' There was a small kitchen area just off the lounge, with a sink, kettle and mugs, and tea and milk in a fridge. She went over to make a pot, leaving Kelly telling Gran how she'd bought the blue dress on eBay. It wasn't an original; it was a forties replica made to appeal to retro-lovers. Like Kelly.

She brought three cups of tea over to Gran and Kelly, and then fetched plates and a knife to cut the cake.

'Lemon drizzle, my favourite,' Gran said, beaming. 'My sister used to make this. Her lemon drizzle cakes were the best I ever tasted.'

'Great-aunt Betty?' Ali frowned. 'I thought you'd always complained she lived on nothing but ready-meals and shop-bought cakes and puddings.'

'Well, er, yes, but I'm talking about the past. A long time ago, when you had to make your own cakes if you wanted any. Come on, Alison. Cut me a slice. Don't leave me here drooling like a puppy over it any longer.'

Ali laughed and cut a large slice for each of them. 'Gran, did you know there was a cellar in the house? We were ripping out the old downstairs toilet and found the door to it, going down under the stairs.'

'Oh yes, the cellar,' Gran said. 'In the war we used it as an air-raid shelter. I hated it. It was so dark and spooky down there, and you couldn't stand up straight. No electrics in it in those days, only an old paraffin lantern Father used to take down. I had my torch, but it didn't always have working batteries in it. Oh, I did hate air raids. You never knew how long you'd have to stay down there. Of course we were better off here than the poor people in London. They had it night after night for months, with no let-up. I don't think I could have put up with that, but of course, they had no choice.'

'It must have been horrible,' Ali said.

'It was.' Gran nodded.

'There's something we wanted to ask you about, Great-gran,' said Kelly. 'Mum found something down there. Look.' She pulled the photograph of the three girls out from her shoulder bag. 'That's you, isn't it, and that's Betty, but who's the third girl, the younger one?'

Gran took the photo, put her glasses that hung from a chain around her neck onto her nose, and peered at it for a moment. Then she laid it down in her lap and sighed. 'Oh, she was such a pretty girl. The prettiest of the three of us. Such a shame.'

'Who was she, Gran?' asked Ali, gently. She could see tears brimming in the old lady's eyes. Whoever the girl was, she'd been important to Gran, that was obvious.

Gran ignored the question and looked at Kelly. 'Kelly, dear, in that dress you look so much like her, you know. When you walked in here today it was almost as though she'd come back to us. After all these years. Oh, you must ignore me. Silly, rambling old lady that I am.' She smiled and passed the photo to Ali. 'Now, Alison, cut me more of that cake. I'm not having just the one slice, you know.'

'Please, Gran, can't you tell us who the girl in the picture is?' said Ali. 'Was she a friend of yours, perhaps, someone you were at school with? She's in the same uniform as you and Betty.'

'It's Joan, isn't it, Great-gran?'

Margaret stared at Kelly. 'Where did you hear that name?'

Kelly stared back. 'I know it's her.'

Gran went white, her hand shaking. Ali quickly took the cup of tea out of her hand and put it down. 'Kelly, shh, you're upsetting her.'

'Poor, dear Joanie.' She leaned back in her chair, her gaze still firmly directed at Kelly. 'I've not heard that name for such a long time.'

'Who was she?' Ali asked again.

'She—she was the youngest of us. Dear, beloved little Joanie.' Gran wiped away a tear.

'The youngest of you?' repeated Ali. She was confused. Or perhaps it was Gran who was confused?

'There were three of us,' Gran went on. 'Betty, Joanie and me. Betty was too stuck up to have much to do with us. Father's favourite, she was, and she knew it. But Joanie and I had each other. We were sisters, but we were best friends as well.' Gran looked at Kelly. 'You look so much like her. Same colour hair and eyes, and your pretty face, just like hers. And—oh! Round your neck—that's Joanie's locket. Where did you find that?'

'It was in the cellar, in a box along with the photo,' Ali said.

Gran shook her head sadly. 'She was such a good person. The dog, she went next door for the dog when no one else would. She could have died then but she saved the dog. The children—they loved her. The little tots all gathered around her for stories and she was the only one who would get on the floor and play with them properly, for hours on end. Such a lively girl, too. The only one of us who'd stand up to our father, even when he was at his most fierce. He was a bully, of course, but she wouldn't put up with it, even if she did get punished for it. Oh, dear Joanie. How I miss her still, after all these long years!' Tears ran down her face, and she fumbled with the sleeve of her jumper, pulling out a tissue she'd tucked up there.

Ali took hold of Gran's hand, and stroked her paper-thin skin. 'So, let me get this straight; you had another sister? You and Betty, another sister, this Joanie?'

'Yes, that's right. Little Joanie. Her birthday was January the first and she was two years younger than me. She was a dear thing. We were so close, right from when she was very little and I mended her teddy's arm. She looked up to me then. She thought I could mend everything that went wrong for her. I wish I could've.' She dabbed at her eyes with the sodden tissue.

'Why have you never mentioned her before?' asked Ali.

'My father said we were never to speak of her again. And Betty did whatever he said. She would get cross if I mentioned Joanie's name, even when Father wasn't there, even after he was dead and gone. So I stopped talking about her. I never forgot her, though. Not for a minute. I've thought of her every day.'

'What happened to her?'

Gran sniffed and shook her head. 'I don't want to talk about that. Not today. I want to remember her how she was, when we all lived together, and when she was young and lively and happy. She was so *very* happy, after she met her young man.'

'Jack,' said Kelly.

'Yes, that was his name. I don't know how you knew it,' said Gran, with a suspicious look at Kelly.

Ali told her about the writing on Kelly's bedroom wall.

'Of course. That room was Joanie's. Funny that you should put Kelly in the same room Joanie had. Father didn't approve of Jack, of course. Well, he never approved of anything poor Joanie did. She might have won a Nobel Prize and he'd not have approved. She couldn't do anything right. He couldn't see the good in her—the way she rescued that dog when the bomb fell so close, the way she was with the children, and all the baking she did. Mother never made cakes; it was always Joanie. She was a whiz at it. Even with all the limitations from rationing, she could turn out the best cakes and biscuits you ever tasted. Her lemon drizzle—oh I remember to this day how wonderful it was. As good as this one. Kelly, you're so like her. I'd never noticed before but with your hair like that, and in that dress, you're the spit of her. Funny how that happens.' She shook her head and lapsed into silence.

Kelly smiled. 'Tell us more about Joanie. She sounds a lovely person.'

'She was. A real darling girl. She worked with little children. The WVS set up a playgroup, so the mothers could queue in the shops without having to worry about their little ones, and Joanie ended up running it. This was in the last year or so of the war. She was too young to have a job before then. Father didn't like it, of course. He thought the children were too common for her to mix with. Some of them didn't have decent, clean clothes. We collected unwanted clothing and gave it to any families in real need. I used to help with sorting out the donations. These days it's all throwaway fashion, isn't it? Shocking, really, when you think of it.' Gran stopped talking and gazed into space. She suddenly looked worn out, and her eyes began to close. 'I'm sorry, Alison, remembering Joanie has quite tired me out. I feel ready for a little nap now.'

Ali nodded. 'We'd probably better go, then. We'll leave the rest of the cake with you. Perhaps you can have some more tomorrow for your tea.'

'They never wanted her mentioned again. Poor Joanie . . .' Gran's eyes had closed, and her voice trailed away.

Ali looked at Kelly. 'You'll have to ask her some more next time. Come on, let's leave her in peace.'

They kissed her gently goodbye, and went out to the car.

* * *

'So, Mum, what do you think happened to Joan? Why did Great-gran's father never let them speak of her again?' Kelly fiddled with the locket as she spoke. 'I knew this was hers, you know. I just knew it.'

'I've no idea. There must have been some sort of scandal. Gran has always said her father was very strict, with Victorian morals. She said he absolutely ruled the household and wouldn't allow anyone to contradict him. Poor Joan must have done something to upset him badly. Though once they were adults, Gran could

69

have ignored her father and stayed in touch with her sister. Her father needn't have known.' Ali opened the car and got in. It was strange. If Gran had been so close to her little sister, why hadn't she stayed in touch with her?

Kelly got in and slammed the car door. 'You're assuming, Mum, that Joan lived. I don't think she did. I think she died young.'

Chapter Eight

January 1944

Joan shook herself free of her father's grip as soon as they were in the house. What had she done that was so bad? Just walked a short way arm in arm with a good, decent boy who had only wanted to see her safely home. Why did Father have to be so draconian? She was seventeen, for goodness' sake. Old enough to look after herself. Her mother had been seventeen when she married Father.

'When you've taken your coat off and changed your shoes I want to see you in my study.' Father wagged his finger at her and left her standing dazed in the hallway.

So she was going to get a lecture. She shrugged herself out of her coat and hung it up in the under-stairs cupboard. Well, she would have to grin and bear it. She knew her father's ways. He would raise his voice enough so that the whole household could hear him. He would threaten to take a belt to her but he never did. All his snobbery and bigotries would come out. And if she so much as said a single word in defence, the whole thing would take twice as long, at twice the volume.

She kicked off her shoes, found her slippers, took a deep breath and knocked on the study door. Mags, who'd seen them come in and was keeping out of the way in the kitchen, grimaced at her and pointed upstairs. Yes, she would go and tell Mags all about it. Whenever either of them got into trouble with Father they always used each other as a sounding board afterwards.

'Come in.' Father's voice sounded particularly stern. Joan turned the doorknob and stepped inside, keeping her head slightly bowed. She stood beside his desk with her hands neatly clasped in front of her. There. Nothing he could complain about regarding her demeanour.

'Who was that boy you were with?'

'Father, his name is Jack McBride.'

'And where did you meet him?'

Time for the lies, or at least economical truths, to start. If Father found out she'd gone to the dance she'd be in even bigger trouble. 'At the WVS. He came in with a message for someone.' It was almost true. She'd met him today at the WVS, and he was delivering a message, albeit one for her.

'And then?'

'We chatted for a short while. He invited me out for a cup of tea when my shift ended.' Best to be truthful about this part.

'And you agreed? You'd only met him for five minutes and you went out with him?' Father's voice was increasing in volume. Soon he would stand, thump his desk, and then specks of spit would appear in the corners of his mouth. When he sat down again she would know the shouting was almost at an end.

'I liked him. I'm sorry, Father. I know it was wrong.' Now she really was lying.

'Anything could have happened to you! Going out alone with a boy like that? You are so young and naive, Joan. You have no idea what could have happened.' Joan thought back to the Canadian airman, Freddie. She had far too good an idea of what could happen when you made a poor judgement call about a man. But she knew she was right about Jack. He had proved himself, beyond any doubt.

'I'm sorry, Father,' she repeated.

He stood up. The desk-thumping couldn't be far off now. 'And by the look of that boy, he's clearly working class. He's not even had the guts to join up. We're better than that, young lady! Better, I tell you.' He struck the desk each time he said 'better'. A pot of paperclips jumped into the air and spilt its contents over the desk and floor. Joan focused on the patterns they'd made. One little jumble of clips had fallen vaguely into the shape of a Spitfire.

'And do you have anything else to say in your defence, young lady?'

Oh, she had plenty that she could say. But better to meekly shake her head, keep her eyes downcast, and let his anger abate. It worked. He sat down.

'I forbid you to see him again. If you do, I shall take my belt to you. You are not too old for a whipping, child.'

'Yes, Father.' If he ever did that she would run away from home, and he would never see her again.

'Right. Well. Go up to your room and consider what I have said. I shall see you at dinnertime and not before.'

'Yes, Father. Thank you, Father.' She gave a small nod. He'd probably prefer her to curtsey, he was that old-fashioned. She backed out of the room and closed the door as softly as she could, then heaved a sigh of relief. It was over.

Mags was waiting in Joan's bedroom upstairs. 'Who was the boy you were seen with, Joanie? Was it that boy from the dance, the Canadian?'

'No! No, not him at all.' Joan shuddered. She shook her head and sat on the bed beside her sister, picking up her old teddy to cuddle. 'Mags, I need to tell you about what happened at the dance, and how I met Jack, the boy Father saw me with in town today.'

Mags's eyes lit up, but her tone was sympathetic as she took Joan's hands. 'Go on, then. Spill the beans.'

Joan told her everything—how her head had been turned by the handsome Freddie, how he'd plied her with gin and then led

73

her to the backstage area, how he'd forced himself on her but Jack had arrived in the nick of time and stopped him. How she'd felt such a fool allowing it to happen.

'I saw the fight—the Canadian, Freddie, and that boy with spectacles. Was he this Jack, then?' Mags's eyes were wide as the story progressed, though she squeezed Joan's hand tightly in support.

'Yes, that was him. And he got into the fight to defend me. Oh, Mags, his poor face, his lip was split and his glasses all broken.'

'So what happened when you went home?'

Joan told her then how Jack had walked her home, and how they'd sat and looked at the moonlight. Then she told how he'd come to the WVS and taken her out to tea, and how Father had caught sight of her and dragged her away.

Mags leaned back against the headboard of the bed and regarded Joan, a smile playing about the corners of her mouth. 'Joanie, darling, I do believe you're in love.'

In love? Was she? Joan considered this carefully. She'd never been in love before, and wasn't sure what it was supposed to feel like. But certainly, just thinking of Jack made her tummy feel as though it was full of fairies dancing, and when she remembered how it felt to snuggle up next to him on the cold promenade bench in the moonlight she couldn't help but smile to herself. And imagining a future in which she never saw him again was, she realised, totally unbearable. 'Oh, Mags. Yes, I think I am. But I am forbidden to ever see him again.'

'Pah. You know what Father's like. He gets all heated about something but he'll forget what it was all about in a day or so. As long as you take care that he never sees you with Jack again, you'll be all right. You were daft going to Lyons—it's far too near Father's offices. Keep away from that part of town, or wear a headscarf. And don't hold hands in public. If you'd been just walking alongside him, Father would not have realised there was anything in it.'

Joan smiled at her sister. Mags had never walked out with a boy, as far as she knew, but she was so much wiser than Joan. This was all good advice. Perhaps, if she followed it and was super careful, she would be able to keep seeing Jack.

'What was all the shouting about?' Elizabeth entered the room, without so much as a tap on the door. 'I heard Father giving a lecture. Who to? What was it about?' She came in and sat on the bed beside Joan. 'Was it to you, Joan? It usually is.'

Joan opened her mouth to speak, but Mags got there first. 'I suppose you want all the juicy details, Betty. Well, you shan't have them. It's nothing to do with you, so you can keep your nose out of it.'

Elizabeth scowled. 'You two are always ganging up on me. It's not fair. I've a good mind to tell Father.'

'What, that we won't tell you why he was shouting? I don't suppose that would go down too well with him, would it?' Mags laughed, and Joan tried to suppress her giggles. She was glad of Mags's support. She didn't want Elizabeth knowing all the details, but sometimes it was hard to stand up to her eldest sister. Betty was far too much like Father, and used her seniority to boss Joan around at times.

'Well, I'll find out one way or another,' said Elizabeth, as she flounced out of the room. Mags jumped up to close the door after her, and then fell onto the bed giggling. Joan joined in, enjoying the feeling of relief after all the unpleasantness. All was not lost. She could count on Mags to help her find a way to see Jack again. She was in love. Oh, what a feeling!

* * *

During dinner Joan kept her head down and said not a word. Father was complaining about their neighbour's dog, who'd apparently got through a loose fence panel at the bottom of the garden, and had dug up some onions. 'Darned nuisance. That fence panel is Mrs Johnson's responsibility. She should get it fixed and keep her dog under control. I'd have it shot if I could.'

Joan fought hard to stop herself saying anything. She was fond of Mrs Johnson's little terrier, Kimmy.

After dinner Father summoned the family into the sitting room for the evening news bulletin, followed by light entertainment programmes on the wireless. It was a family tradition for evenings when they were all at home. They listened to the solemn newsreader recounting news of a huge bombing raid over Berlin.

Mother looked terrified. 'Oh my goodness, what if the Germans retaliate by bombing us here next?' She looked at Father for reassurance.

He scoffed. 'This town is hardly an important target. It's just a small seaside town, of no military importance.'

'We've been a target for plenty of bombing raids, Father. What about that terrible night last May, when the Metropole Hotel was bombed?' Joan couldn't help herself. They may not have been hit as hard as other towns on the south coast but they certainly had not escaped unscathed, and the air-raid sirens still went off occasionally, sending them scurrying to their cellar to take shelter.

'I'm aware of the bomb damage we've had, thank you very much, Joan. I lost a good clerk at work when the cinema was hit. But I believe we are unlikely to be targeted again, for which we should consider ourselves fortunate.'

'Of course, and we do. Don't we, girls?' said Mother. They all nodded, as she went on. 'I must admit I am fed up with the blackout. I wish we could have the streetlamps back on. And wouldn't it be wonderful if the war ended by the summer, and that awful mangled metal was removed from the sea so we could go bathing again.'

'The war will not end by the summer. We've a long way to go yet. You mark my words.'

'Yes, I'm sure you're right, Father, but we can dream of peacetime, can't we?' said Joan. Father glared at her. Time perhaps for her to be quiet again, for fear of incurring his anger once more. Mags, sitting beside her on the sofa, clearly thought so too, for she surreptitiously pinched Joan's inner arm.

'Dreaming is a waste of time. Isn't that so, Father? We should act rather than dream,' said Elizabeth, looking pleased with herself for repeating one of Father's favourite sayings.

'Absolutely. Thank goodness *one* of my daughters has grown up with a modicum of sense. Now then, let's have some hush. It's time for the Tommy Handley programme. We could all do with being cheered up a little.'

The wireless stayed on for another hour, but Joan switched off. She allowed her thoughts to return to Jack, the warmth of his hand in hers, the dimple that appeared in his left cheek when he smiled his lopsided smile at her, the floppy brown fringe falling over his glasses, which he'd mended with sticky tape. His broad shoulders and loping gait. His wishes for a land of peace, somewhere over the sea, which you would reach if you could only follow the moonlight avenue.

The next day, Joan was working at the WVS. Thankfully Father had been pleased by the news of her new job running the play-group. He'd sniffed a little bit when she described herself as 'a kind of nursemaid' but she'd quickly backtracked and rephrased her job as 'managing the children's drop-in centre' and he seemed happy with that. He didn't need to know the job involved getting down on the floor and playing train sets and tea parties with toddlers. If he had the impression she sat at a desk and wrote reports on children under her care, then so be it.

Mags laughed when she told her this. 'You're learning how to handle him, at last! It makes for an easier life. I suppose he can't help being prejudiced. He's from a different generation, and so old-fashioned in his thinking. We can't ever change him, you know, and it's better not to try.' She was right, of course, but Joan couldn't help but imagine an ideal world in which her father treated everyone on their merits, regardless of their gender or class.

At the WVS Mrs Atkins handed her a letter, with a wink and a smile. 'Your young man was here first thing, and left this for you. He's very polite. I rather like him.'

Joan tucked the letter into her bag to open when she had a tea break and a few moments away from the children. It was a brief note, apologising for having got her into trouble with her father, and asking if she could meet him on her day off. He would wait, the note said, on the bench on the promenade where they'd sat before, from ten o'clock. He hoped she would be able to come out, and he very much looked forward to seeing her again.

Joan's heart soared as she read the note. He wanted to see her again! And on her day off, which was in two days' time. That would give them a good number of hours together. She began plotting what her excuse would be to slip away that day. Mags might have some ideas. She would ask her this evening.

* * *

Over breakfast on her day off, with the whole family sitting around the table, Mags suddenly sighed loudly. 'Oh, if only I didn't have to go to work today. I've heard that Flanagan's has got some Seville oranges in stock!'

On cue, Joan spoke up. 'Well, it's my day off. Why don't I go and see if I can get some?'

Father frowned. 'That shop is miles away. It'll take you hours.'

'I can get a bus there. I've nothing else to do today. I'll help Mother with some housework first, then go over and queue for the oranges. If all works out, we'll be making marmalade by the time you come home from work. I know how much you like home-made marmalade.'

'Well, I suppose if you help your mother first, you may go. Do we have enough sugar?'

Mother smiled. 'Yes, we've been very frugal with our rations.

78

I think we can spare enough. It would be marvellous to be able to make some marmalade again.'

Joan grinned at Mags. What a wonderful sister she was! Mags had been over to Flanagan's the day before, taking a long lunch-break from work, following up on the rumour. She'd queued half an hour for the oranges, which were now safely stowed beneath her bed. Joan would sneak them out under her coat, carry them around with her, and then return home triumphantly in the afternoon with tales of queues snaking around the block.

Jack was waiting on the promenade just as he said he would be. His eyes lit up when Joan arrived, and her own tummy-fairies began a little dance of joy. She reached up and kissed his cheek, then stepped back blushing. It had just felt such a natural thing to do. He was blushing too, and she giggled.

'It's so good to see you again, Joan,' he said. 'But why have you brought a bag of oranges?'

She explained her cover story, and he grinned. 'I hope you don't get into trouble again. I'd hate that. I couldn't bear it the other day, when your father dragged you away, knowing I was the cause of it.' He gazed at her with worried eyes. 'He didn't hurt you, did he?'

'No, not at all. He shouted a bit, but it was soon over. Don't worry. I know how to handle him and I won't let him stop me from seeing you, Jack. *Nothing* will stop me.'

Jack smiled, sadly she thought. 'Come on, let's walk,' he said. 'I thought we could walk the length of the promenade and loop round and come back along the riverside.'

'Sounds perfect,' she replied, linking her arm through his and relishing his warmth. 'We can't go over the open ground at the end of the prom though. Isn't it still closed to the public?'

'Yes, they've mined it, sadly. But we can go to the end of the promenade and then cut inland. It's a shame. The top of the hill was always one of my favourite places. I love the way you have a view in every direction from up there. It's like you're on top of the world.'

79

Joan laughed. 'I love it too. My sisters and I used to ride our bikes there in the summer. But did you ever notice how it was always windy on the top? There might be no wind at all at the foot of the hill or on the beach, but it would be blowing a gale on the top. We thought it had its own magic.'

'I think it does. It's a very ancient place. In the Iron Age it was home to a fort.'

'So much history, all around us.'

'Yes, and history being written over in France as we speak. Makes you feel small and insignificant, doesn't it?'

She looked up at him. Jack, a small and insignificant person? No. His was the biggest heart she had ever come across. And in her life, he was fast becoming the most significant person. But it seemed too presumptuous to try to put these thoughts into words. This was, after all, only the third time they had met.

They walked arm in arm eastwards along the prom to the end, with Jack insisting on carrying the bulky oranges, then climbed the small flight of steps up to street level. From here they cut inland across fields towards the river, where they found a bench and rested for a while. A pair of swans were gracefully paddling around near the riverbank, occasionally poking in the weeds in search of food.

'I wish we had something we could feed them,' Joan said. 'We often used to bring stale bread here for the birds.'

Jack laughed. 'I bet there's no such thing as stale bread in your house any more. There certainly isn't in my aunt's house, what with the rationing.'

'No, nothing gets left over now. But I do shake the tablecloth outside so the birds can have any crumbs.'

'That's sweet of you.'

Joan turned to look at Jack. He was biting his lip, as though there was something more he wanted to say. As she watched him, he shook his head as if to clear it of unwelcome thoughts, then took her hand in both of his.

'Joan, I do wish I'd met you earlier. Or later, when we've won the war and we're in peacetime again. It's too bad we had to meet right now.'

'What do you mean? I'm glad I've met you. I love being with you, Jack.' Why was he unhappy to know her? She'd thought he liked her as much as she liked him. She hoped she hadn't got it all wrong.

'Oh, Joan, I love being with you, too. More than you can know. But the thing is, it can't last.'

He had met someone else. It must be that. Joan felt her heart plummet. She withdrew her hand from his. 'Jack, you owe me nothing. If you want to stop seeing me, that's all right. I shan't mind.'

He snatched her hand back again and pulled it to his lips to kiss. 'Joan, it's not that at all. The thing is, I've done it. I've signed up, I've taken the King's shilling, and I'm to leave for my basic training in three days. I'll be home again as soon as I get a pass out, probably after a couple of months, but you won't want to wait for me, will you? A beautiful girl like you, you won't want to wait for someone like me.'

'Oh, Jack! Of course I'll wait for you! And I'll write to you, every day if you like. Two months—that's nothing. You'll be home in no time. Before the end of April. You'll be back again in springtime.'

Jack's face lit up. Joan smiled. He'd seriously believed she wouldn't want to wait for him! She would miss him, but the weeks would pass in a flash and then they would be together again. Joan didn't let herself think beyond then—to the time when Jack would have finished training and would be sent to the war. It was enough—they had a few days now, and then the promise of a few more days together in a little while. Mags had spoken about how in wartime you had to just live in the moment for you did not know what would happen next. For the first time, Joan felt she was beginning to understand what that really meant.

'You'll write? Really? Joan, that would be marvellous! And may I write to you? Would it cause a problem with your father?'

She pulled a face. 'He would never allow it. But I'll think of some way you can write to me.' She thought for a moment. 'I wonder if Mrs Atkins at the WVS would allow the letters to be sent via her. She likes you. I'll ask her.'

Jack smiled at her, then put his arm around her shoulders and pulled her close to him. She relished the feeling of his strength and warmth beneath his tweed coat, and laid her head against his shoulder. He leaned his head onto hers. She wondered if he might kiss her, but he didn't, and they sat like that until they both began to feel cold.

Chapter Nine

October 2014

'Let's get inside and make some coffee,' Ali said, as they got out of the car after returning from the visit to Great-gran. Kelly nodded, her thoughts still on what Great-gran had said about Joanie. She'd guessed the third girl in the photo was Joan, and that she'd been Great-gran's sister. She couldn't say how she knew this, but she just knew. There was something about this house. She'd felt it ever since she moved in, and even more so after they'd found the writing on her wall and the box in the cellar. She couldn't say anything to Mum or anyone else—they'd think she was mad—but she felt as though there was a presence in the house. Like a ghost, or a spirit. It was Joan, of course. Hanging around in the house where she'd grown up. Why would she do that? Kelly felt as though she couldn't rest until she found out the full story.

'Ladies, how are you?' Jason Bergmann's head appeared over the fence that divided his house from theirs. He had a broom in his hand, and had been sweeping autumn leaves into a pile. 'It's a glorious day. I'm just trying to get this garden in a fit state to face the winter. I must say, your pampas grass looks amazing at this time of year.'

'Yes, it is lovely,' said Ali. 'We were just going to make some coffee. Do you want to come and join us?'

'Thanks, I'd love to. Give me five minutes to get these leaves cleared up, and I'll be round.'

Kelly smiled at him. He was a good neighbour to have. She wondered if her mum possibly fancied him a little. He was her type—all twinkly eyes and smooth manners. Unlike her dad who was a little rougher round the edges. 'See you in a minute, then,' she called to him, as she followed Ali inside.

As soon as she stepped into the hallway she felt the familiar prickly sensation that Joan's presence was around. Looking down at herself she remembered she was in one of her retro 1940s frocks. She wondered why she bought them—it was as though Joan influenced her taste in clothes. 'Just nipping upstairs to change,' she said. Sometimes she felt better if she was in her own stuff.

By the time she came back downstairs, in jeans and hoodie, Jason was sitting at the kitchen table drinking his coffee. 'Hi again, Kelly,' he said. 'Oh, you've changed. I was going to say, I love that retro look you wear. Really suits you.'

Kelly flashed him a brief smile at the compliment.

'Kelly's very interested in the 1940s,' Ali said to Jason.

'Yeah, well, between doing A level history where we're doing stuff about the war, and trying to find out more about my great-great-aunt who used to live here, sometimes it feels like the forties are all around me. Can't get away from it.' Kelly smiled wryly. The forties weren't just all around her, but in her head too. Sometimes it felt as though she was going mad.

'Your great-great-aunt?' said Jason. He raised his eyebrows. 'Do you mean Betty Perkins? You were related to her?'

Kelly opened her mouth to answer, but her mother got in there first.

'Betty Perkins was my great-aunt,' Ali said. 'She left the house to me in her will.'

'Wow. That's just . . . well.' He looked as though he was about to say something else, then shook his head briefly as though he'd thought better of it. 'You must have been close to her, Ali.'

'Not at all, really, but she had no one else to leave it to, I suppose. I must admit, it's a fabulous place to live.'

Kelly rolled her eyes. Might be nice for the rest of them, but they weren't plagued by the other great-great-aunt's presence. Jason noticed her expression and laughed. 'Hey, I've just remembered, I found something you might like, Kelly. I was sorting through Mum's old costume jewellery, and there was a little brooch, kind of forties style I'd guess. Would you like it? It'd go with your retro stuff. I thought of you when I found it, but forgot to bring it round.'

'Yes, I'd love to see it,' Kelly replied. 'But I can't possibly take it from you.'

'Yes you can. It's not worth anything, and if you don't want it, I'll just give it to a charity shop or something. But I'd like you to have it.' He reached into his pocket and pulled out his front door key. 'Here, why don't you pop round and get it now. It's on the sideboard in the hallway; you can't miss it.'

She took the key from him, intrigued to see the brooch, and went next door. Jason's house was different from all the others on the street. It was a chalet-style house, red brick with dormer windows. The exterior of the upper floor was tile-hung. Every other house in the street was more like theirs, rendered and painted, with bay windows. As she let herself in, she vaguely wondered why Jason's house was so different. It was obviously much more recent than the others.

The brooch was on the hall table as he'd said, a pretty piece made of marcasite, in the shape of a butterfly. One or two stones were missing but they barely showed. It would look lovely pinned at the neck of her blue forties dress, she thought.

Kelly had never been in Jason's house before. She looked around, at the peach-coloured carpet and floral wallpaper. Not the kind of decor you'd expect from a single man. She remembered he'd inherited it from his mother. That made more sense.

Something Great-gran had said about Joan, and her saving a dog from next door when a bomb fell came back to her. That must be it—this must be where the bomb had fallen. Great-gran had said it was close. That would explain why Jason's house was a more recent style than the other houses in the street—it must have been built on a bomb site. She wondered whether Joan and her family had been hiding in their cellar when the bomb fell. How terrifying that must have been! And according to Great-gran, Joan had rescued a dog from the bombed house. She must have been so brave. Kelly felt a surge of respect for her newly discovered great-great-aunt.

* * *

Later that evening, Ali was sitting with Pete in the living room, finishing a bottle of wine. The kids were both upstairs in their rooms. Ali told Pete what Gran had told her and Kelly that afternoon.

'So the third girl in the photo is your gran's sister?' said Pete. 'Wow. Why had she never mentioned her before? And why do you think this Joan's stuff was all hidden away in the cellar? There's nothing down there for either your gran or Betty. Just Joan's things.'

'I don't know,' Ali replied. 'It's all a bit of a mystery. We couldn't stay and ask Gran too much about it—it was obviously upsetting and tiring for her to be asked about Joan after all these years. But we do need to find out. Kelly's desperate to know more about what happened. She seems to be more and more obsessed with the war years and especially this Joan.'

'She'll forget it all soon enough and move on to a new obsession. You know how teenagers are.' Pete picked up the bottle and topped up both their glasses. 'It wasn't all that long ago when she refused to wear anything but Barbie pink and insisted when she grew up she was going to be a fashion model. It's a phase and it'll pass.'

'I hope so. I'm beginning to find it a little creepy, though, when she dresses up in her forties gear with her hair pinned in curls. I prefer her when she's being a twenty-first-century teen. Mind you, it's all good input to her A level courses I suppose.' Ali took a sip of her wine. 'Can't believe the weekend's over already and I'm back at work tomorrow.'

'Poor you,' Pete said, planting a kiss on her head. 'I'll be working hard on the DIY as usual. Every day's a work day for me.'

'Talking of work,' Ali said quietly, 'how's your job-hunting going? You've not said much about it recently.'

'It's on hold, for the moment, love. You know that. I'm too busy doing up this house.'

'But—we're running out of money, Pete! Your redundancy pay has pretty much all gone, and my salary can only just cover our regular living expenses. Unless you start bringing in some money soon, we'll be broke.'

'We're fine. I'll get this house finished and then look in earnest for a new job. I can't do both things at the same time.'

Ali bit her tongue. She had to work full time and do all the shopping and cooking and general chores around the house. She could manage more than one thing at once. Surely Pete could find time to do a few application forms and attend some interviews in between working on the house?

'What worries me, Pete, is that we won't be able to afford to finish the house. We'll have to live in it half completed. So you'd be better off looking for a job so we can afford to finish it.'

'Ali, how on earth do you think I could finish doing up the house if I had a full-time job? Like I said, I can only do one thing at once. We could mortgage the house—that would give us some money to finish the work.'

'And how do you think we'd be able to afford the mortgage

repayments? My salary barely covers our day-to-day expenses, as you know. I can't do any more hours than I already do. If you got a job, we'd just have to accept that the renovations will take a lot longer to finish. I'm beginning to wonder if we did the right thing moving in here. The way we're going, I'm scared we might have to sell the house and buy ourselves somewhere cheaper after all.'

Pete stood up and turned to face her. 'Don't be ridiculous. This is our home now. It'll be a struggle for a while—we knew that when we moved in. We'll need to be careful with our finances, but once the house is complete, I'll find a job. Then you'll be glad we stuck it out here. We'll have a gorgeous house in a great location, and plenty of money to enjoy life. Stop fretting about it. It'll be fine.'

She shook her head. 'I can't help fretting, as you put it. I hate having to scrimp and save. I'd rather work fewer hours myself, and have more time to spend with Gran and the kids.'

'Won't be for long. Next year, love, it'll all be done, and I'll be back in work. You'll see.' Pete sat down again and put his arm around her shoulders, giving her a reassuring squeeze. 'Hang on in there.'

Hang on in there, he said. All very well for him to say that, but what with the money worries and the stress of living in a building site, Ali was finding life hard at present. She snuggled up to him. 'I hope you're right, love. I really do.'

Chapter Ten

February 1944

'When will your young man be here to fetch you?' asked Mrs Atkins, with a wink.

Joan blushed. 'He said he'd come at three o'clock. Are you sure it's all right for me to leave early today?'

'Of course it is, love. It's a special day, as it's the last time you'll be able to see him for a while. I do believe you have to grasp every opportunity for happiness that comes your way. One never knows quite what is around the corner.' Mrs Atkins stared off into the middle distance, then shook her head and turned back to Joan. 'And it's perfectly all right if he sends his letters to you via me. I can bring them to you here. No need for your father to know anything about it.'

'I can't thank you enough, Mrs Atkins. You've been very kind to us.'

'Not at all. It's hard, being young and in love when there's a war on. I'll do anything I can to make things easier for you.'

There was a shimmer of unshed tears in her eyes. Joan suddenly felt a rush of love and gratitude towards the older woman, and flung her arms around her. It was so good to have someone on their side, who understood. Mrs Atkins had never said anything, but Joan knew from WVS gossip that she'd lost her husband in the Great War, and had never married again.

'Now, now, that's enough. Be off with you, back to your work. You're leaving early but that doesn't mean you can shirk your duties this afternoon. You've three little ones all wanting their noses wiped by the looks of things.' Mrs Atkins unwound Joan's arms from her neck and pushed her away gently.

There were two hours to go until Jack was due to arrive. The afternoon dragged—Joan could have sworn the hands on the clock were not moving, but it matched her watch, and she supposed it was unlikely that both had stopped at exactly the same time. She took her mind off things by getting down on the floor with the toddlers and inventing a riotous imaginative game involving all the dolls and teddies from the toy box.

Finally the clock creaked its way to three o'clock, and Mrs Atkins came to take over running the playgroup for the last hour. 'I do believe your young man is already waiting outside,' she told Joan. 'And give him this slip of paper—that's my address for the letters.'

Joan kissed her, fetched her coat and ran outside. Jack was indeed already waiting on the steps of the church hall. When she saw him, she felt suddenly shy. Was he really her 'young man' as Mrs Atkins had said? It seemed so grown-up to have a boyfriend. She still felt so young, so inexperienced in these things. She really wasn't sure how she was supposed to behave.

'Hello, you,' Jack said, taking her hand. 'My aunt has invited you to tea today. We could catch the bus, or walk if you prefer?'

'Oh, let's walk,' said Joan. It wasn't raining and she felt she would have Jack more to herself walking than if they were sitting on a bus.

He smiled at her. 'I hoped you'd say that. We can cut through the parks. Come on.'

* * *

The time and miles passed quickly though Joan was alert to everything, trying to savour every moment with Jack. She couldn't bear to think about the weeks ahead, when he would be away training to be a soldier.

All too soon they arrived at a pleasant-looking Edwardian semi-detached house, with a neat front garden and net curtains at the windows. A couple of houses opposite showed evidence of bomb damage.

'They were hit last year,' Jack said, nodding at them. 'Thankfully no one was hurt, as the occupants were all out at the pub that evening, celebrating someone's birthday.'

'That was lucky.'

'Well, here we are.' Jack took out his key, opened the door and ushered her into a tidy hallway, with gleaming floor tiles and polished wood panels on the lower half of the walls. 'Aunt Marion! We're home!'

A tall, neat-looking woman came out into the hallway, kissed Jack and held out her hand to Joan. 'You must be Joan. Welcome! I've heard a lot about you, all good, and I've been longing to meet you. Please, go inside and take a seat. I'll bring the tea things in shortly.'

'Thank you, it's lovely to meet you too, Mrs Simmons.'

'Call me Marion, please. Or Aunt Marion if you prefer. Right then, give me five minutes in the kitchen and I'll join you.'

'May I help you at all, Marion?'

'No, dear. You sit down with Jack and make the most of him. I can't believe he's going away . . .' Marion bit her lip, and turned abruptly away, heading down the hall to where Joan supposed the kitchen must be. She followed Jack into the front sitting room.

'Sorry about that. Poor Aunt Marion. She didn't want me to sign up. I could have got a college place studying engineering and made myself exempt from the call-up but I didn't want to. I'm all she has, and she's terrified I'll get myself shot or blown up.'

'I don't blame her. I'm terrified of that, too.'

Jack took her hands in his, and gazed into her eyes. 'Don't be scared. I'll keep myself safe, and I'll come back to you, I promise. And for now, let's not think ahead. Let's just live for the moment. All right? Promise me you won't worry about me while I'm away? I don't want to be worrying about you worrying about me, if you see what I mean.'

She laughed. 'No, and I wouldn't want to be worrying about you worrying about me worrying about you. So we won't either of us worry about the other one, then.'

'It's a deal!'

'What's a deal?' asked Marion, coming in pushing a tea trolley laden with scones and cakes.

'We've agreed we're not going to worry about each other while I'm away,' Jack explained. 'Gosh, look at all that food!'

'Well, it's your last night here, so I've splashed out with the ration book. I'll be dining off worms and grit for the rest of the week but never mind. Nothing but the best for my favourite nephew.'

Jack stood and gave her a hug. 'Your only nephew, but I'll accept the accolade. Now then, shall I pour?'

'Thanks, love.' Aunt Marion smiled at him and patted his shoulder. Joan felt a pang of jealousy. How wonderful it must be to have a parent or guardian who really cared about you and was proud of you. Her father was a bully who only cared about his favourite, Elizabeth, and her mother was weak and spineless and seemed only to want to get through life without making her husband cross. Jack may not have his parents around but Aunt Marion had clearly more than made up for his loss. Joan warmed to her instantly.

Teatime passed pleasantly, and after Joan had helped wash up, Marion announced she needed to go out on an errand. She slipped on her coat, kissed Joan and left, calling after her that she'd be at least an hour.

'Bless her, she's giving us a bit of time alone,' Jack said. 'You don't mind, do you, being alone in the house with me? I wouldn't . . . well . . . you know. Take advantage or anything.'

'Of course you wouldn't!' Joan took his hand and squeezed it. 'I think I know you better than that, now. I really like your aunt. She's lovely.'

'She is, yes. She's wonderful. Oh, I almost forgot. I have something for you. Stay here.' He pulled his hand from hers, leapt off the sofa and ran out of the room and up the stairs. Joan could hear him moving around upstairs, and a moment later he was back, his hands behind him.

'Close your eyes.'

She did, and he placed something in them. A small square box. With her eyes still closed she ran her fingers over it. It seemed to be made of leather. What was he giving her? She couldn't guess.

'All right, open your eyes now. And open the box.' Jack was grinning at her, but behind the grin he looked nervous, as though he was scared she wouldn't like the present.

The box was maroon leather, quite worn with scuff marks on the corners. Carefully she hinged it open. Inside was a small gold locket, set with mother-of-pearl in the shape of a flower, hung on a delicate chain. She gasped. 'It's beautiful!'

'It was my mother's. Aunt Marion kept it for me, and suggested I give it to a special girl.' He sat beside her, took the locket from her and gently fastened it around her neck. 'Joan, darling, you're the special girl. The only person I could imagine wearing my mother's locket.'

'Oh, Jack, I . . . I'm flattered! Won't Aunt Marion mind you giving it to me?'

'Not at all—she knows how much I care about you. Will you promise me you'll wear it always? You said you'd wait for me to come back. This is to remind you of me when I'm not here.'

'Of course I'll wear it always. It's lovely, really lovely, and I can see how much it means to you. But now I feel guilty, because I've nothing to give you.'

'I don't need a gift. I can just close my eyes and bring you to mind.'

'Even so, I wish I had something . . . Ah! I know!' Joan had a sudden idea. She pulled out her handkerchief, which was, thankfully, clean. 'Do you have some scissors?'

Jack fetched a pair from his aunt's sewing basket. Joan first cut away part of the lace edging of the handkerchief. Then she snipped a lock of her hair, from underneath at the back, placed it on the hanky, and bound one end of it with the lace edging. She folded the hanky around the hair, tucking one corner inside the other so it would stay in a neat parcel, and gave it to Jack.

'There. It's not much, but I give it to you with love.'

He received it reverently, and held it to his face. 'It smells of you, too. Your perfume. And it contains a part of you. It's the perfect present.' He put it into his inside jacket pocket. 'There. I shall keep it next to my heart at all times. But wait! I have your hair—you need a piece of mine, inside that locket. Cut a piece off—it'll all be shorn short tomorrow anyway.'

She did as he asked, twisted the hair into a ring around her finger, and tucked it inside the locket. 'We're bound together, now. We should seal our bond . . . with a kiss.' She leaned into him, and felt herself melt as he snaked his arms around her back and pulled her close. His lips were warm and soft on hers, and the longer the kiss went on the more she felt as though she were part of him.

Finally he broke away, and she smiled shyly at him. 'You must think me very forward, being the one to ask for a kiss first.'

'I think you're beautiful,' he replied. 'And I'm glad you asked, as I was being too shy. I've wanted to do that since the moment we first met, but after . . . well, after what happened with that Canadian I thought you might have been put off that kind of thing.'

'I was put off the Canadian, not kissing!' she giggled. 'Kissing you is lovely.'

'Yes, it really is,' he murmured, as she covered his mouth with hers for a second time.

* * *

94

All too soon they were disturbed by the sound of a key being jiggled noisily in the lock, the front door opening, and a lot of stomping on the doormat and coughing.

'She's back,' whispered Joan with a grin, as she reluctantly untwined her arms from around Jack's neck. 'And I suppose it is time I went home.'

'You mustn't get into trouble with your father,' said Jack. 'Write to me, won't you? I leave tomorrow morning. I'll be home again in a couple of months.'

She sighed. 'So long! Of course I'll write. Every day. Don't forget me, will you?'

'Never. Come on then, I'll walk you home.'

Chapter Eleven

October 2014

As Kelly sat on the train on her way to college, she couldn't stop thinking about the letters. She'd read them over and over—the little bundle of brittle yellowed papers tied with a ribbon they'd found in the box in the cellar. They were all from Jack, to Joan, and had apparently been sent while he was doing his basic training after joining the Army in 1944. The letters reminisced about their time together, and mentioned a kind-hearted Mrs Atkins who seemed to be championing their relationship. There were mentions of Jack's Aunt Marion, and descriptions of the barracks, the training regime and the other young recruits, in particular a boy named Mikey, who seemed to have become Jack's best friend over the time period the letters covered.

She envied Joan her closeness with Jack. She could tell from the way he'd written his letters that she was the world to him. Theirs was a deep and lasting love, one which survived separation and the hardships of war, and which would continue for ever. Kelly considered her own relationship with Matt. It was good; at least it had been good. She hadn't seen much of him lately—she'd been too tied up with other things. Matt was a lovely boy, but they certainly didn't have the intensity of Joan and Jack's romance. There was definitely something missing. She sighed. Life in the twenty-first century seemed so much more superficial than in the 1940s. Things were too easy now—there was nothing to test and deepen a love.

The letters also mentioned Joan's job, looking after small children at a playgroup, and Jack wished her good luck with all the little ones. 'You're doing so much good,' Jack had written. 'Such a useful job. I'm proud of you, my darling.' How wonderful to be doing a useful job and to be making your loved ones proud!

What had happened to Joan and Jack? The last letter was dated 5th June 1944. The day before D-Day. Kelly was fascinated by Joan and Jack. She couldn't wait to go to visit Great-gran again, to hear the end of their story. What was this dark secret, which meant Great-gran's father had forbidden everyone to ever mention her again?

She was studying the Second World War in history—the effects of the war on daily life and how it influenced that generation's politics and beliefs for years afterwards. These letters were a wonderful insight into that period. But increasingly, studying at college seemed a bit of a pointless activity. She envied Joan and her meaningful job looking after small children. If only she could do something like that. Make a difference to other people's lives, give something back, become a valued and useful member of society. Well, there might be something she could do about it. She spent the rest of the journey mulling it over, and came to a decision, a big one, just as the train pulled into the station near her college.

She was due to have lunch with Matt today. Once a week they treated each other to a cooked lunch from the college café, rather than the usual sandwiches or snacks. She realised she hadn't seen him since the previous week's lunch date, and hadn't replied to his last few texts. Should she tell him her decision? Maybe. She'd see how he was at lunchtime. It wasn't as easy to talk to him these days. She couldn't talk about the one thing that was uppermost on her mind—Leanne's reaction to her mention of the presence of Joan in the house had put her off telling anyone else about it. They'd think she was going mad.

* * *

'OK, everyone, homework for today is to write an essay on the ethics of the Milgram electric shock obedience experiment. I want you to cover the background of the experiment, with reference to Nazi war criminals' defence of their actions during the Holocaust. Three pages, to be handed in after half-term.' The bell for the end of the lesson had gone, and the psychology teacher had to shout the last words over the sound of books being snapped shut and chairs being scraped back. Kelly smiled. Everything these days seemed to have some kind of connection to the war and the 1940s. She stuffed her books in her bag, pulled her cardigan off the back of her chair and draped it over her shoulders.

Matt was already waiting in the queue. She eased past a few people to join him. 'What's on the menu? Oh. Pizza or pasta. Why don't they ever have any English food?'

'Like what? Thought you liked Italian.'

'I do, but it'd be nice to have something more traditionally English. Beef and dumplings. Rabbit pie—that kind of thing. It's what they'd have eaten during the war. Never mind. I'll go for the fish and chips.'

Matt stared at her. 'Rabbit pie? No one here would eat that. Who'd have eaten it during the war?'

'Joan. And the rest of them.'

'Who?' He rolled his eyes. 'Never mind. You get a table—I'll bring the food.'

A few minutes later he arrived bearing a laden tray. 'I got you a milkshake to drink. It goes with that fifties hairstyle you've got.'

'Fifties?' Kelly frowned at him.

'Fifties, forties, whatever this new look you're wearing is. I don't know anything about fashion. You know me.' Matt shrugged and speared a chip. 'So, shall I come over on Saturday? We could go to see a movie. There's a new thriller out. It'd be a good start to half-term.'

'Yeah, maybe, though I don't know whether I'll be free on Saturday.'

Matt looked puzzled. 'What's up, Kells? We didn't see each other last weekend either. Have I done something wrong?'

She shook her head. 'No, no. It's just I've got stuff to do.' Should she tell him her decision? She supposed she'd have to, sooner or later, so why not now? 'Thing is, Matt, I'm probably going to leave college, and get a job. I need to try to sort it out this weekend.'

'What? Why? Thought you liked college?'

'I do, but it seems so pointless. I want to be more useful—to society, I mean. Being a student is a selfish way to live. I'd like to be giving something back.'

Matt was staring at her wide-eyed. 'But studying means you'll be able to get a better job in the future and can give something back to society then. What do you want to do—work for a charity or something? You'd earn very little, so I hope this isn't about making money.'

'No. You're not getting this, are you? It's about becoming a worthwhile member of the community. Instead of sponging off the state and my parents.'

'What do your parents think about this? Can't imagine they'd be happy with you jacking in your A levels.'

Kelly looked down at her lap. No, they wouldn't be very happy but she'd cross that bridge when she reached it. 'Haven't told them yet.'

'Well you'll have to talk to them first, won't you, before you go off looking for a job. Got anything in mind?'

'I want to work in a day nursery. Look after little children, so their parents can go to work. There's one up the road from us that I pass on the way to the station. They're advertising for more staff. I could do an NVQ in childcare on day release, so I'd still be studying as well as working.' She speared a chip and ate it, awaiting his reaction. He was being so stuffy about it all. As if he was her strict Victorian father, rather than her twenty-first-century boyfriend.

'Well, whatever floats your boat, I suppose. I'll hardly see you if you're not at college. Hardly see you as it is, these days. What have you been up to?'

'Thinking about Jack, mostly,' Kelly said. The words just slipped out of her mouth before she'd realised what she was saying.

'Jack?' A look of confusion passed across Matt's face.

'Yeah, well, he just fascinates me, that's all. I can't help it. I just wish I knew more about him.'

'*Fascinates* you? Well, what about me? Do *I* fascinate you too, or am I not good enough any more? What is up with you? Who is this Jack guy anyway? There's a Jack in your psychology classes, isn't there? Is it him? Hmm? Is that why you won't see me at weekends—you're seeing Jack instead?' Matt was standing now, shouting at her. 'Well you've got to choose, Kelly. I'm not sharing you. Is it me or him?'

She stacked her plate, cutlery and glass onto her tray and stood up slowly, lifting the tray. 'It's not the Jack in psychology. Don't be silly. But I can't help thinking about him. I suppose I'm obsessed by him,' she said, quietly.

Matt knocked the tray out of her hands. Crockery and leftover food went flying and a couple of girls at the next table leapt up squealing as they were showered with debris. 'For fuck's sake, Kelly. We've been together nearly a year and you do this to me? Well, that's it. I've had enough. It's over. Over! Happy now?' He stormed out of the café.

Kelly bent to pick up her plate and cutlery. Thankfully nothing had broken but there was quite a mess. 'I'm so sorry,' she said to the member of staff who'd come hurrying over with a dustpan, brush and cloth. 'I don't really know what upset him so much.'

'You don't know?' said a girl from the next table. 'You told him you were obsessed by someone else. That'd be enough to piss off any bloke.'

Kelly frowned and turned away. Yes, she was obsessed, but by a bloke who was either long dead or at least ancient by now. Had she not explained to Matt who Jack was? And Joan? She had; she was sure. For goodness' sake, he'd even been there when she discovered the writing on the wall. Well, if he wanted to dump her over a ghost, that was his loss. Not hers. Obviously she was right not to tell anyone about the presence of Joan. No one seemed to understand.

* * *

Ali looked at her watch as Kelly entered the house. Funny, she was back from college early today.

'Hello, love. Had a good day? You're back early. Did you have a free period this afternoon?' She watched as Kelly dumped her bag on the bottom stair and kicked off her shoes.

'I had a terrible day. Matt dumped me.' Kelly went through to the kitchen and flicked on the kettle.

'Oh no, love. Why? I thought you two were getting on so well!' Ali felt a pang of real regret. Matt was such a lovely lad, and had been very good for Kelly.

'I thought we were as well. But he seems to think I'm two-timing him. Which I'm not. I never would.' Kelly threw a teabag angrily into a cup.

'Why on earth would he think that? Can't you talk to him? Do you want me to have a word perhaps?'

'God, no, Mum. You having a word wouldn't work. I don't know why he thinks it. Anyway, it's over, and I need to get on with my life now.'

'Is this why you're home early from college?' Kelly seemed so fierce. Ali would have expected tears from her, after being dumped.

'Kind of. No, not really. The thing is . . .' She looked sheepish.

Ali frowned, wondering what else was going on with her. Seventeen was such a difficult age. 'What?'

'There's a job going at the day nursery up the road. I'm going to apply for it.' Kelly kept her eyes fixed on her tea-making as she spoke.

Ali couldn't believe what she was hearing. 'So, what about college? Your A levels?'

'I'm giving up college. Might do an NVQ on day release from the nursery, assuming I get the job.'

'Giving up? Is this because of Matt?' Ali ran her hands through her hair. Just a month or so ago Kelly had seemed so settled and sensible. A normal teenager, going out with her boyfriend and mates, studying for her A levels and considering what degree course to do. And now here she was, dressed like something out of a wartime drama, saying she wanted to give up her studies.

'No. Nothing to do with Matt. I was kind of making the decision anyway. It doesn't seem right—me going to college each day and giving nothing back. Joan worked with small children. I want to do that too. Studying seems pointless when there are more useful jobs I could do. Like Joan did.'

'What's this about more useful jobs?' Pete had just walked in. He looked from Ali to Kelly and back.

'She's not making much sense, Pete,' Ali said. 'She's talking about leaving college and going to work at a nursery. And Matt's packed her in.' Ali hoped Pete might be able to make more sense of it all. Kelly had always been a bit of a daddy's girl.

'Hold on, one thing at a time. Giving up college? That's surely nonsense, Kelly?' Pete pulled a chair out from under the kitchen table and sat down, motioning for Kelly to do the same.

'I'm sick of sponging off you. I know you and Mum are running out of money. If I earn, I can pay you rent.'

Pete snorted. 'I may be currently out of work but we're not

so poor we need to send you out to work. And what . . . should we send Ryan out as well, as a chimney sweep or something?'

'He could perhaps get a paper round, so you don't have to give him pocket money.'

'Don't be silly. He's not old enough. What did you say about Matt, Ali?'

'He's packed her in.'

'Oh. Hardly surprising though, is it, the way she's been acting?'

Ali stared at him. 'Pete! Have a heart.'

Pete frowned. 'So are you wanting to quit college because it's all ended with Matt? To avoid having to see him? Is that what this is about?'

Ali rolled her eyes. That's what she had just asked Kelly.

'Not at all. It's my own decision. I just think it's time for me to grow up, stop being a student and do something more useful with my life. Something like Joan did. She was able to help the war effort indirectly by making it easier for other women to do their bit.'

Pete gaped. Ali shook her head. 'What are you talking about— war effort? And what's Joan got to do with any of it? Kelly, you are acting very strangely. Go upstairs and lie down for a bit. I'll do dinner and then I think you need an early night.' Ali expected protests but Kelly simply got up from the table and went upstairs without another word.

'What was all that about?' said Pete.

Ali bit her lip. 'I don't know. She is behaving very oddly. Let's see how she is in the morning. Perhaps this is all her idea of a joke. It's like she's obsessed with the war years.'

'Is that because she's doing it in history? She's taking it to an extreme, isn't she, for someone who wants to give up college?' Pete laughed and shook his head. 'Yeah, you're right. She's having a laugh. Tomorrow she'll be back to her jeans and stroppy teenage attitude, and we'll be wishing we had the forties chick back again. And she'll be staying on at college no matter what. She can get a Saturday job at the nursery if she really wants to, and maybe work in the holidays.'

Ali smiled. She hoped he was right.

Chapter Twelve

February 1944

It was a foul evening—rain lashed at the windows and the wind howled in the chimney. Supper was over and Joan and Mags were sitting cross-legged on Joan's bed.

'Has he written to you yet?' Mags asked.

Joan blushed. She'd collected the third of Jack's letters from Mrs Atkins only that morning. She knew the contents of the first two almost off by heart, but she hadn't yet confided in Mags. The most recent letter contained a photo of him in uniform, which she'd tucked with the letters under her mattress.

'What makes you think he will?' she said.

'Oh, come off it, Joanie. You know that I know that you're sweet on him, and he's sweet on you. Now that he's gone away to train up, of course he'll be writing to you. And you'll be writing back to him. I don't know what arrangements you have for collecting letters from him—I guess he's not sending them here. But I reckon you'll have received at least one or two from him by now. I'm right, aren't I? Or I'll eat my stockings!'

'Don't do that. You know how hard they are to come by.' Joan picked up a pillow and swung it at Mags's head.

Mags ducked. 'Hey! I only asked. You used to tell me everything. So, have you?'

Joan fiddled with her locket, and considered for a moment. Mags was right—she always used to tell her sister everything. So what was different now? Her friendship with Jack felt special, more grown-up than any previous crushes on boys. There were elements of it she wanted to keep to herself. But it would be lovely to be able to have someone to talk to again, about how much she was already missing Jack, even though he'd only been gone a fortnight.

'Well, yes, all right then. He has written.'

'He has?' squealed Mags, clapping her hands in delight. 'I knew he would! Go on, do tell—what did he put in his letter? And have you written back to him?'

'He's written three times. I've written one letter back and I think I'll write another this evening.'

'Three! Cor, he is properly smitten with you, isn't he? How lovely, but to think you, the youngest, would be the first to find a proper sweetheart—who'd have guessed it? Go on then, read them out to me, do!'

Joan smiled, reached under her mattress and pulled out the little bundle of letters. She passed the photo to Mags.

'He looks very handsome with short hair and in his uniform,' she said. 'But surely you're not keeping the letters under your mattress, are you? Mother might find them when she's changing your sheets. You'll need to find somewhere better to hide them.'

'You're right,' Joan said. 'This was only temporary until I thought of a better place. I need a loose floorboard I could lift up, or a secret panel at the back of a wardrobe.'

'You've been reading too many novels,' said Mags. 'I would suggest putting them in a shoebox at the back of your wardrobe. Even if she's spring-cleaning Mother wouldn't open shoeboxes.'

'Good idea. Trouble is, I haven't any shoeboxes.'

'I have. I'll get one for you. But not till you've read me those letters! I'm dying to know what's in them.'

You'll not hear *everything* that's in them, thought Joan. She unfolded the first one and began to read Jack's description of his journey to the training barracks, how he'd been issued with his uniform, gas mask and rifle, how his first allocated task had been to scrub the floor of the dormitory hut.

'Scrubbing a floor? I thought he was off to be a soldier.'

'They've to learn discipline first, he says, and that means doing any task assigned, immediately and without question.' Joan read on—Jack had talked about the basic living conditions in the huts, the straw mattresses and thin blankets, the food rations, the other recruits, in particular his new friend Mikey.

'All a bit dull,' Mags said. 'I mean, I'm sure it's very interesting but where's the really juicy bits? Where he tells you he loves you and can't live without you?'

Joan put down the letter and glared at Mags. 'Those bits are there, but don't think I'm reading them out to you. A girl's got to keep some things to herself.'

'Oh, you're growing up too fast, Joanie. But I suppose I understand you want to keep some secrets. Just don't get in any trouble with him, will you? I mean, when his training's over he'll get some leave, and—'

She broke off as a deafening screech drowned her words, followed by a huge explosion that rocked the house. Pictures fell from the walls, a little vase of snowdrops crashed from Joan's dressing table, and the girls were showered with plaster dust.

'What was that? There was no air-raid warning, was there? What's happening?' Mags screamed.

'Bomb. Must be close. Come on.' Joan stuffed Jack's letters, which she was still holding, into her pocket, grabbed Mags's hand and pulled her out of the room, and down the stairs. Mags screamed again when she saw the window on the half landing—it had been blown inwards and glass was everywhere. Joan was thankful they were both wearing shoes. 'We have to get to the cellar. Come on!'

Downstairs Mother, Father and Elizabeth were also rushing down to the cellar that the family used as an air-raid shelter. Joan and Mags were right behind them. Father grabbed the torch he kept beside the cellar door, and flicked it on to light the way down the steep cellar steps. Once the door was closed he lit a paraffin lantern and they all collapsed onto the scraps of carpet and piles of old blankets he'd put down there at the start of the war.

'Why was there no warning, Father?' asked Mags. 'There should have been a warning. That bomb was close.'

'There haven't been any bombers over here since last summer. Maybe they've stopped watching out for planes,' said Joan.

'Rubbish, the war's still on, so they'll still be watching out. I don't know why there was no warning. Now sit quietly, girls.'

'Where do you think the bomb landed, Father? It did sound close.' Joan ignored her father's instructions to stay quiet.

'I think it may have been on this street,' he said.

'I do hope our neighbours are all safe,' said Mother, wringing her hands.

* * *

It was only fifteen minutes until the all-clear sounded. Father went up first, and ushered the women out. He opened the front door to survey the damage in the street. Joan and Mags went out with him, while Mother and Elizabeth went to make tea.

'Goodness, it was Mrs Johnson's house that was hit!'

Joan looked where Father was pointing and saw their next-door neighbour's house had a gaping hole in its roof, and half the front blown off. Flames flickered from the remains of the first floor.

'Oh my goodness! So close! Where's Mrs Johnson? There was no warning . . .' Joan had a horrible feeling about this. With no air-raid warning Mrs Johnson could have been inside. 'We must look for her. Father, come on, please help!'

She ran towards the wrecked house, clambering over the piles of rubble that filled the front garden and pavement.

'Joan, get back here this instant. It's not safe! Come back. I order you to come back.'

Joan ignored him. If Mrs Johnson was inside, she could be trapped somewhere. 'Mrs Johnson? Can you hear me? Are you in there?' She climbed over the remains of the front wall of the house, into what had been the sitting room. The door to the hallway was still in place, and she tugged it open, showering herself with ceiling plaster. Coughing, she went through to the hallway. She could hear the fire crackling upstairs, and smoke was beginning to billow downwards into the hallway. She yelled up the stairs. 'Mrs Johnson? Are you there? Shout out if you can. I'm coming to help.' She listened hard, and over the sound of the fire she could just make out a pitiful whine, coming from under the stairs. She pulled aside a wrecked sideboard and wrenched open the under-stairs cupboard. Mrs Johnson's terrier, Kimmy, was cowering inside on his dog-basket.

'Oh, Kimmy, you poor dear. Come here. I'll get you out.' She grabbed the dog by his scruff and pulled him into her arms. She glanced up the stairs—they were now impassable. Mrs Johnson only put Kimmy in his under-stairs bed when she left the house, as she didn't trust him not to chew the furniture. Joan prayed that meant she'd been away from the house when the bomb fell.

She tried to go out the same way she'd come in—via the living room—but one look told her more of the front of the house had fallen and the way was blocked. Instead she went through the kitchen, which was relatively undamaged, and to the back door. It was locked but a key hung on a peg. Tucking a struggling Kimmy under one arm she managed to unlock the door, and went out to the side passage. There was no way back to the street from here—too much rubble from a fallen chimney blocked the way.

Remembering the loose fence panel at the end of the garden between her own house and Mrs Johnson's, she ran down the garden, wanting to get away from the ruined house before more of it fell. Thankfully her father had still not fixed the panel. The last fence post had rotted, and the panel hung loose, not attached at one end. With Kimmy still in her arms Joan heaved her shoulder against it and easily pushed through. She ran across her own garden and out to the street along the side passage.

As she approached the street she could hear Mrs Johnson screaming. 'Kimmy, my darling Kimmy, he's inside! Someone, oh please, my darling boy, someone get him!' She was safe, then. Thank goodness. Joan could see the fire brigade had arrived, and were setting up their hoses, attaching them to a nearby fire hydrant. Joan's family stood across the road, her father in front of her mother and sisters.

'I've got Kimmy; he's all right,' she called as she picked her way through the gathering crowds towards Mrs Johnson, who was being restrained by an air-raid warden.

'Kimmy! My darling!' Mrs Johnson took the dog from Joan and buried her face in his fur. 'Thank you, my dear. But look at the state of you!'

Joan looked down at herself. She was filthy—covered in dust and grime, her skirt was torn, her jumper matted with plaster dust, and somewhere along the way she'd lost a shoe without noticing it.

Father was striding across the road towards her. 'You stupid girl. I forbade you from going in there but you disobeyed me. You will be punished for this. Severely.'

Joan looked towards Mrs Johnson for support, but the old woman turned away, still snuggling her face into Kimmy's matted coat.

'Father, I went in because I thought perhaps Mrs Johnson was still in there, and someone needed to do something.'

'There are professionals to go into bombed houses to rescue people. Not disobedient girls.'

'The authorities weren't here when I went in, and surely every minute counts?'

'That's enough. You put yourself in danger and what for? A mangy dog? What would your mother have done if the house had collapsed on you?'

'Well it didn't, did it? I'm glad I went inside. You didn't know Mrs Johnson wasn't in there. And I rescued her dog. Kimmy means the world to her. She's got no one else.' Joan turned her back on her father and strode across the street towards her sisters and mother.

'You're for it now,' Mags muttered to her.

Father was a step behind. He grabbed Joan roughly by her upper arm. 'Inside, girl. Now. And you are confined to your room until I decide how to punish you.'

She tried to shake him off but his grip was too firm. She was frogmarched inside, and pushed towards the stairs.

'There's glass, Father, on the half landing. And I've no shoe on . . .'

'Get up those stairs now, girl!'

She had no choice but to obey, tiptoeing carefully over the shattered window glass. In her room she pulled off her ruined clothes and threw herself onto the bed, tugging the eiderdown over her and cuddling her battered old teddy bear. The shock of the evening's events was catching up with her. It was so unfair. She'd done what she thought was right. Maybe she'd been a little reckless but she'd really thought Mrs Johnson might be in there, cowering terrified in a corner, waiting for rescue. More of the house had collapsed and if she'd not gone in when she did, it would have been impossible to get anyone out. And she'd rescued Kimmy—that was worth it, wasn't it? Mrs Johnson was scared of Father. That much was obvious, so Joan didn't blame her for not backing her up. But she knew the old lady was grateful. That little dog was all she had—her husband had died in the Great War and her son, a fighter pilot, had died during the Battle of Britain. She didn't deserve to lose anyone else. No, Joan was glad she'd gone inside. No matter how Father decided to punish her, she was glad of what she'd done. It was the right thing.

If only she could see Jack, and tell him all about it. But he was miles away in his training camp and it would be weeks before she could see him again. He'd be worried, she supposed, that she'd risked herself going into the bombed house, but he'd understand and he'd praise her for her courage. He'd hold her, kiss her hair and stop her shaking. Everything would be all right if only Jack were here now.

Joan lifted her head and regarded her pillow. It was stained—her tears had mixed with the dust and grime on her face and been smeared across the cotton. So now she'd be in trouble with Mother as well. She heaved herself out of bed and went into the bathroom, where she ran herself a shallow bath. Father would probably complain about the use of hot water when it wasn't bath night, but too bad. She didn't care what he might say.

As she eased herself into the comforting water she felt as though a switch had flicked across in her head. She no longer cared what Father said or thought of her. As long as *she herself* knew she'd done the right thing, the best thing, she was happy. She realised it mattered too what Jack thought, but she knew that he would side with her, in everything that she did. That idea gave her a warm glow, and she felt her shaking begin to subside. Oh, if only he was here now!

She washed her hair in the bath water, giving it a final rinse with clean water from the tap. The bath was filthy when she drained it, and she had to wipe it round with a rag. Wrapping herself in her candlewick dressing gown, she went back to her room. Jack couldn't be with her, but she could look at his photo, reread his letters and write one back to him, to tell him what had happened. She'd play down the danger to herself—no sense in worrying him, but it felt essential that he should know. How many more weeks until he came home on leave? She counted off on her fingers and sighed. Too many.

Chapter Thirteen

October 2014

'Coffee?' Ali asked Jason. It was Sunday morning and he'd called round for a chat. It was becoming a regular occurrence—he was often popping round. Ali enjoyed his company. He was easy to chat to.

'Lovely, thanks,' he said, taking a seat at the kitchen table. Pete was outside chopping up some firewood—now that the days were becoming colder Ali wanted to start making use of their open fireplaces during the long dark evenings. Ryan was playing some computer game or other, and Kelly was upstairs, still pottering around in her dressing gown. Despite Ali and Pete's misgivings, she'd got herself a job at the nursery, started immediately on a trial basis and had worked a full week during half-term. Ali felt she deserved a rest. Whether or not she returned to college after half-term was still being debated.

She put on a jug of filter coffee, found a packet of biscuits and sat opposite Jason at the table. 'So, how are things? Is there much more of your mum's old stuff to clear out?'

Jason had been making regular weekend trips to the charity shops or recycling centre as he cleared out his mother's stuff. 'I'm getting there. I've still got all her old china to do, and then there's the loft to explore. I've dealt with her clothes and books though. Then I need to decide about the furniture—I'll keep some of it but it's not all to my taste.'

Ali poured him his coffee, adding milk and one sugar as she knew he liked. 'It must be hard, doing all this. Your mum wasn't that old, was she?'

'No. Just sixty-eight. She was born in January 1945. But cancer doesn't care what age a person is, does it?' He sipped his coffee.

Ali felt a pang of guilt at upsetting him. 'Sorry, Jason. Tell me to shut up if you don't want to talk about it.'

'No, it's fine. I've been meaning to talk to you about her a bit anyway. There is something you should know about me, and Mum.' He picked up a biscuit and ate it thoughtfully.

'What? You're sounding all mysterious!'

'I suppose I should have said something when you told me you'd inherited your house from Betty Perkins. But somehow I couldn't seem to find the words then. It was a bit unexpected, finding out you were Betty's great-niece. Lovely biscuits, Ali.'

'Unexpected? How so?' Would he please get on with it!

'Yes, well, the thing is, Ali, we're actually related, you and I.'

'What? What do you mean?'

'My mum was adopted. When she was in her forties, after my dad died, she went through the process of tracing her birth parents. She'd been given up for adoption as a baby, during the war. So many were, of course, war babies whose mothers had got pregnant by soldiers on leave, who perhaps never came home. Mum was one of those. Dad was German, hence my surname—Bergmann.'

'So how does that make us related?'

'It turned out Mum's mother was Joan Perkins, Betty's sister. And your grandmother's sister, too, of course.'

Ali gasped. 'Joan was your grandmother?'

'Yes, which makes us, Ali, second cousins. Pleased to meet you, cousin!' He stood and held out his hand.

114

She shook it and laughed. 'Wow. I have no brothers or sisters, or first cousins. Thought I had no second cousins either. The weird thing is, Jason, we only heard a week or so ago of Joan's existence. We'd always thought there was only the two sisters, Betty and my gran, Margaret. Gran had never once mentioned Joan. But I don't understand. How did your mum end up living next door to Betty?'

Jason sat down again and took a sip of his coffee before answering. 'When she traced her birth mother, Mum found Joan had died years before, but she couldn't believe it when she found out Betty was still living in the family home, here. She came to visit one day, on a pretext of doing some charity work for the Red Cross. Mum didn't let on who she was, but every time she tried to gently question Betty about her sisters, Betty would talk about Margaret only. She never mentioned Joan. She hinted that Margaret might be senile, which is why Mum never tried to meet her, after finding Betty. Anyway, she befriended Betty and came to visit quite often. At the time she lived thirty miles away. Then number seven came up for sale, and Mum had always fancied living by the coast, so she bought it. As Betty aged, Mum did more and more for her—all her shopping, some cooking—and saw her every day. But in all those years Betty never acknowledged she'd had another sister, and Mum never admitted she was Betty's niece. She didn't want to upset her, or stir things up. Betty was very frail.'

Ali was amazed, and touched that Jason's mum had done so much for Betty, without ever revealing who she was. 'That's so sad, and so selfless. Your mother must have been a wonderful woman. Look, we found this in a box in the cellar.' Ali fetched the photo of the three girls in the chequered school frocks and plaits. 'That's Betty, that's my Gran, and that's Joan. Your grandmother.'

'Oh my word. That is the first photograph I have ever seen of my grandmother. Oh, how Mum would have loved to have seen this!' Jason took the photo and gazed at it in awe.

A thought struck Ali. 'Gran—who's not at all senile, by the way—said her father had forbidden them to speak of Joan. We guessed there must have been some kind of scandal but Gran didn't want to talk about it any more the other day. I wonder if this was it—perhaps she was ostracised because she got pregnant?'

'Who was pregnant?' Kelly had come downstairs and was standing at the kitchen door, still in her dressing gown.

'You'll never guess,' Ali said, and quickly filled her in on what Jason had said.

Kelly sat down at the table. 'Wow. Why didn't Great-gran tell us Joan had a baby? Do you think perhaps she didn't even know?'

Ali considered. 'Hard to keep that sort of thing secret, I'd have thought. And even if Joan was sent away to have the baby, Gran said they were close, and so Joan would have told her. I think Gran did know. Something more to ask her about next time we see her, if she's feeling up to it.'

'Mum, do you think Jack might have been . . .' Kelly glanced over at Ali.

She realised what her daughter was hinting at, and got up to retrieve the other photo they'd found in the cellar—the one of Jack in his uniform. 'This man was Joan's sweetheart. It's possible, I guess, he may have been your grandfather.'

Jason took the photo and studied it. 'There was no father's name recorded. It could have been this chap but we'll never know.'

'What was your mother's date of birth?' Kelly asked.

'January 1945,' Jason replied. He was still holding both photos, looking from one to the other.

Kelly counted back on her fingers. 'April 1944. That fits with when Jack came home on leave.'

Jason stared at her. 'What do you mean? How do you know the dates?'

'There were some letters in the box as well,' Kelly told him. 'Letters from Jack to Joan. It does all tie in—I think Jack McBride was your grandfather.'

'My word,' Jason said, quietly. 'I thought I'd be astounding you with this news, but you've managed to go one better. Do you know what happened to either of them? All I know is that Joan died young. I don't know when or how.'

'I knew she must have died young,' Kelly said. 'I think Great-gran ought to meet Jason. He's her . . . What relation is he to her?'

'Great-nephew. I'd love to meet her, if you think that would be OK, Ali?'

'Yes, I think you should meet her eventually, but I'd like us to ask her more about Joan first. I kind of think it'd be better if she told us herself about Joan's pregnancy before we go springing Joan's descendants on her.' That didn't come out quite as she'd intended. She shrugged and put her hand on Jason's shoulder. 'If you see what I mean.'

'Of course. I'll leave it up to you to judge when the time is right.' Jason smiled reassuringly at her. He was definitely a good bloke. Ali felt a rush of pride that he was her cousin. She'd never had any siblings or cousins, and now she had the nicest one ever.

'Mum, I'm desperate to hear more from Great-gran. Especially now I know about the baby. When can we see her again?' Kelly was bouncing around like a five-year-old at a birthday party.

'Well, I'm fetching her here on Friday,' Ali said. 'For tea and cake. We'll have a chat with her then.'

'Yes!' Kelly punched the air. 'At last we'll find out what happened to them.'

'It's Halloween on Friday,' Jason said.

'Yes. And Ryan's asked if he can have a few friends for a sleepover that night as well. We'll have a full house.'

'Sounds like fun,' Jason said. He picked up the two photos again. 'She's so pretty. He's good-looking too, in his way. I wonder if they were very much in love.'

'Definitely. Head over heels, judging by those letters,' said Kelly. 'How old do you think she was, when she had my mum?'

Ali considered. 'She was about seventeen when she met Jack,

117

Gran said. I suppose eighteen by the time the baby came along. Yes, because Gran said her birthday was January the first. So if your mum's birthday was also January Joan would have been just eighteen.'

'So young. I guess that's why she couldn't keep the baby, and why her father thought it such a scandal.'

'They were horrible back then, weren't they? I mean, if I got pregnant, you wouldn't chuck me out and refuse to ever speak of me again, would you?' Kelly took a gulp of coffee and stared at Ali over the rim of the cup.

'Of course we wouldn't. Though please don't. You're a bit young for all that.' Ali put an arm around her daughter's shoulders and gave her a squeeze. The idea of a pregnant Kelly was too much to contemplate. They didn't have enough money to cope with a baby in the family. Besides, at forty-two Ali felt far too young to become a grandmother.

Kelly snorted. 'I'm hardly likely to. Haven't even got a boyfriend, have I?'

Ali was about to say something about it being Kelly's fault she had no boyfriend—her forties obsession having pushed away the lovely Matt—but at the last minute thought better of it and pressed her lips together. She noticed Jason raise his eyebrows at her, but he too said nothing.

'More coffee?' Ali said, to break the tension.

'Not for me. I should go and get on,' Jason said, as he stood to leave. Then he seemed to change his mind, and turned back to them. 'I've just had a thought. My mum is buried in the cemetery. Would you, I mean, are you at all interested in seeing her grave? I was going to go and put some flowers on it today in any case.'

'I'd love to,' Kelly said. 'I want to find out all I can about Joan and Jack. Even more so now that I know they had a baby. Can we go today?'

'Why not? I'll drive us,' Ali said. 'You'll need to get dressed first, though.'

* * *

118

An hour later Kelly got out of her mum's car and the three of them went through the cemetery gates and threaded their way along the neatly tended paths. It was a blustery autumnal day, sunny but with occasional clouds blocking the sunlight. Crisp brown leaves blew around, settling on graves as though to provide winter warmth for the occupants. Kelly felt a strange excitement at the prospect of seeing Joan's daughter's grave. Joan, that strange presence that seemed to be always with her—was it Joan's influence making her feel excited to see a grave?

'She's over here,' Jason said, clutching a hastily bought bunch of carnations. Kelly followed him, scurrying to catch up. Cemeteries were weird places. To think of all those dead bodies lying under the earth, slowly rotting away. She shivered a little.

'Are you cold?' asked Ali.

'No. Stop fussing, Mum.' Just a bit spooked by this place, Kelly was going to add, but thought better of it.

Jason's mother's headstone was made of Purbeck limestone, a pleasant mid-grey colour. It bore a simple inscription: *Constance Bergmann, beloved mother and wife, you will never be forgotten. 12th January 1945–3rd February 2014.* Kelly watched solemnly as Jason laid the flowers gently down on the grave, and bowed his head for a moment's quiet contemplation. Never forgotten. Yet Great-gran, her aunt, had never mentioned her existence. And she and her mum, Constance's relatives, hadn't known she was even born until earlier that morning.

Maybe that's what Joan's ghost wanted. To not be forgotten. To be remembered by her relatives. Kelly fingered the pearl locket that as always was around her neck. It felt warm to her touch, despite the chill of the autumn day. Yes, that was what Joan wanted. For her story to be known. Recognition. With Great-gran coming on Friday for tea, then surely she'd be able to find out the end of Joan and Jack's story? Especially now that they knew the big secret of Joan's pregnancy. That had to be the scandal Great-gran had alluded to. There couldn't be anything more, could there?

Chapter Fourteen

April 1944

Joan stood on the platform anxiously awaiting the incoming train. She was scanning the faces of the other waiting people, hoping no one she knew, or rather, no one who knew Father, would arrive. She'd managed to keep Jack's letters secret—they'd all been delivered via Mrs Atkins, so it had been easy to bring them home smuggled in her coat, and read them in private in her bedroom. Only Mags knew of their correspondence, and had even brought a letter home from the WVS once, when Joan had been sick and unable to go to work.

And now he was coming home! He'd be here on the next train, her Jack, in the flesh again at last! How the weeks had dragged since he'd joined up. He'd written about his training, about his friend Mikey and the other lads in his platoon, about the rations they received, the duties they had to perform. And then he'd written to say he had three days' leave, before his next posting. Three whole days! Joan would have been excited at the prospect of just one hour in his company. With luck they'd be able to see a lot of each other. She'd managed to have a whispered conversation with Mags about it, who had agreed to cover for her where possible. And the wonderful Mrs Atkins had told her to take as much time off from the playgroup as she needed. Someone else could run it for three days. It was more important for Joan to spend time with her sweetheart, for you never knew what was just around the corner. She'd smiled and hugged Joan, and there'd been the tiniest glint of a tear in her eye as she sent Joan off to the station.

The sound of a train whistle brought her back to the moment. It wasn't far away now. There was an air of excitement on the platform—women with small children in tow telling them to look for Daddy's train; middle-aged couples awaiting the return of a son; young girls like her, lipstick in place, best stockings on, waiting for their sweethearts. Finally the train rounded the last corner and pulled into the station with a squeal of brakes and a whoosh of steam—the engine dark and fierce, swathed in steam like a fire-breathing dragon. The olive-green coaches were dusted with soot, and the soldiers were already hanging out of every door, waiting till the train slowed enough for them to jump out. Joan looked up and down the platform, peering at each man who jumped out and ran into a woman's arms. Whether the woman was wife, mother or girlfriend, the emotion was the same. Fierce hugs and a plethora of kisses bestowed, tears dashed away, and children scooped into loving arms. Where was Jack? Her arms ached, her lips tingled, she longed to be the next one to be kissed. Where was he? Oh, what if he'd missed the train, or his leave had been cancelled? She bit her lip, wondering how she would cope with the disappointment.

'Penny for them?'

She spun around, and into his arms. 'Oh, Jack! I thought perhaps you weren't on the train! I was looking and looking . . .'

'I was in the last carriage. Fought my way through these crowds—so many people on the train! God, it's good to see you, Joanie. I've missed you so much.' He bent down, and covered her face with kisses.

121

She no longer cared who might be watching and reporting back to Father. It felt so good to be in his arms. 'I've missed you too, Jack. So very much! And now you're here again. I can hardly believe you're real!' To her surprise she found tears were streaming down her face.

'Sweetheart, don't cry. I'm here now, and I have three full days. Don't think about the time we had apart; don't think about me leaving again. Just think about the here and the now, and let's make the most of every minute we can be together.'

He kissed away her tears, and she smiled up at him. 'You're right. The here and now.'

'The only place and time we can ever be.'

'So let's get going. Let's get away from all these people.' He hoisted his kit bag onto his shoulder, took her hand and led her out of the station. She walked proudly by his side—her young, handsome soldier, now fully trained to fight for his country.

Out of the station, it had begun to rain heavily. Joan grimaced as raindrops trickled down her neck. 'Oh, that's a shame. I'd hoped we could walk to your aunt's house. I suppose we'll have to get the bus now.'

'She's not expecting me till later. She'll be out at work right now. Why don't we go to the pictures while it's raining? What time do you need to be home?'

Joan grinned. 'Not till ten. The parents think I'm at the WVS this evening. Mags and Mrs Atkins will cover for me.'

Jack put his arm around her shoulder and gave her a squeeze. 'Thank goodness for Mags and Mrs Atkins, then! Right, off to the cinema. What's on, do you know? It's ages since I was able to go.'

'*Rhythm Serenade* is on at the Odeon. It's got Vera Lynn in it.'

'Perfect!'

Joan linked arms with him and they ran from the station to the cinema. Thankfully it wasn't too far, and the main feature hadn't started when they arrived. Jack bought two tickets and they crept in while the newsreels played, and chose seats at the back, far away from the other cinema-goers. Joan hadn't sat at the back before. She and Mags had giggled at the girls who did, and wondered just exactly what they'd got up to with their sweethearts, under the cover of darkness. Well, she hoped she was about to find out. She already knew that Jack was the love of her life. No matter what, she wanted to be with him. Now and always. And whatever he wanted to do with her, she wanted it too.

The film was wonderful. Uplifting and warm, and with Vera Lynn singing some splendid songs. At least that's the impression Joan left the theatre with, although she couldn't have said much about the plot. She'd snuggled up against Jack, and spent the entire time breathing in his warmth, relishing the strength of his arm around her shoulders, enjoying the many kisses they shared. One had been particularly deep and lingering, and afterwards Jack had groaned and pulled himself away from her for a moment.

'It's all right. I don't mind, whatever you want . . .' Joan had begun.

But Jack had shaken his head. 'Not here, not now.'

* * *

Dusk was falling by the time they left the theatre. The rain clouds had gone, and the sky was a riot of colour in the west, fading to a deep purple in the east. A silvery moon was rising over the sea.

Joan looked at her watch. 'I'm going to have to start heading home,' she said. 'I daren't be late, in case Father forbids me going out for the next few days.'

'Let's walk back along the prom,' Jack said. 'Like we did on the evening we met. The moon's as bright as it was then. Do you remember?'

'Of course, I remember every second of that evening.' She leaned her head against his shoulder. Who would have thought it? If that horrible Canadian airman hadn't assaulted her, bringing Jack to her rescue, maybe they wouldn't be together now. And a life without Jack by her side was not one she wanted to contemplate. She smiled to herself, happy to have him close for now, and a beautiful moonlit walk ahead of them.

They strolled along the prom, commenting on the way the low moon lit a pathway across the sea. Just like it had on that cold crisp night back in January. This evening it was mild, the air fresh after the rain, the sea lapping gently on the shore. Joan looked forward to the days when the beach would be back in use again, with the invasion defences removed. When the war was over, and Jack would no longer need to go away to fight. She shuddered. Mustn't think about that. Live in the here and now, he'd said. The only place and time we can ever be.

'What's wrong?' said Jack, stopping to pull her into his arms.

'I'm trying not to think about it, but the truth is, when you leave next time you'll be going away to fight in the war.' She buried her face against his chest. 'I'm scared, Jack, of what might happen to you.'

'Oh, my love. Don't be frightened. I'll be perfectly all right, you'll see. In any case, that's ages away. I've three days here, then I'm to be sent somewhere in Dorset for some more training. It'll be weeks yet before I actually have to go and fight at all. But you're right—you mustn't think about it. Look, here's our bench.'

It was indeed—the bench in the Victorian shelter where they'd sat in January. Joan liked thinking of it as 'theirs'. It gave their relationship a history, a little past. She hoped fervently it would have a long future as well. But she mustn't, *mustn't* look ahead.

'Damn this war!' she blurted out. 'Keeping us apart. Why can't it be peacetime? Why did you have to join up? You told me before you don't believe in countries having borders. The world should be free. Why are you fighting for England if you think that way?'

He sighed, and pulled her close. 'My love, I *have* to do my part. It's not just England I'll be fighting for. It's Europe. We must keep Britain free for the British, France free for the French, Poland free for the Polish. Jews free, wherever they live. I see it differently now.

You're right. I wish there were no borders between countries, and everyone could live happily wherever they wanted to. But when people like Hitler come along and want to take over, the rest of the world must and *shall* stop them. I'm a citizen of the world, and I must do my part to make the world a better place. Right now, that means I must fight, and do my bit to stop Hitler. God knows I wish it was peacetime too, and you and I could walk out together like any other couple did, before this blasted war began. But we can't sit here wishing we had different lives. We can only make the most of what we have. We're luckier than many—we live in a country that is still free, we are healthy, we have homes and people who love us, and we have each other. So please, let's enjoy these next few days and not fret about what might happen. It might not happen. The war might end next week, or next month or next year, and we'll be able to be together. But I want to be able to tell our children I played my part in it all, that I did what I could.'

Joan sat quietly for a moment, letting his words sink in. She knew she was being selfish wanting to keep him home, away from the war, but she did understand his need to do what was right. For the greater good. She gazed across the sea, at the shimmering pathway to the moon. 'Our children', he had said. He wanted to be able to tell 'our children'. Not 'his children'. She turned to look at him. His eyes were shining with love, love for her. His lips were slightly parted, as though he was about to speak. She wanted to kiss him, and leaned forward, but he put his finger on her lips.

'Joan, there's something I must ask you. I want you to think carefully about the answer. You don't have to answer immediately, and I'll understand . . .' He trailed off, then took her hands in his. 'Joan, my sweet, darling girl, would you . . . will you . . . the thing is, I'm asking you . . .'

'Yes,' she said, and leaned forward once more to kiss him. This time he allowed it, a gentle sweet kiss. Joan felt as though she was melting in the warmth of his love.

He broke off the kiss, and breathed deeply. 'Let me try again. I want to do this properly.' He slipped off the bench, onto one knee on the sandy promenade, still holding her hands. 'Joan, darling, I love you and will always love you. Would you do me the greatest honour, make me the happiest man alive, and consent to be my wife?'

She smiled, her heart swelling with love for him. 'Of course, my darling boy, that's what I meant when I said yes before! I love you too, so very, very much. To be your wife would be the greatest honour for *me*. Oh, Jack, but *when* will we be able to marry?'

He climbed back on the bench and enfolded her in his arms. 'Well, not this week, I guess. On my next leave, perhaps, if it can be arranged. Or at the latest, on the very day the war ends. Thank you, my sweet love! I am so proud, so happy!' He kissed her, full and deep and long.

She sighed happily. She was engaged to be married! 'Wait till I tell Mags! She'll be so thrilled for us!'

'I'll come to see your father tomorrow,' said Jack, 'to ask for your hand in marriage. The old-fashioned way. Do you think he'll appreciate that?'

'No, love. Let's keep it secret for now. I'm frightened that even though you're my fiancé—oh, what a lovely word!—he might try to stop us from seeing each other. I couldn't bear for that to happen this week, when we have so little time. After you've gone, I'll tell him and Mother and the rest of the family. But for now I only want to tell Mags. And that's only because I know I shall never be able to keep such a wonderful secret all to myself!'

He laughed and hugged her. 'You should have a ring. I can't afford a good one, at present, but . . .'

'You gave me your mother's locket. That can be the symbol of our engagement. I need nothing more. I have you.'

She checked her watch. It was a quarter to ten. Reluctantly she pulled Jack to his feet, kissed him again and with a final glance at *their* bench, linked arms to continue the walk home, now as an engaged woman.

Chapter Fifteen

October 2014

It was Halloween and preparations were in full swing for Ryan's Halloween sleepover. Ali had taken a few hours off work to get the house ready and some food prepared. Pete was out raiding B&Q for the stuff he needed to decorate Ryan's room, which was next on the list. Gran was coming to tea—'I always love seeing the jack-o'-lanterns,' she'd said—and Ali had collected her at three p.m. As soon as Ryan got in from his half-term holiday club he had charged off to 'sort stuff out', decorating the house with Halloween bunting and fairy lights and choosing a selection of spooky DVDs for his friends to watch late into the night. Ali was carving pumpkin lanterns. Even Kelly was home, baking biscuits in the shape of cauldrons and witches' hats, wearing an apron tied neatly over her forties-style skirt and blouse. When they'd finished the preparations, Ali had promised Kelly they could gently ask Gran to tell them more about Joan and Jack.

'Lovely shortbread, Kelly, dear,' Gran said, as she sat at the kitchen table and tucked into a biscuit warm from the oven. 'Truly melt in your mouth. You are so like poor dear Joan in some ways. Dressed like that, and with your skills at baking. If I believed in reincarnation I would almost think—' She broke off as Ali glared at her. Kelly was far too obsessed by Joan and Jack, and everything to do with the Second World War and the 1940s, for her liking. She wished she could have her regular twenty-first-century teenager back, in jeans, a hoodie and an attitude.

'Hey, you guys, come and see what I've done.' Ryan burst in through the kitchen door, his face shining with excitement.

Ali wiped her hands on a tea towel and went out to the hallway. Ryan was pointing proudly up the stairs. He'd hung a full-sized blow-up skeleton, dressed in a shirt and a pair of old jogging trousers, from the newel post on the half landing. A thick rope tied in a hangman's knot was draped around the skeleton's head and looped over the newel post.

'Wow, that's really effective,' said Ali.

Ryan looked pleased and proud. 'I was thinking of putting some ketchup in a mesh bag under its shirt so it would gradually ooze through and drip down on people like the skeleton is bleeding. What do you think?'

'I think not. Unless you're going to pay for the carpet cleaning bill?'

'Oh. Yeah, didn't think of the carpet. Kelly! Great-gran! Come and look!'

Ali went back to the kitchen to help Gran to her feet, and pass her the walking frame. Gran was so unsteady on her feet these days. It'd be awful if she fell.

'That's quite disturbing,' Kelly said, reaching the hallway first. 'Ugh. Not sure I like it at all.'

'What am I supposed to be looking at?' asked Gran.

Ryan pointed. 'There, look, over the stairs. What do you think?'

'Oh, oh my, no! That's where . . . No!' Gran was shaking uncontrollably. Ali rushed to her side, but wasn't quick enough. Gran's legs seemed to buckle under her, and despite still holding on to the walking frame she crumpled in a heap on the floor, sobbing and shaking.

'Gran! What's the matter? What is it?' Ali crouched beside her.

'That . . . that thing, oh, take it down, oh, it's so awful . . . too terrible . . .' She curled onto her side on the floor, facing away from the stairs, making little mewling noises.

'Gran, dear, let me help you up and onto the sofa.' Ali tried to pull her up but Gran didn't seem able to help herself at all.

'What's wrong with her?' Kelly asked, her face ashen.

'I don't know. That skeleton has upset her badly for some reason.' Ali didn't understand it. It was effective but clearly only a blow-up model. She stroked Gran's forehead. She felt cool to the touch—too cool. Her breathing was irregular. 'I'm worried about her. Ryan, take it down, now. In case she looks at it again. Kelly, go next door and see if Jason can come and help. I think he's at home.'

Both leapt to their designated tasks. Gran was barely conscious. Ali fetched a cushion and rug for her, from the sitting room, and made her comfortable. Should she call a doctor? An ambulance? 'Come on, Gran. Speak to me. I wish we could get you off the floor.'

'Terrible, terrible, that thing,' Gran kept muttering.

'It's all right, Gran darling. Ryan's taking it down.' Ali held her hand, gently caressing the cool, papery skin. Gran was still trembling, and her eyes were rolling back in her head.

Kelly was back in a moment with Jason at her heels. He immediately rushed over to Gran and knelt beside her. 'Oh Christ, what's happened? Did she fall?'

Ali explained about the skeleton and Gran's collapse. He placed his fingers on the pulse at her neck, and leaned over her, her breath blowing on his neck. Gran moaned slightly and shifted her position. 'I think we should call an ambulance. It's probably nothing much but she'll need to be checked over, to find what caused this and whether she hurt herself at all when she fell.'

He didn't wait for an answer but stood up, pulled out his phone, stepped into the kitchen out of the way and made the call. Ali was grateful for his support. She knew she would probably just break down and sob on the phone to the emergency operator. Better that she stay by Gran's side. At least the mock hanging was down now. She glanced over, to where Ryan was sitting on the stairs, head in hands.

'It's all right, love. It's not your fault. You weren't to know it would upset her like this.' She kept stroking Gran's hair. The old lady was still making faint whimpering noises. Kelly sat beside her, and held Gran's hand.

'Oh, Mum. It's awful seeing her like this. It's this bloody house. She didn't want us to move in, did she? She knew there was something wrong about this place. And now it's done this to her. You'll say it's rubbish but I think the house is haunted. Probably by Joan. I can feel her. I've always been able to.'

Ali did not want to hear this. What on earth was she blathering about? 'Kelly, shut up. You are right, you are talking rubbish and this is really not the time. Poor Gran was just frightened by Ryan's Halloween decorations and fell. You're not helping saying things like that, so please, don't.'

'Knew you wouldn't listen. You never do.' Kelly got up and stomped upstairs, pushing past Ryan.

'Well, thanks for helping,' Ali said to her retreating back. 'Ryan, go outside and wait for the ambulance. Show them where to come.' He dashed off, apparently happy to have an excuse to get away from the drama.

'They'll be here any moment,' said Jason, returning from the kitchen. He looked down at Gran. 'She's got more colour now than when I arrived. Don't worry, Ali. She'll be fine.'

She smiled gratefully at him. 'I hope so.'

'This is not quite how I imagined the first meeting with my long lost great-aunt would go,' he said, with a wry smile.

'No. God, not at all. She's never done this before.'

Jason put a comforting arm around her shoulder. 'Don't worry,' he said, again.

'Ambulance is here,' announced Ryan, bursting in through the front door.

Ali stood and stepped back, allowing the experts to take over. 'Listen, Ryan, I'm sorry but you'll need to cancel the sleepover. Can you go and contact your friends? We'll do it some other time.' He nodded, biting back tears, and went off to make the calls. 'Jason, would you stay and tell Pete what's happened? I don't want to tell him on the phone. He'll be back soon. Get him to drive up to the hospital. I'll go in the ambulance with Gran.'

'I'll go with you.' Kelly came downstairs, untying her apron and with a cardigan now on over her dress.

That was a surprise, after Kelly's outburst of a few minutes earlier. But Ali had to admit she'd be grateful for the company and support. 'Thanks, love. Fetch her coat and handbag, will you? Looks like we're almost ready to go.'

* * *

Kelly fidgeted in the cheap plastic chair. You'd think they'd supply more comfortable ones in hospital waiting rooms. This one was doing her back in. She was beginning to regret having offered to come with Mum and Great-gran to the hospital, but at least it had got her away from the house. And she had been worried about Great-gran. What on earth had happened to make her collapse like that? She may be frail and old but she never just fell like that, or passed out, or had a fit or whatever it was. It was something to do with the house. Kelly knew it. Perhaps Great-gran had felt that spooky weird feeling she often felt. Joan's presence.

She looked at Ali. Her face was drawn and worried, and she was picking at the rim of her polystyrene teacup, gradually reducing it to tiny white balls, which she dropped into the dregs of the tea. 'What do you think they're doing now?' she asked.

'More tests of some sort, I suppose. We'll be allowed in to see her soon. God, I hope she's all right.'

131

'She will be, Mum. It's just that house that—' Kelly broke off as Mum glared at her. She wouldn't listen. She never listened. Kelly rolled her eyes.

'Sorry, love. I just don't want to hear your theories about the house right now. Not with Gran lying there hooked up to drips and God knows what. It just doesn't help. I'm glad you came here with me, though. I'd have been in pieces sitting here on my own. Ooh, hey, think I got a text. Maybe it's your dad . . .' She took out her phone and read the text. 'Dad's outside trying to get a car park ticket but he has no money. Do me a favour, love, and run outside to give him some change?' She pulled her purse from her bag and emptied a handful of coins into Kelly's hands.

'Sure, will do, Mum. Back soon, then.' Kelly got up, stretched her aching back and walked quickly along the corridor towards the main hospital entrance. The car park was opposite, and she could just see Dad standing by the pay-and-display machine. She jogged over to him and gave him the money.

'Thanks, Kelly. How is she?' said Pete as he fed the coins into the machine.

'Having tests. We haven't been able to sit with her yet. Mum's pretty upset. She'll be glad you're here.'

'I couldn't believe it when Jason told me. Poor Mrs E.' Kelly followed him to the car to put the ticket inside, then showed him the way into the hospital.

'Follow that corridor towards A&E. There's a waiting room on the left. Mum's there. I'll just go and get you both a cup of tea. Won't be long.'

'You're the best daughter.' Dad gave her a squeeze before striding off in the direction she'd indicated.

Was she, though? She headed towards the bank of vending machines, fed in a pound coin and selected tea with milk, no sugar. If she stayed here at the hospital now, she'd end up going back to the house with her parents later that evening. That bloody house and its ghosts. After what had happened to Great-gran she didn't

132

think she could bear going back. She put the first cup of tea to one side and selected the same again. But what else could she do?

If only there was somewhere else she could stay. Just for a while, until she got her head straight. Sometimes it felt as though she was going mad in that house, with voices in her head and the feeling that someone was looking over her shoulder all the time. And she'd never even had the chance to ask Great-gran more about what happened to Joan. No, she didn't want to go back there tonight. The second cup of tea was dispensed, and she removed it from the machine and put it beside the first. A third, for herself? Or not? No. She didn't want tea. She wanted to get away. And not go home. An idea struck her. On impulse she left the cups of tea on a table beside the vending machine, walked back towards the main entrance, and jumped into the first available taxi.

Chapter Sixteen

April 1944

How could it be the last evening of Jack's leave already? It didn't seem five minutes since Joan had met him at the station, and here she was walking along the prom to meet him at 'their' bench for their last few hours together. Jack had to leave in the morning, on the first train out. Joan was trying to live in the moment, as he'd said she must, but it was so hard, knowing their parting this evening would be the last time she would see him for ages. As if in sympathy, the weather, which had been so good throughout his leave, had turned. There was a chill breeze and a light drizzle. She shivered. It wouldn't be as pleasant sitting on the bench as it usually was. Though she'd be warm enough with Jack's arms around her.

Jack was already there, and stood to greet her.

'I'm so sorry I'm late. Mother wanted me to wash up, Father called us into the sitting room to listen to the radio news, and Betty got suspicious, threatening to tell Father I wasn't really going to the WVS.' Joan kissed him on the lips. 'Still, never mind all that. I'm here now.'

Jack took her hands and sat down, pulling her close beside him. 'I hope you don't get into trouble on my account.'

134

She shook her head. 'Mags stood up for me. She dared Betty to go and ask Mrs Atkins if she didn't believe me. Anyway, I don't care any more if I do get into trouble. We're in love, we're engaged, we're going to be married, and before you come home the next time, I'm going to tell them all. They can't stop us.' She stuck her chin out defiantly.

Jack laughed. 'That's my girl. We have our love and each other. Nothing can stop us.'

'Not even German soldiers,' whispered Joan, snuggling close to him.

Jack put his finger to her lips. 'Shh. That's for tomorrow. We don't think about tomorrow, remember? Now then, what would you like to do this evening? The night is young, and so are we! Shall we go to the pictures, or walk in the rain, or see if my aunt has baked a cake?'

Joan thought for a moment. This was their last evening together. She had spent much of the previous night lying awake, thinking about Jack, about how little time they'd had together, and how to make the most of what was left to them. Who knew what would happen in the future? She couldn't bring herself to consider the worst, but it was a very real possibility. After a little more training Jack would be posted to the battlefields. She wanted to make his last evening with her special. She'd eventually drifted off to sleep having made a decision, and now it was time to tell him.

'Jack, I want us to . . . to do what we would do if we were . . . already married.' She felt herself blushing furiously, but forced herself to lift her head and look directly at him. He must know she meant this, she wanted this, with every part of her.

'Joan, what are you saying? We can't . . . We should wait . . .'

She shook her head. 'No, let's not wait. There's a war on, and we must make the most of every opportunity. We must live in the moment—you said so yourself. We don't know what will happen next, and we mustn't waste the chances we have. I've thought this

135

through, Jack, honestly I have. I know, without a doubt, it's what I want. Don't you want it, too?'

His mouth had dropped open as she spoke. She almost couldn't believe it herself; who'd have thought she could be so forward? But it felt so right. They were meant to be together. In peacetime they'd have waited until they married, but this wasn't peacetime and there were no signs that the war would end soon.

'Oh, Joan, my dear sweet girl! Of course I want to, with you. I just need to be certain that you are certain . . .'

In answer she leaned in and kissed him, long and deep, pressing herself against him. She could feel him tense against her, his mouth on hers more urgent, and she felt herself respond.

But all too soon he pushed her away. 'Darling, not here. The rain is getting heavier, and who knows if someone might come along.'

'Where, then?'

He thought for a moment, his gaze fixed on the meeting of sea and sky. 'I know. Follow me. I don't know how comfortable we'll be but . . .' He stood up and held out his hand to her.

Joan grinned and took his offered hand, allowing him to pull her to her feet. Who cared about comfort if you were in the arms of the man you loved with all your heart?

* * *

The air-raid shelter was in the back garden of an empty house. It was an Anderson shelter, half buried in the earth, with a rough wooden door. Inside was damp, but they were sheltered from the rain. There was a low wooden bench along one side, on which a couple of woollen blankets were folded. Jack found a paraffin lantern and some matches under the bench.

'Perfect,' said Joan. 'We have all we need.'

Jack shook his head. 'Not quite. I know—would you mind just walking once around the block while I make things ready? This is our first time. It has to be right.' He kissed her, and gave her a gentle push out of the shelter.

Joan giggled, feeling nervous now that the moment was near. She retraced their steps across the back garden of the house, down the side passage and out to the street. She hoped no one had seen them go in. The worst thing would be for them to be interrupted. She walked to the end of the road and back. She was about to cross a line—there would be no going back once this was done. She would be a woman, and for better or for worse she would belong to Jack.

The shelter was in the garden of a house not far from Jack's aunt's. The house, so Jack had told her as they walked there from the prom, belonged to an elderly couple whose son had been killed in France the previous year. His wife had been left with four young children, and the couple had moved to Shropshire to help her with them. Joan glanced up at the boarded-up windows, and wondered if the couple would ever be able to move back. Perhaps they could bring their daughter-in-law and grandchildren to live here, once the war ended. It would be nice for the children to be beside the sea.

Jack waved to her from the side passage. She took a deep breath, and followed him back to the shelter.

Inside, he'd laid out the blankets to make a bed on the floor. The lamp was lit, casting a warm glow over everything. Flowers— primula, thrift, forget-me-not—were strewn along the bench, delicately scenting the air. He'd removed his jacket, and made a pillow out of it.

'I thought they wouldn't mind if we took a few flowers. They're growing wild in the garden,' he said.

Joan smiled. He looked as nervous as she felt. 'It's beautiful. Come here; kiss me.'

He stepped forward and took her in his arms. She relaxed against him and her nerves dissipated immediately. Being in his arms felt so right. She belonged there. They kissed, and she ran her hands over his back, relishing the feel of his muscles through his thin shirt. He shuddered at her touch, and pulled her closer. His own hands explored her shoulders, neck, and down, brushing her breasts lightly, sending a tingle down her spine. She groaned, and he let go of her. 'What's wrong? If you've changed your mind, that's all right of course. We can just . . .'

'I haven't changed my mind, my love.' She slipped off her coat and pulled him down onto the makeshift bed he'd made for them. Soon they were unclothed and between the blankets. A thought flitted through Joan's mind—what would Mags say when she told her? And immediately a second thought—she would not tell Mags, or anyone. This was for her and Jack alone to know about. She was brought back to the moment by Jack's touch, delicate and light, but sending shivers throughout her body. Funny how although she'd never done anything like this before, she instinctively knew what to do and how to respond to him.

He hesitated once again before entering her. 'You're sure?'

She smiled and pulled him onto her. 'I've never been more sure of anything, Jack.'

It was magical. She felt as though she'd been living in a dream, and only now was she fully alive. Past and future melted away; there was only the moment they were in. The air-raid shelter, its muddy floor, corrugated iron roof and rough bench, faded into the distance, leaving just the two of them, entwined in the blankets and each other's arms. Nothing mattered any more, only Jack and her and this wonderful, intense feeling of absolute joy mingled with deep, pure love.

* * *

Afterwards, she lay in his arms, and they pulled their coats on top of the blankets for extra warmth. 'You'll have to go soon,' Jack murmured. 'Don't be late home. I don't want to let you go, but you mustn't get into trouble.'

'I don't care,' Joan replied. 'Nothing else matters, only us. Let's stay here, all night.'

'But what will your family say? They'll worry about you.'

'I'll think of something to tell them. Perhaps I'll even tell them the truth. Don't fret about it, Jack.' She snuggled closer, laying her head on his shoulder. She felt so warm, loved, protected. If only this night could last for always, and they could stay here, in their own little world, together, for ever.

Chapter Seventeen

October 2014

Kelly slammed the taxi door, leaned forward and gave the driver an address. Not her parents' address. She couldn't go back there. But there was one place she thought she might feel safe. It was a bit of a gamble perhaps, but she had to try it. Luckily there was a tenner in her cardigan pocket. It might not be enough to get her there, but it would do for now.

The taxi meter read £11.40 by the time it pulled up outside the familiar semi-detached house.

'Uh, I've only got ten pounds on me,' Kelly stuttered, as the taxi driver glared at her. 'Hold on while I knock on the door. I should be able to borrow the rest from my, uh, friend.'

'Please be in, please be in,' Kelly muttered, as she hurried up the garden path. If he wasn't, she was in big trouble. Miles from home, no money, no phone, and in any case, she didn't want to go home. She rang the doorbell with crossed fingers.

Someone was coming to the door, thank goodness. But was it him, or one of his parents? She peered through the frosted glass trying to make out who the blurred figure was. The door opened.

'Matt, I am so glad you are in. Look, can I borrow a couple

of quid? To pay for this taxi? I'll pay you back, soon as I can. And can I come in?'

'Kelly. Hello. Is something wrong?' He frowned, his eyes sad and hurt, and she remembered how he'd thought she was two-timing him with Jack. She'd been so obsessed by Joan and Jack, she'd allowed him to think Jack was someone real, someone alive, and not just a product of her imagination. Or had Joan's influence made her let him think that? Right now all Kelly wanted was to be held in Matt's warm, friendly arms. Where she belonged.

'Yeah, kind of. It's a long story. Can I just get rid of the taxi? Then I'll explain. If it's OK to come in . . . Thing is, I can't go home, and I've no money and no phone . . .'

'For fuck's sake, Kelly.' Matt dug in his pocket and pulled out a two-pound coin. He thrust it at her then turned and walked back into the house, leaving the front door open.

So he wasn't turning her away, at least. She paid the taxi driver, took a deep breath and followed Matt inside, closing the door behind her. He was in the kitchen, sitting at the table with his head in his hands.

'Thanks, Matt. I didn't know where else to go.'

'What, have you run away from home or something? Acting the drama queen as usual? And you thought your ex-boyfriend's house was the best place to turn up? Why didn't you go to Leanne's?'

Kelly shrugged. 'I'm not really friends with Leanne any more. Besides' – she put her hand tentatively on his shoulder – 'I wanted to see you. I want to tell you everything, to try to explain what happened. It's, well, it's kind of weird and you might not believe me, but please, hear me out.'

He stared at her, his eyes still full of hurt. She met his gaze, willing him to soften and listen to her. She didn't know why, but she had the strongest feeling that Matt was the only person who would understand. If she explained it well enough. Her stomach lurched every time she recalled how she'd treated him—kind, gentle Matt who'd adored her, and who she'd pushed away by her obsession with events from seventy years ago.

'Go on then. Tell me.' Matt leaned back in his chair, arms folded.

'Should we go upstairs? For privacy, I mean. This could take some time. I don't want your parents interrupting in the middle of it.'

'They're on holiday till next week. I'm home alone, poor me.' He pulled a face. Kelly smiled. That was more like it, her old, funny Matt back again.

'Can I make us a cup of tea?' she said, already filling the kettle.

'Go on, then. You remember where everything is?'

'Of course. It's only been a month or so since I was last here.'

'Feels like for ever,' he said, quietly.

* * *

Kelly made the tea in silence, then took the cups through to the living room. She sat at one end of the sofa, while Matt chose an overstuffed armchair. Memories of evenings spent watching DVDs while cuddled together on the sofa ran through her mind, but she pushed them aside. Maybe, if he understood, and if he could somehow help her, there could be another chance for them, in time.

'Go on, then,' he said, taking a sip of his tea. 'I'm listening.'

She took a deep breath, and told him everything. How she'd had a strange feeling about the house the very first time she entered it. How she'd become obsessed with the past ever since they discovered the 'Joan loves Jack' writing on her bedroom wall and the box of photos and letters in the cellar. How she'd felt a cold draught on the stairs, and the feeling that someone—Joan—was watching her, influencing her, persuading her to dress in clothes from the 1940s. How she'd felt as though she couldn't get on with her life until she'd found out everything she could about Joan and Jack, and what had happened to them.

142

Matt listened in silence. 'So when you told me you were obsessed by Jack, you meant this Joan's boyfriend?'

Kelly nodded. 'Her sweetheart, yes.'

'Sweetheart? That sounds like one of her words, not yours.'

She shrugged. 'It's just that word sounds right for describing their relationship. Boyfriend sounds weird. If they were still alive today, they'd be really old. And it's strange, but now I'm here she feels more distant. I don't feel as though she's so much in my head. She's still there, but it's like she's looking over my shoulder and maybe whispering in my ear, rather than right inside my head.' She stared at him. 'Matt, you're the only person I've told all this to. Tell me honestly, do you think I'm going mad?'

He was slow to answer, regarding her carefully with his sad grey eyes. She wished she could put that look of love back in them, the special look he'd always had for her, since they'd started going out together.

'No, Kelly. I don't think you're going mad. And I don't think you're making it up, either. Do you believe in ghosts?'

She opened her mouth to answer, but he didn't give her the chance.

'Because I do. And I think some can't rest, until they've resolved something, or found something. I reckon this Joan is dead, but can't sleep quietly for some reason. And for some reason she thinks you can help.'

'But why me?' Kelly felt she already knew the answer, but wanted to hear more of Matt's theory.

'I suppose because you live in that house, where she must once have lived. I wonder who she was?'

'We showed Great-gran the photos we found in the cellar. The one of the three girls and the other one of the soldier. She told us the third girl was her little sister, Joan, and the soldier was her boyfriend, Jack. I'd already guessed who they were, from having read Jack's letters to Joan. Something bad happened, but I don't know all the details, and Great-gran said their father had forbidden them ever to speak of Joan again.'

143

'Why? Was there some scandal or something?'

'Yes—Joan got pregnant, by Jack when she was still a teenager, and had to give the baby up for adoption. But I think something else happened as well.'

'Don't you know? Haven't you asked your Great-gran?'

Kelly finished the remains of her tea as she considered the question. She did need to ask Great-gran more about what happened; she knew it. But when would she be able to, with Great-gran ill in hospital?

'No, and right now I can't. She's not well.' She quickly told Matt what had happened earlier that day. Was it only that afternoon that Great-gran had collapsed when she saw Ryan's hanging skeleton? It seemed like ages ago.

'Oh, babe. That's, well, horrible. What do you think caused her to fall?'

'She didn't fall. It was more of a collapse. She took one look at Ryan's Halloween decorations and it freaked her out.' She shook her head. It was so weird. 'The thing is, Matt, it freaked me out a bit as well. I mean, when I saw it I felt as though I could hear Joan screaming in my head. Really screaming. If I'd been old and frail like Great-gran I reckon I might have collapsed as well. And now she's in hospital.' She didn't want to tell him yet that she'd come straight from there, leaving her parents. He would lecture her about that; she knew it. Right now, he was staring at her, quizzically.

'Your parents know you're here, right?'

'No. Not exactly.'

'It's, uh,' he looked at the mantelpiece clock, 'getting on for nine p.m. Do you still have that eleven o'clock curfew? I guess I can lend you the taxi fare home, when you're ready.'

Kelly leaned back in the sofa, kicked off her shoes and curled her legs up underneath her. 'I don't want to go home, Matt. Can't I stay here? Like, in your mum's spare room or something?'

'Well, I guess so . . . You'll have to phone your mum and tell her, though. She'll worry.'

'She'll come and get me and make me go home.' Kelly stuck her chin out, defiantly.

'She might . . .'

'And I'm not going back there. I can't, Matt! Haven't you been listening to me? That house freaks me out. It's spooky. Filled with Joan's presence, or ghost, or whatever you want to call it. I can feel her there the whole time. She's influencing me—making me do stuff, wear stuff I don't really like, listen to that retro Amelia Fay music I'm not really into. What if she gets stronger, and takes over completely? It scares me. I hate it. It's horrible, Matt. I can't go back there!' She buried her face in her hands and sobbed. He had to understand. There was nowhere else she could go, no one else she could talk to.

'Shh, babe, it's all right. I'm here.' Kelly felt him sit beside her on the sofa, and then his strong arms were wrapped around her. How she'd missed him! She nestled against his shoulder, his familiar aftershave making her feel at home. He kissed the top of her head. She wondered whether to lift her face, kiss him back, or might he pull away? Was she misconstruing his actions? Perhaps he was only offering sympathy, but more and more she realised she wanted him back, as her boyfriend.

But there was still more of the story to tell. She took a deep breath, then sat upright again, putting space between her and Matt.

'I haven't told you it all, yet.'

'Go on,' he said, his eyes deep with worry.

She told him how she'd gone to the hospital with Mum and Great-gran. How they'd sat and waited while Great-gran was checked over. He sat listening in silence, and when she got to the part about how she'd just left in a taxi without telling her parents, he groaned and held his head in his hands.

'Kells, you shouldn't have left. Not just like that. They'll be worried sick, and they've got your poor great-gran to worry about as well. You'll have to go back home tonight.'

She stood up angrily. 'I knew when I told you this part you'd get cross. I suppose you think I'm mad, going on about Joan in my head. Mum won't even listen to me when I try to tell her about it. But I just need to be away from that frigging house and all the memories floating around in it. I reckon if I never went back there, I'd be OK.'

'You can't stay here,' Matt began.

'Not for ever, no. Obviously. But just for a night or two, can't I? Your parents are away; they don't even need to know. I'll wash the sheets tomorrow.'

'Then what?'

'I don't know. I'll think of something.' She paced up and down the room.

Matt sighed, got to his feet and stood in front of her. 'Come here, babe. I'm sorry. I do believe you, I think. It's weird, but if you say that's what's happening then I'll buy it. You've never lied to me.' He wrapped his arms around her. She felt safe in his arms. She buried her face against his shoulder, and hooked her thumbs in his belt loops.

'I'm scared if I go back there, Joan might take me over completely. Or I'll go completely mad or something.'

'Shh, babe. You don't need to go back. But I do think you need to call your mum and tell her you're safe.'

She shook her head. 'No. She'd come and get me.'

'But if you don't, she'll be frantic. It's bad enough already, as you never went back with the cups of tea. The longer it goes on the more frantic she'll become. Don't do that to her.'

'I'll call her tomorrow.'

He pushed her away from him, and held her by the shoulders. 'No, Kelly. If you want to stay here tonight, you call her now. You don't need to say where you are, just tell her you're OK, and that you'll phone her again in the morning. It's not fair on her or your dad otherwise. It's not their fault.'

He was right, and she knew it. He'd always been the sensible one, the one who thought through consequences in detail. The one who knew what others would be thinking. She'd mocked him in the past, for being too straight, too grown-up, when after all, they were only seventeen. But she didn't want to cause her mum pain. She'd been worried enough by Great-gran's collapse. 'All right,' she said. 'I'll do it. But I don't have my phone on me and if I use your house phone she'll know where I am.'

'Use my mobile. She doesn't have my number—I changed it last week when I switched contracts.' He pulled it out of his pocket and handed it to her. 'Then, *after* you've talked to her, I'll dig out a pair of jeans and a hoodie, so you can dress like Kelly rather than Joan.'

She grinned, took the mobile and tapped in her mother's number.

Chapter Eighteen

June 1944

As the landing craft drew near to the beach Jack scanned left and right. He was nervous, of course he was, but relieved that at least he hadn't been part of the first wave. What must it have been like, three days earlier, on D-Day itself? The beach they were landing on was secured, the debris of battle still scarring it, but thankfully the fallen soldiers' bodies had been removed and hastily buried. He could feel Mikey shaking beside him.

'It'll be all right, kid,' he said. 'We'll get through this, you'll see.' Mikey grinned nervously at him, but carried on shaking. He was just seventeen, but had lied about his age so he could join up early. Too young for this, Jack thought, forgetting for a moment that he was himself only eighteen. He slipped his hand inside his pocket and felt the now-grubby handkerchief containing a lock of Joan's hair. It was his lucky talisman. He'd kept it with him always, whenever he was away from her.

Closer in now, they could see the remnants of barbed-wire defences along the tops of the dunes. There were deep craters in the beach where shells had exploded above the high water line. Burst boxes of supplies and ammunition, broken armoured vehicles that had been hit, a landing craft nose down, filled with water. Anti-tank defences were still in evidence, some knocked out of line but still there, jagged shards of metal thrusting out of the sand like arms of part-buried soldiers, reaching skywards for help. Jack shook his head, banishing the image from his mind.

Ahead, the first few landing craft of their wave had reached the shore, and soldiers were splashing through the water and regrouping on the beach. Jack squeezed Mikey's shoulder. 'Almost there, kid. You ready?'

'As I'll ever be,' Mikey replied, his eyes fixed on the dunes ahead.

And then the landing craft grounded, the ramps were lowered, and Jack and Mikey along with the rest of their squad disgorged into the shallows. The water was cold and murky, the sand beneath his feet shifting and unstable. Mikey, beside him, lost his footing and fell, floundering in the surf. Jack caught his arm and hauled him to his feet. Thank God they weren't under fire. What must it have been like, for the first few to land? How many even made it to the beach? He shuddered. Some things did not bear thinking about.

Knee deep now, and his uniform weighed twice as much as it had done on the boat. Still clinging on to Mikey's arm he struggled up the beach, pulling the boy after him. Sergeant Crane was already out of the water, waving his arms around and shouting orders. Jack emerged from the surf and let go of Mikey's arm. 'All right?'

'Yeah.' Mikey shrugged, and joined the chain of soldiers unloading boxes from the landing craft. Jack nodded. Mikey hadn't liked the crossing, admitting he was not much of a sailor. Now his feet were on solid ground he'd be fine. He was a plucky lad, and Jack had liked him instantly. They'd teamed up in training and had made a pact to look after each other once they were on the Normandy battlefields. Jack had told Mikey about Joan, though he'd left out the details of their night together in the air-raid shelter. Mikey told Jack about his childhood sweetheart, Eileen, the girl next door who he'd grown up with and who he hoped would marry him once the war was over. Jack had wondered how many more couples there were, waiting for the war to finish so they could marry and get on with their lives.

The boxes of supplies were heavy and came thick and fast from the boat. Jack's arms were aching long before they'd finished unloading. At last it was done, and the boxes were stacked in the dunes. The lads who'd arrived over the previous three days fell upon the new rations eagerly—chocolate and cigarettes being the most popular items. In the field behind the dunes, a makeshift camp had been set up. Here, wounded men lay waiting to be loaded onto the landing craft for the return journey to the hospital ship sitting out at anchor. Jack and Mikey's next job was to help with the stretchers, carrying them across the beach and on to the boats. There were distant sounds of warfare—the occasional crump of shells exploding—thankfully they were out of range.

'Good luck, mate,' said one private, whose mangled leg was bound to a makeshift splint. 'I'm glad to be getting out of here. Go and liberate France for us.'

'We will,' Jack replied, clapping the fellow on the shoulder. 'You've done a great job, made it easy for us.'

'Did our best,' said the man, groaning with pain as Jack and Mikey hauled his stretcher onto the landing craft.

'Did you see his leg?' said Mikey, as they waded back to shore. 'They won't be able to mend that for him.'

'He'll be all right. Once he's in an English hospital they'll patch him up just fine.' Jack suspected the man would have to lose his leg but didn't want to think about it. This was what war was about. The myriad individual acts of bravery and sacrifice. What would he be called upon to do? Would there be a big moment, in which he would have to prove himself? He hoped he would be up to the job, whatever it would be.

It was a long and tough day, and they hadn't even seen any battle action yet. Jack was impressed with the scale of the operation. So many men, so much material and supplies, all brought across the channel by boat or plane. The big push was well underway: forcing the Germans off the beaches, out of the fields, back towards the towns and cities; then they would fight to regain the towns, push towards Paris, give France back to the French. They must and *would* prevail. There was a feeling of confidence—news from the last three days had been positive, and with temporary harbours now being constructed to help with offloading supplies, it could only be a matter of weeks before the Allied forces reached Paris. For a moment Jack imagined himself marching into that great city, with French children cheering and waving flags. No, it wouldn't be like that, he knew. It would be a long and bloody battle, with many losses on both sides. Who knew whether he would be a part of it or not? First, his unit had a more immediate battle—to take the little village of Sainte-Marie, which lay a couple of miles inland. There was a bridge over the river there, strategically placed, and the Allies needed to gain control of it. Which meant liberating the village first.

They worked till darkness fell, shipping out the injured men, organising the incoming supplies and equipment. Jack collapsed exhausted onto his bedding roll, in the makeshift encampment his battalion had set up in a captured German gun emplacement. He took out the locket of Joan's hair, wrapped in her handkerchief, and breathed in its scent, as he lay staring up at the just-past-full moon. Perhaps Joan was looking up at the moon too—the same moon. Was she thinking of him? Was she wearing his locket? Not a moment went by when she was not forefront of his mind. He felt she was with him in spirit, always and for ever. The idea comforted him and kept him going. He was fighting this war for her, so that she could live her life in a free country, with him by her side. The harder he worked the sooner this war would be over and they could be together. He drifted off to sleep under the moonlight, dreaming of Joan.

* * *

The next day was cloudy with intermittent sunshine. At least it wasn't raining, Jack thought. He awoke stiff and aching but well rested. The squad breakfasted off tinned pork and tea before being briefed by Sergeant Crane. The objective for the morning was to launch an attack on the village of Sainte-Marie from the northeast, with other units approaching it from different directions. The village lay in a shallow valley among farmland. Just short of the village there was a large barn, which the Germans had used as an ammunition dump. That needed to be destroyed, and most of the squad led by Sergeant Crane were to attack it first and go on to take the village. There was also a German machine gun emplacement on a slight rise to the east, and that needed to be taken out in a simultaneous attack. Jack and Mikey were assigned the task of setting up a mortar under cover of a hedgerow, to destroy the machine gun.

'This is it, kid,' said Jack. 'The real thing. What we did all that training for.'

'I'm ready for it.' Mikey's fists were clenched and his gaze, across the fields in the direction of the German emplacement, hidden from their view by the lie of the land, was steady.

'Good lad. Keep low and quiet in the ditches and you won't be seen. Get that mortar set up, and fire it once you see my signal. We'll attack the barn at the same time. Good luck.' Sergeant Crane nodded curtly and sent them on their way.

Jack led, carrying the mortar, crouching low beside the hedgerows. Mikey carried a bag of mortar shells. There was a drainage ditch running along the edge of the field, which meant they had good cover but their feet were wet. Halfway across the first field they disturbed a pheasant, which flew up vertically making a terrible clacking racket.

'Might as well send up a flare to tell Jerry we're here,' muttered Jack. He flung himself face down in the muddy ditch and gestured to Mikey to follow suit. Any moment now there could be the rattle of machine-gun fire, strafing the ditch. But none came.

Cautiously he raised his head. They were still just out of range. The machine-gun placement was over the next field, and couldn't be seen from where they were. Which meant the Germans couldn't see them either, though they would have seen the pheasant's frantic flapping.

'We're all right,' he whispered to Mikey. 'Let's get going.' He resumed crawling along the ditch, the heavy mortar gun making progress difficult. At the corner of the field he pulled out a pair of wire cutters and used them to snip a way through the hedge at ground level. Using elbows and knees he wormed his way through, pulling the equipment after him. Mikey followed.

This field's ditch was shallower than the last, and drier, not much more than an indentation. Jack grimaced. It wouldn't give them much cover. And from here, the tops of the sandbags surrounding the German machine gun were just visible, over the next hedgerow.

'On your belly. Right in close to the hedge. We can set up the mortar once we're through to the next field.' Jack moved forward, crawling commando-style and praying that the Germans' attention was elsewhere. Was the machine-gun post even manned? They had to assume so, but from here they couldn't tell. Not without standing upright and advertising their presence, which Jack had no intention of doing.

The sudden rattle of machine-gun fire provided an answer. It was definitely manned. And the Germans had seen something they didn't like. Jack flattened himself completely and rolled into the hedge. He could see Mikey had done the same, and was lying there shaking with fear. But the firing had not been aimed at them. It was something else, further up the field. A flash of red, a movement in the hedge. Something was there. Something that shouldn't be there.

'I'm going to check out that movement. Wait here. Keep still,' he said to Mikey. He offloaded the equipment he was dragging. It was easier going without it, and he'd be less noticeable. He made quick progress, until another burst of fire sent him rolling into the hedge again. Cursing the tangle of brambles he found himself ensnared in, he glanced up and down the field, trying to work out where the fire had been targeted. Up the field, again a flash of red, just a few yards away from him now. Down the field, a slight movement, back where he'd left Mikey. Another burst of gunfire. Dear God don't let it be Mikey they've spotted. Keep still, kid. That red, it was clothing. It was moving, crawling through the hedge. He elbowed his way quickly over the remaining yards, and through the same gap in the hedge. On the other side, crouched in the next drainage ditch and sobbing, was a small child in a tattered scarlet dress. She flinched and hid her eyes when he followed her through the hedge.

'It's all right. I won't hurt you,' he said, quietly. She began to wail, but he caught her quickly and put his hand over her mouth. He racked his brain to remember the French he'd learned at grammar school. 'Shh, little one. *Tiens-toi tranquille.* We're playing a game. We must be quiet as mice. *Fais comme une petite souris. Compris?*' Thankfully the child nodded, and stopped crying. She was probably about four years old, he estimated. Jack held her tightly and looked around. This field was thigh deep with wheat and fell away sharply to his left. At the bottom was a farmhouse. Was that where the child had come from? Or was it occupied by the Germans? He should get back to Mikey, set up the rocket launcher, destroy the machine-gun post. But in his arms the little girl whimpered and shook. He couldn't leave her. An image flashed through his mind of Joan, sitting on the floor at the WVS, playing with the little children. She wouldn't leave a vulnerable child. Neither would he.

'*D'où viens-tu?* Where've you come from, pet?'

She pointed, down towards the farmhouse.

'*Ta maman? Ton papa?*'

'*Oui.*' Tears streamed down her face, making pale tracks in the grime.

So she was from the farmhouse. He had to take her back. Perhaps her parents were there, safe, hiding from the battle. One thing was for certain, she wasn't safe out in this field. Not until the machine-gun post was destroyed and even then, not till the village was secured. There was no choice. He had to get across the field with her, find somewhere safe at the farmhouse for her, and only then could he get back to Mikey. The distant crump of shells told him the battle for the village had begun. He needed to complete his mission, to do his part so that Sainte-Marie could be liberated quickly and with minimal loss of life. But first, the child.

'*Allons-y.*' He scooped her up under one arm, and began running around the edge of the field, keeping close to the hedge. He couldn't crawl while holding her. The sooner he got to the farmhouse, the safer they would both be. He had to take a chance and run. At any moment he expected machine-gun fire at his heels. He prayed there wasn't also a sniper holed up somewhere. He ran faster, gasping for breath, the child screaming now. No point hushing her. He must have been spotted by now. But there was no rattle of machine-gun fire. Perhaps Jerry could see he was saving the child, and perhaps Jerry was human too, not wanting to kill an innocent. He had to believe so. At least as he crossed the field he was moving out of their range.

The farmhouse was positioned on one side of a small yard, opposite a tumbledown, empty barn and deserted chicken coop. The door stood partly open.

'Hello? *Quelqu'un?* Anyone there?' God, please don't let there be Germans here. The door opened into a kitchen, a large table in the centre of the room, debris from the last meal the family had eaten here strewn across it. A jug of milk, gone off in the June heat, sat beside the deep sink. Flies buzzed around a dish of jam.

'*Maman!*' the little girl wailed.

Where indeed was Maman? Jack hoped Maman or Papa were nearby, and more to the point, alive. What if the Germans had killed them, as they retreated from the first wave of the Allied invasion? He glanced around. Where would they have hidden?

A door in the corner of the room looked promising. It was tightly shut. He crossed over to it, and tried the handle. Locked. Was this the door to the cellar? The little girl pounded her tiny fists against it, shouting for her maman.

There was a noise behind the door. Jack offered up a swift prayer that it was the child's family, and not holed-up German soldiers. Some whispered speech, one person shushing another, steps, the sound of a scuffle.

'*Maman!*' squealed the child, growing frantic.

He should take no chances. He crouched behind the table, pushing the child behind him, and pulled out his Browning pistol. Aiming it at the cellar door he held his breath as he heard a key turn in the lock. The door opened slowly, and a man, wearing a rough shirt and trousers tied with a piece of rope, peered out. He was holding a poker as a weapon.

Jack sighed with relief. '*Je suis soldat anglais,*' he said, and the man broke into a grin, talking quickly to someone behind him.

A woman, her face lined with worry, pushed past the man. '*Véronique, ma petite, où es-tu? Véronique!*'

Jack stood aside and pushed the little girl towards her. He watched as the woman scooped her up and covered her face with desperate kisses. He couldn't imagine what they'd been through, wondering where their child was, with battles raging in their fields. Battles that weren't over yet. He gestured for them to go back into the cellar, and lock the door. Until the village was secure, they would have to stay in hiding.

The man ushered the woman and child down the cellar steps, then turned to shake Jack's hand. '*Merci, merci, merci,*' he said, his eyes conveying even more thanks than his words. Jack nodded silently, then turned to leave. It was all nothing more than one tiny drama in the enormous theatre of war. And he still had a job to do.

He made it back across the lower field, keeping lower than

before. Jerry might have spared him while he carried a small child, but he had no such talisman now. He dived back through the gap in the hedge where he'd followed little Véronique. Keeping low and quiet, he crawled back to where he'd left Mikey and the equipment.

The mortar and bag of shells was there, but no Mikey. Only a smear of blood along the bottom of the ditch. 'Shit, Mikey, what's happened?' Jack muttered. He followed the trail of blood a few yards further along the ditch, and found Mikey, lying on his back, clutching at wounds in his thigh and side.

'Mikey, oh Christ, Mikey. Hang on, kid. I'll soon patch you up.' The thigh wound was pumping blood. Jack pulled out his knife and cut off the lower part of Mikey's trouser leg. He tore a strip of it and tied it tightly above the leg wound, wadding the rest against the hole in Mikey's side. He placed Mikey's hand over this. 'Push hard. Keep the pressure on. I'll get you home.'

'Never coming home,' Mikey mumbled.

'Yes you are, kid. You're not fighting any more with those injuries. We'll have you back on a boat in no time. Shit!' Jack ducked as more machine-gun fire rattled across the field. He felt the whoosh of a bullet right past the side of his head. 'Too close. Mikey, look, I've got to get that mortar set up. We've no hope unless I can take out the machine gun. Keep that pressure on, and hang on in there.'

Mikey mumbled some more, but kept his hand on the wad of fabric. Jack crawled back to the equipment, and working quickly, set it up. Using his binoculars he scanned the hedgerows. Yes, over there, higher up the hill he could see the wall of sandbags. He needed one single direct hit. To his left, back the way they'd come, was the barn from which Sergeant Crane would give the signal. Could he wait for a signal? What if it never came? With the mortar set up and loaded, he scanned the barn. A glint of sunlight on something. And again. That was the signal. He aimed and fired, one, two, three shells in quick succession, wincing with ear pain as each one fired. 'Be a direct hit, please. Take them out,' he muttered.

Part of him felt shocked at this, the first time he'd actively tried to kill another human, but he knew those Germans had badly injured Mikey and had tried to kill him. He'd been lucky to have escaped so far. The machine gun would do so much more damage if it were left. Pointing the other way it could cover the whole village.

The third shell hit its target. Bingo! A scream, and a ball of fire shot into the air, flaming orange and red against the dull clouds. He'd aimed well. Now for Mikey.

He crawled back to Mikey. 'How are you doing, kid?'

Mikey's lips moved but no sound came out. He'd let go of the wad of fabric against his side. Jack pressed it back tight again. 'Hang on, kid. I'll get you home.'

'Eileen . . . Tell Eileen . . .'

'You'll tell her yourself, when you're back in Blighty,' Jack said.

Mikey shook his head feebly. 'No, never coming home. Tell Eileen . . .'

'Go on then, what should I tell her?'

'Tell her . . . Tell Eileen . . .' Mikey's voice trailed away. Blood bubbled between his lips.

'No, kid. No. Stay with me.' Jack cradled his friend's head. He had to get him down off the hill, back to their makeshift camp. He pulled Mikey to a sitting position, hoisted his arm over his shoulder, and stood, hauling Mikey over his back in a fireman's lift. With the machine gun neutralised it'd be safe, and quicker, to do this on foot. Staggering under the weight he began to half walk, half run, down the field. In the distance he could see Sergeant Crane organising the men. The munitions dump in the barn was engulfed in flames. They could advance on the village now. Jack had done his job, and taken out that machine gun. He'd saved a child too. All that remained was to get Mikey back, to save him as well. He imagined telling Joan the story of this, his first real action. She'd be proud of him. So proud. He fell to one knee under Mikey's weight, then hauled himself back to his feet. Not far to go.

* * *

158

Jack never saw the sniper, nor heard the shot. There was a searing pain, a vision of Joan smiling and holding out her hands to him, and then blackness as he fell, still clutching the dead body of Mikey.

Chapter Nineteen

November 2014

'I don't know why you agreed she could stay here last night,' said Pete, as he parked in front of Matt's house. 'We should have brought her home last night.'

'I know. But she was so upset. I've never heard her react like that.' Ali shook her head at the memory of Kelly's anguished wailing on the phone the previous night, when Ali had suggested driving over from the hospital to collect her there and then. She unclipped her seat belt and climbed out of the car.

'We were *all* upset, Ali, with what happened to your gran. Thank goodness *she's* OK at least. It was just thoughtless and irresponsible for Kelly to run out on us like that, while we were waiting at the hospital.'

Ali waited for him to lock the car and they approached the house together. 'Calm down, Pete. Please. We need to be a united front here, find out what's wrong and why she won't come home. Remember what Matt said to us, about there being a good reason, though one we'd find hard to believe. He promised us he'd persuade her to tell us everything this morning.'

'She'd better do,' growled Pete, as he leaned on the doorbell.

'His parents aren't at home, are they? And we let her stay the night with him?'

Ali sighed. 'She's seventeen. Old enough. I trust her. And him. Besides, they're not an item any more.'

As Matt opened the door, Pete barged past him into the hallway. 'Kelly? Where are you? Listen, girl, you'd better not ever pull a stunt like this again. Have you any idea how frantic your mum was when we couldn't find you at the hospital? Thoughtless, that's what you are. She was worried sick.'

Kelly emerged from the kitchen, her eyes downcast at her father's tirade but her chin slightly jutted in at attitude of defiance. Ali knew that expression. It meant that she would take whatever was coming to her, but that she would not give in.

'Pete, go easy on her. Come on, let's sit down and talk about this properly. Matt, dear, any chance of a cup of tea?'

'Of course, Mrs Bradshaw. I'll get the kettle on. Go through to the living room, please.'

Kelly led the way, and curled herself up on an oversized armchair. Ali took one end of the sofa and gestured for Pete to sit beside her. But he remained standing, hands on hips. 'So. What happened? Why did you run off from the hospital? Why were you so upset last night, and why are you refusing to come home?'

Ali reached for his hand and pulled him towards her. 'Pete, give her a chance to answer one question at a time.'

'Kells, tell them what you told me last night,' said Matt, quietly, from the doorway.

Ali watched as Kelly made eye contact with him, and he nodded encouragingly. Matt was such a good influence on her daughter. Maybe this would bring them back together again. She hoped so. She'd always liked Matt.

'All right. I'll tell them. But I bet they won't believe me.'

Matt crossed the room and leaned over to whisper something to her. She nodded, took a deep breath and began to speak.

*   *   *

'Oh, what rubbish, Kelly. Ghosts? In our house? And you think you're hearing the voices of the dead? That's ridiculous. Crazy.' Pete had stood up again, and was pacing the room, waving his arms around.

'Sit down, Pete, you'll knock something over,' Ali said. She didn't believe in ghosts either, but was prepared to listen to more.

'Our daughter is babbling about the house being haunted by the ghost of your gran's dead sister and you're worried I might break an ornament?' Despite his words, Pete sat down, and stared at Kelly. 'So what happened to them? To Joan and her fellow?'

Kelly shook her head. 'I don't know. When we asked Great-gran about it she got too tired to tell us the end of their story. We were going to ask her more about it yesterday, but then she collapsed before we had the chance to.'

Matt came back in with a tray of tea and biscuits, which he put down on the coffee table and handed round. 'So, she's told you then? About Joan?'

'She's told us, yes. Though I don't understand why it means she can't come home,' grumbled Pete. Ali pinched her lips together. He was always like this with things he didn't understand or couldn't control.

'Because it's worse in our house, Dad. It was her house too; she lived there when she was my age, during the war. And when I'm there, I can feel her all the time, and hear her voice in my head, and she makes me want to wear clothes like she would have worn, and talk like she would have. It's frightening, Mum. What if she took over completely and I couldn't stop her? I'm scared, Mum. That's why I didn't want to come home last night. Why I still don't want to come home. If I'm away from home it's easier—she feels more distant. I can control it more, and feel more like myself. Please, don't make me come home!' Tears ran down Kelly's face.

Ali jumped up and went to sit on the arm of Kelly's chair, hugging her. 'Oh, love, we're not going to make you if it scares

162

you that much.' She glared at Pete. 'And your dad agrees. We'll think of something.'

'She can stay here. In the spare room, I mean. I'll call my parents to ask them but I'm sure they wouldn't mind.'

'Thanks, Matt. But yes, you must check with your parents first.' Ali had only met Matt's mum and dad once but they'd seemed like good people. She'd have done the same for Matt if needed. Any time.

'Hang on, do I get a say in this?' Pete said. Ali shook her head in warning, but Pete ignored her and carried on. 'She can stay here if it helps—I'm not an ogre; I don't want to see my little girl all upset. But we need to find a solution to this. Kelly has to be able to come home soon. I think we have to find out what happened to this Joan and her boyfriend. Maybe that'll help Kelly move on. There must be some reason. Ghosts don't just haunt people for the hell of it.'

'Dad, you're talking as though you believe me.'

'I don't believe in ghosts, sweetheart. But you're right about Joan's presence being in the house—it is. There was her writing on the wall in your room, and her belongings in the basement. Then your imagination has got going with all that, your quest to find out the full story—*that's* what's allowed her to get inside your head. You're not possessed by her; you're obsessed. But we do need to lay it all to rest, one way or another. We have to find the truth.'

'Thanks, Dad. Mum?'

'I don't know, love. I just don't know.' Ali wanted to believe everything her daughter said, but how could she? Ghosts, voices in her head? It was all too much. She considered what Pete had said. He was talking sense—whether or not you believed in ghosts, something had got inside Kelly's head. Even if it was just her overactive teenage imagination. 'We'll have to ask Gran. As soon as possible. She must know what happened to her sister. She didn't want to talk about it last time we asked her, but she'll have to, now. We do need to know. Your dad's right.'

Kelly stared at her. 'But Great-gran's surely not well enough?'

'She was much better when we left her last night. I think they'll probably discharge her today. Like you, I think she is perfectly all right if she's away from our house. I'll be taking her home, and I'll arrange for us to visit her at the nursing home tomorrow.' Ali looked at Pete and shook her head. 'We should have listened to Gran. She never wanted us to move into the house in the first place. We should have just sold up and bought somewhere else.'

'Now's not the time for that discussion, Ali,' Pete said, firmly.

* * *

Gran was looking tired and drawn when they arrived at the nursing home the next day. She seemed to be shrinking—every time Ali saw her she was smaller, frailer and more hunched. They must make the effort to see her more while they still had her, Ali thought, sadly.

'How's things, Gran?' she said, bending over to give the old lady a kiss. This time she was in her own room, sitting quietly in the armchair beside her bed. The TV was on—some documentary about a seventy-something Frenchwoman, Véronique Dupont, who'd spent her life leading humanitarian relief efforts across the globe, was playing at full volume. 'Do you mind if I turn this off?'

'No, not at all. I wasn't really watching it. I'm not so bad, Alison, love. I've got over that nasty turn from Halloween. Was that only two days ago? It feels like longer.' She lifted her gaze and widened her eyes when she saw Pete, Matt and Kelly. 'Gosh, you've brought a lot of people with you. Is it a special day? Is it my birthday?'

'No, Gran, not your birthday. That's not till next month. It's November now.'

'I know it's November, love. I'm not going cuckoo just yet, you know. But you don't normally bring so many people. And who is this handsome young man?' She pointed a wavering finger at Matt.

'I'm Matt. Kelly's, um, friend. Pleased to meet you, Mrs Eliot. I've heard a lot about you.' Matt took her hand in his, and gave it a gentle shake. Gran smiled up at him, clearly delighted by him. Good old Matt, always behaving impeccably. Ali wondered again if there was a chance he and Kelly might resume their relationship. That would be a good thing all round.

'Gran, we've come to ask you to tell us a little bit more about your sister Joan,' said Ali, gently. 'You see, Kelly's been, um, fascinated by her, ever since she found that photo of the three of you. And the other photo, of the young soldier.'

'Oh dear.' Gran sighed and then took a deep breath. 'I thought you might come back and ask about her again. Especially after what happened at your house the other day. All these years, and I said nothing, as Father and then Betty advised. But now they're gone, and I suppose there's no harm in telling you about her.'

'Please do, Great-gran. I'm longing to hear more about her. It's funny, but I feel as though I've got some kind of connection with her.' Ali threw her daughter a warning glance. No point in frightening the old lady with talk of ghosts. She'd already warned them all to say nothing of this. Gran was too old and frail to be worried by such things.

'All right. Well. That soldier, his name was Jack. I told you about him last time, didn't I? He was Joanie's sweetheart. She loved him, so much. It nearly broke her heart when he signed up and went away to the war. He could have trained as an engineer, stayed out of it and got himself a civilian job, but she knew he felt he had to do something for his country. Is it time for tea? I don't suppose Kelly's made another lovely lemon drizzle cake, has she? I did enjoy the last one.'

'Sorry, no cakes this time. I'll make you one next time I come, I promise, Great-gran,' said Kelly.

Gran continued her story. 'Anyway, Jack came home on leave, after his training and before being posted to France. Joanie was so happy to have him back. I covered for her, lied through my teeth to Father, I did. But it was worth it to see her happy. But, oh dear me, it was to be the last time she saw him.' She broke off, and shook her head sadly.

'What happened to him?' Ali asked, gently. Kelly was sitting absolutely still, barely breathing.

'He was involved in the Normandy landings,' Gran went on. 'Not actually on D-Day, but a few days later. His aunt came round with the telegram. Oh, poor Joanie . . .' Again, she shook her head.

'She must have been devastated,' Pete commented.

'Yes, and even more so because of . . .'

'Because of?' It would be the pregnancy. Ali was sure of it.

Another sigh. Gran was clearly having difficulty breaking her silence after all these years. 'They'd got engaged, you see. While he was home on leave, he'd asked her to marry him once the war was over.'

'So sad. Did your father know?' Joan had been seventeen. The same age Kelly was now. Ali tried to imagine how she'd react if Kelly and Matt got engaged. However much she liked Matt, she was sure she would feel they were far too young for such a step.

'Not straight away,' Gran replied. 'Joanie had kept it secret to start with. She only told them to try to make them understand . . . about the other thing . . .'

'Great-gran, please go on. What was the other thing?' Kelly's eyes were wet with unshed tears.

'Well, the thing was, as they had planned to marry, they'd, well, jumped the gun a bit. When he was home on leave. And of course, these things happen, and Joanie found herself . . . pregnant. There, I've said it. Father was furious. You can imagine. Poor Joanie. A baby on the way, and Jack dead in France. It was a terrible, terrible time.'

Ali caught Kelly's eye. So Jack was the father of Joan's baby then, as they had guessed. And therefore he was Jason's grandfather. But they couldn't mention Jason to her yet. It would be too much of a shock. 'Gran, oh, I'm sorry. We didn't mean to distress you asking about all this.' She jumped up and hugged the old lady, who had tears streaming down her cheeks. 'Pete, pass me a tissue. There, Gran. Poor Joan. How awful, and she was so young.'

'Yes, so very, very young. Don't ask me to remember any more, Alison. Not today, love. I'm so tired. I think I need to rest now.' She leaned back in her chair, looking even more old and worn than when they arrived. Ali glanced at Kelly. She too was looking worn, but there was a light gleaming in her eye. It was helping her, finding out the truth, hearing their guesses confirmed by Gran. They would have to come to see her again soon, Ali realised. There was more to the story, she was sure, but Gran wasn't able to talk about it today.

'We'll leave you in peace then,' she said, kissing Gran goodbye. The old lady's eyes were almost closed. Ali pulled a knitted rug from the bed and tucked it around her. 'Enjoy your nap. We'll be back with lemon drizzle cake soon. Come on, troops.'

* * *

'Did it help, talking to your great-gran?' Matt asked.

Kelly nodded. 'Yes, definitely. I'd kind of guessed something tragic like that must have happened to Jack. And at least we've confirmed that Jack was the father of her baby. Jason's mum. I mean, we'd guessed but it was good to hear it for certain.'

Ali and Pete had dropped Kelly and Matt off at Matt's house after the visit. Pete had agreed that Kelly could stay with him, as long as Matt okayed it with his parents, which he'd done while Ali and Pete were still there. As expected, they hadn't minded at all. Ali had given Kelly twenty quid towards her food bill, and promised to call round again the next day. Then they'd left.

Matt had cooked them a pizza, and they'd shared a couple of cans of lager before curling up on the sofa in front of the TV. This must be what being married is like, Kelly thought. Sitting companionably with the curtains drawn and the heating on, while rain lashes down outside, but we're warm and safe here in our little nest. She patted the sofa beside her. 'Come and sit with me?'

Matt gave her a questioning look, but picked up his can and moved over. Kelly snuggled up against him. 'You don't mind, do you?'

'Not at all.' He put his arm around her shoulders and pulled her close. 'Like old times, isn't it?'

'Mmm.' She laid her head against him, enjoying the feeling of warmth and security. She turned her face upwards, to see Matt gazing down at her, a slight crease between his eyes.

'What's happening here, babe?' he whispered.

In answer, she shifted position so that she could kiss him, full on the lips, long and deep, as they used to do. He responded cautiously at first, then eagerly, his hands stroking her face, her neck, running down her back and around to her breasts.

'God, I've missed you,' he said throatily, as she pulled him down on top of her, sensing his mounting excitement as she slipped a hand down the back of his jeans.

They could do it, right here, right now, she realised. They never had, before. There hadn't been the opportunity. You could hardly go for it in a bedroom when your parents were sitting downstairs. And she'd always wanted her first time to be special, not rushed or uncomfortable, not down a side alley or on top of a pile of coats at a party. This was the perfect chance. And she did love Matt. She wanted him back. She fumbled with his jeans buttons and slipped her hand inside. He groaned.

'Do you want to . . . you know?'

'Yes. And I think you do, too.' She giggled, giving him a squeeze which elicited another groan.

He undid her jeans, and used both hands to tug them down over her hips, while she rolled her T-shirt off over her head. There was a fleece throw folded on the back of the sofa, which he pulled down over them.

Suddenly, he stopped. 'Um, babe, I don't suppose you've got any—'

'Shit. No. Have you?'

'No.'

An image of Joan, swollen with Jack's baby, flashed through Kelly's mind. Joan had become pregnant by Jack and then lost him, and had to give her baby up for adoption. What if the same happened to Kelly? No. It wouldn't happen. They couldn't risk it. She pushed him away and rolled off the sofa, retrieving her jeans and T-shirt. 'Sorry, Matt. I can't. We shouldn't.'

'You're right. Sorry. I got a bit carried away there.' Matt stood up and re-buttoned his jeans. He ran a hand through his hair, and looked around the room, as if unsure what to do next.

'It was my fault,' Kelly said. 'I started it. But then I thought of Joan, and her baby, and, well, that kind of stopped me.'

'Just as well, I guess. You getting pregnant would be disastrous.' He sat down again beside her and put an arm around her shoulders. 'Another time, perhaps?'

'Yeah.' She smiled, and picked up the TV remote control. A sitcom was about to start. That would take their minds off what they'd been about to do.

'What do you think happened to Joan?' Matt asked.

Kelly shook her head. 'I don't know. But I have a feeling it was something terribly sad.'

Chapter Twenty

June 1944

Joan knelt on her bed, holding her curtain slightly open. An almost-full moon shone into her room, casting its silvery light across her bed. It was a beautiful, peaceful sight. She remembered the moonshine across the sea that she and Jack had gazed upon on the night they met, and again on the night they'd become engaged. It was as though the full moon was smiling on them, being there at their most significant moments, watching over them. She shook her head. No, that was too fanciful a thought. But was the moon watching now over Jack? Or, at least, was he lying somewhere in France, looking up at the moon just as she was? Thinking of her just as she was thinking of him? It was the very same moon. If they were both gazing at it at the same moment, then however far apart they were, that gave them some kind of connection. That was a comforting thought. She tucked the edge of the curtain behind her bookcase, so that the moonlight shone across her bed, and lay down.

After her secret visit to the doctor that morning, she missed Jack more than ever. How different things would be if it were peacetime, if she'd been able to tell him her news today. But he was away fighting the war in France, part of the Normandy landings. And she was alone in England, with her momentous news held tightly within her belly. She placed a hand on her lower abdomen, imagining it swelling and growing, the baby wriggling and kicking. She wondered whether it would look more like her or Jack. Like Jack, she hoped. He'd be delighted with her news, she knew. It may be a bit early in their relationship—ideally they'd have married first and had a child later—but when there was a war on things didn't always happen as they should. They'd taken a chance sleeping together, that one night in the air-raid shelter. They wouldn't have done that if it had been peacetime. But it *had* happened, and she didn't regret it for a moment. Not even now she'd found out she was carrying his baby. *Especially* not now. There was something of Jack, growing inside her. How could she ever regret that?

She lay back on her pillow, the moonlight streaming silkily across her bed, and settled down to sleep with a secret smile on her face.

* * *

The following day Joan was due to run the playgroup at the WVS for a few hours, from late morning till mid-afternoon. One small girl, wearing a red dress and with a matching ribbon in her hair, was being left for the first time.

'Her name's Olive,' said the child's mother. 'I'll only be an hour. I hope she'll be good for you.'

'I'm sure she will. Olive. What a pretty name!' said Joan. 'Come on, Olive. Sit down with me. Do you like to play with dolls? We have a lovely one here. Her name is Annabel.' The little girl shyly put out a hand to touch the doll's dress. Her mother smiled, and waved goodbye as Joan settled down with Olive on her lap, already happily undressing the doll.

The hours passed quickly, with up to half a dozen children being left with Joan at any time. She was lucky today—they were all easy children, happy to play with the selection of toys she'd brought out of the cupboard. Sometimes it wasn't so easy if the children fretted for their mothers, or mistreated the toys. Mrs Atkins brought her tea and biscuits, and squash for the children. She sat beside Joan for a few moments with her own cup of tea.

'You do so well with the little ones,' she commented.

'It's an easy job,' Joan replied, laughing. 'All I have to do is play!'

'Yes, but not everyone has the rapport with children that you do. You'll make a wonderful mother, some day.'

Joan blushed. Surely Mrs Atkins couldn't have guessed her secret?

'Have you heard from your young man lately?' the older woman went on.

'Not for over a week. In his last letter he said he was being sent to France. I believe he's been involved in the D-Day landings. So many soldiers have been sent over.'

'Yes, and they are doing a marvellous job. We should be very proud of them. And don't you worry about him. When he's in the thick of it, remember that no news is good news.' Mrs Atkins's eyes were misty. 'And you too, you're doing your bit for the war effort here. These mothers rely on you, you know, to give them a bit of time to do everything else. Especially those whose menfolk are away at the front.'

'I'm glad there is something I can do to help,' Joan replied. 'In some ways I'd rather be out there, fighting alongside Jack, getting shot at, and—oh!' She broke off speaking and clutched at her forehead. She'd felt a sudden, sharp pain, through the back of her head, and between her eyes. It vanished as quickly as it had arrived, but she was left feeling decidedly queasy.

'What is it, dear? Are you all right?'

'Yes, um, no. Sorry, Mrs Atkins, I just feel a little peculiar . . .' She got up and rushed to the cloakrooms, where she vomited into the toilet. This wasn't morning sickness. This was something else. A terrible feeling of dread and foreboding sat at the pit of her stomach. Oh God, was she losing the baby? No, it felt worse even than that. Jack, it was Jack. Where was he? What was he doing? Something felt horribly, sickeningly wrong . . .

There was a tap at the door of the cubicle. It was Mrs Atkins. 'Is everything all right, dear?'

Joan pushed open the door and went out. Mrs Atkins instantly folded her in her arms and rocked her, like a baby. 'There, now. Shh, don't upset yourself. Now, tell me, what can the matter be?'

Should she tell her? About the baby? About the feeling of horror that had just washed over her? No, it was all too private, and although Mrs Atkins felt more like a mother to her than her own mother, she didn't feel she could confide any of this to her. 'It's nothing, Mrs Atkins. I just felt a bit dizzy for a moment. I should get back to the children.'

'They're perfectly all right. I've asked one of the other girls to keep an eye for a few minutes. Are you sure there is nothing you want to talk to me about? I do understand, you know. My Arthur went away to fight in the trenches, back in 1916. He never came back. I was pregnant when he left. My poor Johnny never knew his father. And now he's away fighting in France as well, like your Jack. Come, sit in the kitchen with me for a moment. I'll make us a nice cup of tea.'

Joan followed her obediently into the kitchen and sipped the sweet tea Mrs Atkins made for her. Poor Mrs Atkins. It must be particularly hard to bear having a son fighting in this war after having lost her husband in the Great War.

'Joan, what happened out there just now? You jolted so violently, almost as though you'd been shot.'

Joan regarded the older woman carefully. What harm was there in confiding? 'It did feel as though I was shot. A sudden pain, right through my head, and then a terrible sickness. And, oh Mrs Atkins, there is something else but I am not sure I should say . . .'

'You can tell me anything, my dear. I'm not sure if you realise it, but I'm actually a Miss. My Arthur and I never got the chance to marry. I moved away from my hometown when I heard he'd died, and pretended I was a widow. Being a young mother, it was much more acceptable if people thought I'd been married before getting pregnant.'

Joan stared at her. 'Oh! No, I never knew that. I'm so sorry. It must have been so awful for you.' A thought struck her. What if Jack never came back? What if her sudden pain was a premonition of his death? She gulped.

Mrs Atkins took her hand and patted it. 'It was all a long time ago. No one knows the truth here, but I thought it might help you to . . . well, to confide in me. If you want to, of course.'

'You've guessed?' Joan whispered.

Mrs Atkins nodded. 'Don't worry; your secret is safe with me. I've been in your shoes, my dear, as I've now told you. Things will be different for you, though. Your Jack will come back and marry you, the war will be over soon, and you'll have such a happy life together, the two of you and your little one, and perhaps many more after that. And you won't forget me, of course—I would *love* an invitation to your wedding.'

Joan smiled weakly at her. She still had that terrifying feeling that something was very badly wrong with Jack. But Mrs Atkins was so sure that Joan's story would have a happy ending, not like her own, that she didn't feel she could say anything more. Too late, she felt the bile rising again and she rushed to the kitchen sink.

'Oh, you are definitely not well today. There, now. After the first few weeks all this stops, you know.' Mrs Atkins rubbed her back gently. 'Listen, why don't you go home? We've enough people here to cover for you today. Go home and rest. Come back when you're feeling better. If you can get hold of some ginger biscuits they'll help with the sickness. Go on, off you go now.'

Joan hugged her. 'Thank you. Yes, I think I will feel a bit better at home. I'll come back tomorrow.'

'Only if you feel up to it, mind. And, Joan, I think you should tell your parents. They need to know, and the sooner you tell them the better.'

* * *

174

The following morning Joan woke up early, turned over in bed and instantly felt sick. She rushed to the bathroom and vomited into the toilet.

'Joan? Are you all right?' Mags was standing behind her. 'Are you ill?'

'Yes, well, no, not ill exactly . . .' she replied, as she rinsed her mouth over the sink.

'Oh my God, Joanie, you're not . . .'

Joan straightened up, dried her face and looked her sister in the eye. 'Yes, I'm afraid I am.'

Mags clapped a hand over her mouth. 'What are you going to do? Does Father know?'

'Not yet. I'll tell him and Mother today. Oh, Mags, will you stand by me while I tell them? Father's going to be furious.'

'Of course I will. But, Joanie, dear Joanie, you shouldn't have . . .' Mags was shaking her head, her eyes wide with shock.

'Please don't tell me off. I couldn't bear it if I felt you, of all people, disapproved. I know we shouldn't have, but in wartime you have to take every chance you have at happiness.' Joan clutched her sister's arms. 'Please say you don't think badly of me.'

Mags put her arms around Joan. 'Of course I don't. I was shaking my head in disbelief rather than disapproval. I'll be an aunty! That's marvellous! And I will be right by your side when you tell the parents. Don't you worry about that.'

Joan hugged her back. Thank goodness for Mags. With her sister and Mrs Atkins on her side, she felt she could cope with anything until Jack came back to her.

* * *

It was breakfast time before Joan pulled together the courage to tell her parents. It was a Saturday, so Father was not due at work, and the whole family had breakfasted together in the breakfast

175

room. As Father laid down his newspaper to pour himself a second cup of tea, Joan took a deep breath.

'Father, Mother, I have something I need to tell you both.' Under the table Mags grabbed her hand and squeezed tight.

'Go on, then,' said Father.

'The thing is, I . . . I met a boy, and we're very much in love, and he has asked me to marry him . . .' She'd decided on the spur of the moment to start with this, rather than her pregnancy. Mags smiled at her supportively. Across the table, Betty snorted dismissively. Jealous, Joan thought. As the oldest it ought to be Betty who was first to announce an engagement.

'You're too young. I forbid it,' said Father, picking up his newspaper again.

'Father, please, there's more I need to say. I accepted him. I love him with all my heart, and when the war is over there is no one else I would rather be with. I would like your blessing, of course I would, but I'm afraid I will go ahead and marry him when it is possible regardless.'

'And where is this boy now? Why has he not come to ask my permission?'

'He's in France, fighting the war.' And pray God that he is safe, Joan thought.

'Well, dear, this is all very sudden, and I must agree with your father that you are rather young for such a big step, and if your chap is away in France I can't see how you can get married for some time. I don't think the war is likely to finish any time soon, is it, Herbert?' said Mother.

'Not a chance.' Father opened up his newspaper and held it up, a barrier between himself and Joan. Usually that was to be taken as a sign that the subject was closed and not to be reopened. But Joan had to go on.

'Also—' she began, but broke off as Father lowered his paper and glared at her.

'There's nothing more to say, girl. I've said no, and with the boy away at war and maybe not even coming back, there's no point discussing it further at this stage anyway.'

Mother gazed at Joan, her eyes compassionate. 'Perhaps when or if he does come back, he can come to speak with your father then.'

'Yes, thank you. I'm sure he will.' Joan wished they would stop saying 'if' he comes back. He had to come back; he had to!

'What's the boy's name?' Father barked.

'Jack McBride. You met him once. I was walking home with him and you caught us up.'

'That working-class fellow? I thought I forbade you from seeing him again?'

'You did, but . . .'

'You disobeyed me? That settles it. You will be kept in, every evening and every day off. You will not see him again.'

Joan looked down at her empty plate. This was not going the way she had intended, and she had yet to voice the news that would really make him explode with rage. 'Sorry, Father. I love him so much. I can't stop myself from seeing him whenever we get the chance.'

Betty looked at Joan's hands and sneered. 'How can you be engaged? You haven't even got a ring.'

'I have my locket. That's just as good. Better because it belonged to his mother,' Joan replied.

'Rings, lockets, all mean nothing. You will not see him again,' Father repeated, thumping the table.

'She's young, Herbert. Remember when we were courting and my father tried to stop us?' Mother was standing up for her for once. Joan couldn't believe what she was hearing. Beside her, Mags made wide eyes at her, obviously also astounded.

Mother was silenced by a stern glare from Father. 'You were older than Joan is now. It was quite different.'

'Was it, though?' Mother spoke quietly. 'You were away fighting, and we disobeyed my father to spend time together whenever

177

you were home on leave. Just as Joan is doing now. Let them have their time together. Lord knows what will happen to the boy, in France.'

'Thank you, Mother,' Joan said. Now. It was now or never. She'd won her mother's support but she was well aware she was almost certainly about to lose that with her next announcement. Mags squeezed her hand again, in support. 'The other thing is, I seem to be, well, that is, I am—with child.' Such an old-fashioned, stuffy phrase. Why had she used that?

'You are *what*?' Father stood up, knocking the teapot over. It smashed onto the floor, splashing over Mother's legs. She leapt up and went for a cloth at once. Had she even heard what Joan had said? Probably—and clearing up the mess was her way of blocking it out for a few moments more.

'Pregnant, Father. With Jack's child.'

'Oh my Lord, Joan. What have you gone and done now?' said Betty. There was a slight smirk playing at the corners of her mouth. Mags kicked her under the table.

'I should think it is pretty obvious what she has "done", Elizabeth, and we don't require your comments on the situation. Go up to your room. You too, Margaret. Your mother and I need to talk to Joan.'

'You're for it, now,' whispered Betty as she left the room. Mags gave her hand one last squeeze and smiled sympathetically as she obeyed.

'Stop that cleaning up,' Father snapped at his wife.

'My favourite teapot,' Mother wailed.

'Leave the bloody teapot, woman! Your daughter has brought shame on her family and you're fussing about a bloody teapot! Joan, I'm appalled at you. I thought we'd brought you up better than that. To become a fallen woman, and at your age! Did he force himself on you? Is that it? I'll give him what-for, I will, when I lay hands on him.'

'No, Father, it wasn't like that at all. We both wanted to. It

178

was just the once, while he was home on leave. After we got engaged. It was . . . it was beautiful, Father, and I don't regret it for a moment.'

'You shameless hussy. I cannot believe what you are saying. Beautiful? Pah. It was fornication, outside of wedlock, and that is an ugly, sinful thing. So now we need to decide what we are going to do about your predicament.'

'When he comes home, we'll get married.' Joan stuck her chin out defiantly.

'I said before, and I will stick by what I said even with this disgusting twist in the proceedings—you are too young. You will not marry him.'

'But, Herbert, she must marry if she has a child! She can't be left on her own with the baby.'

'She won't be.'

For one brief moment Joan thought he was going to say that he and Mother would support her, that she wouldn't be alone because she had her family. But no. Her father stared straight at her as he spoke his next words. 'You'll go away to have the child. To my sister's, perhaps, in Shropshire. When the baby is born you will give it up for adoption.' He thumped the table. 'You will *not* marry this boy who thinks it is all right to take a girl's virtue and then run off. I will not have such a coward as a son-in-law.'

'He hasn't run off!' Joan screamed at him. 'He's gone to war, to fight for our country and for our freedom. As you did, Father, in the last war. He's not a coward; he's a hero!'

'Is there no way, Herbert, perhaps if the war ends before the child is born and this boy comes back . . .' Mother began, wringing her hands.

'Chances are he won't come back,' sniffed Father. 'He'll either cop it out there, or think twice about taking on a child and a girl who knows nothing of life. Does he know about this, Joan?'

'No, I've only just found out myself, and I wouldn't want to worry him while he's away. Oh, please don't say he might not make it home. I can't bear that thought.' Tears streamed down Joan's face. Father couldn't make her give up the child, could he? No. She would fight him all the way. When Jack came home, and he *would*, he *must* come home, he would fight Father too. They would be a family, the three of them, one way or another.

'You should have thought of that before you gave yourself to him so wantonly. You've only yourself to blame.'

'Was that the doorbell?' said Mother. 'I'll go. Goodness me, whoever it is we mustn't show them in here with all the mess from that teapot. Dry your eyes, Joan, dear. Your father is right, of course.' She bustled off to the front door.

Joan was left with her father, each glaring at the other. She would stand her ground. She would not be bullied into giving up this child, her child, Jack's child. She'd run away if need be, somewhere Father couldn't find her.

The breakfast room door opened, and Mother entered. The look of horror on her face hit Joan like a fist in her gut. Behind her was Marion Simmons, Jack's aunt. Her face was drawn and grief-stricken, and she was clutching a telegram.

'No,' Joan whispered. 'No, it can't be, it isn't . . .'

'Oh, my dear, I'm so very sorry.' Marion rushed forward and took Joan in her arms, the two of them sinking to the floor amid the wreckage of the teapot. Joan howled with anguish, and buried her face against Marion's shoulder. Not Jack, no, not her Jack!

Sobbing, Marion read out the telegram. '*Regret to inform you Jack McBride missing presumed killed by enemy action tenth June stop*. Oh, Joanie, he's gone, but he's a hero, do you understand? He has died a hero, fighting for his country. We must take some comfort from that.'

'No! My Jack, taken from me! So young, so beautiful, I cannot believe it, Marion. Tell me they've made a mistake, a horrible, terrible mistake!' Let it be some other boy killed, someone else called Jack McBride perhaps, not her Jack.

'Oh, love, there's no mistake. I'm so sorry. I came as soon as I got the telegram. I know how close you were to him. He told me, you know, that he planned to marry you as soon as the war was over.'

All their plans, all their dreams, all smashed to pieces by a telegram of a dozen words. Life was so unfair. And the baby, the baby! Marion didn't know about the child. Joan opened her mouth to tell her, but Father interrupted.

'Thank you for informing us. I'm very sorry for your loss, Mrs McBride . . .'

'Simmons. I am—was—Jack's aunt. I brought him up. His mother died and his father went to America when he was a baby. He has—had—lived with me ever since.'

'Mrs Simmons, I apologise. Ahem. As I was saying, we're sorry for your loss. Now, if you'll excuse us, as you can see we had a small accident in here earlier, which we must clear up. And I'm sure you have much you need to do.' Father was standing stiffly to attention beside the open breakfast room door. Through it, Joan could see Mags sitting on the turn of the stairs. She wanted to run to her. She wanted Mags to make everything better, the way she had when they were children and Joan's teddy's arm came off—Joan had thought the world was ending but Mags had fixed the toy. If only she could fix this, too.

Mrs Simmons got stiffly to her feet. She stroked Joan's hair as she still knelt on the floor. 'Joan, dear, you know where I am. Come and talk to me, whenever you need a friend, or if you just want to remember Jack. Our poor boy. Our poor, darling boy.' She stifled a sob, and followed Father out.

The front door closed, and Father came back into the breakfast room. 'Well, that makes our decisions a little easier now, doesn't it? There's no question of you keeping the baby now that your chap is dead. You'll go to my sister as I suggested, and come back after the child has been adopted. We'll tell no one here of your trouble. I'll write to my sister at once, and you can be on the train to Shropshire within a few days. Until then, you are to stay in the house. No running off to the WVS or to that Simmons woman. I don't want you blabbing to anyone about your predicament.'

Chapter Twenty-One

July 1944–May 1945

Joan lay in the narrow bed at her Aunt Doris's house and stared at a brown stain on the ceiling. It was a humid night, so she kicked off the worn cotton bedspread and lay under only the sheet, a hand on her lower abdomen, over her growing baby. She'd been living in this room for three weeks, but already it felt like for ever. True to his word, her father had packed her off to Shropshire at the earliest opportunity.

Aunt Doris, tall and thin-faced with an expression of permanent disappointment, had not exactly welcomed her with open arms. 'You poor love,' she'd said, when she met Joan off the train. 'How terrible to have lost the boy you loved. Well, I promised your father you could stay until you're . . . well . . . until you're back to normal, as it were. I hope you'll be no trouble.'

At least she had shown a touch more sympathy for her regarding Jack's death than her family had. Except Mags, of course. Mags had been the one person who had got her through those first horrendous days after Marion Simmons had called with that horrible telegram. Father and Betty had seemed irritated by the inconvenience of her grief. And Mother, after a brief 'there, there, dear,' had resorted to her usual behaviour of doing and saying the same as her husband.

Joan had become numb. It was a survival instinct. If she thought about Jack, what had happened to him, and the devastation of their plans, she found herself crumpling with pain, able to do nothing but curl up into a ball in her bed and sob. The same happened if she thought about their baby, growing inside her, and wondered what its future might hold. So she had closed herself off, shut her mind down, and was going through life in a kind of daze, doing whatever she was bid, thinking about nothing, just getting herself from one end of the day to the other.

Aunt Doris had recognised she needed to be kept busy, and had set her to work cleaning rooms, baking, preserving. She kept chickens in a coop in the garden, and it was now Joan's responsibility to feed the hens and collect the eggs each day, and clean the coop each week. The company of the chickens was surprisingly therapeutic. They had quickly begun to recognise Joan and associate her with feeding time, and she liked the way they clucked and fussed around her feet when she let them out of the coop. She enjoyed, too, the endless supply of fresh eggs. So much better than the powdered rations she'd had at home.

But it was at night, when she had nothing to do but lie in bed and stare at the ceiling, when sleep would not come, that she could not stop herself from endlessly replaying every moment she'd ever had with Jack. From that first dance when he'd taken on that pushy Canadian airman, to their one and only night together in the air-raid shelter. She would take out Jack's letters and reread every one of them, and spend hours poring over his photo. She inevitably ended up sobbing, wiping her eyes on the edge of her sheet, and eventually falling asleep exhausted once again with grief.

Why Jack? Why did it have to be Jack? Couldn't some other poor boy have been killed instead? That was a terrible wish to have, she knew, and she was disgusted at herself for thinking it, but she couldn't help herself. Jack had been such a good man, with his life ahead of him, and he'd have been a wonderful husband and father. Not only had his death ended all that, it had also destroyed her chances of happiness, and left their baby without a father.

When she thought of the baby she was gripped with yet more anguish. What would become of it? In her brighter moments she thought perhaps she would somehow keep it, bring the child up on her own as Mrs Atkins had done, pass herself off as a widow somewhere new. Perhaps once the child was born she could run away from Aunt Doris and Shropshire, find some other place and make a new life for herself and the child. But then, a more rational, depressed part of her brain would ask how she could possibly manage that, in wartime, at her age, with no skills and no money. In those moments she would acknowledge that her father was right—the best choice for the child would be adoption. All she could do was to pray that a good and kind couple would take the child.

* * *

The weeks and months passed slowly at Aunt Doris's. When the baby began to move around inside her, every twitch, every kick, every hiccup was a reminder of what might have been. Every letter from home made her think of the letters she'd loved to receive from Jack, when he was away training for the war that would kill him. When the dark cold nights of autumn arrived, they reminded her of the winter when she'd met Jack, and he'd loaned her his coat as they walked home along the promenade. When Christmas came, a quiet affair with just herself and Aunt Doris sitting down to a meal of roast chicken—one of the hens that had stopped laying—the meagre present-giving put her in mind of the gifts she'd had from Jack. New Year's Eve and then her birthday passed, almost unmarked except for a card and present of a paperback book from Mags. She fingered the locket

185

Jack had given her and which she always wore, no matter what she was doing. If only she could go back to that moment and tell him not to join up, persuade him to take up the college place to study engineering and let others go to war, not him. If only they could go back in time and change things. If only they could be together again.

* * *

At last her time came. It was mid-January, a cold and blustery day, and just over a year since Joan first met Jack, that she felt the first twinges while she was outside feeding the chickens. She straightened up and groaned, then shooed the chickens back into their coop and went indoors. A few hours later, in the nearby cottage hospital, her daughter was born. The tiny, angry little bundle was placed in her arms, swaddled in a blanket, and she felt a surge of love for the helpless creature, and sorrow that she'd been born into such a mess. 'I would have been a good mother, and he'd have been the best father, little one,' she whispered. 'I am so sorry. So very sorry. Be well, be happy, be good.' The midwife gently took the baby from her, and at once a wailing noise started up, a sound so anguished it was as though someone's heart was being ripped from their body. It was a sound she'd last heard when Marion Simmons came with the telegram. It was a moment before Joan realised the wailing was coming from herself.

* * *

Four days later, her breasts still producing unwanted milk, she travelled back home by train. 'You'll be better off among your family,' Aunt Doris had said. 'Thank you for your help with the chickens. Now off you go, and forget all about this little period of your life. Move on, find new ways to be happy.' She'd hugged Joan. 'I'll miss you.'

Father met her off the train. 'We said you went away to be part of the land army,' he told her. 'We told people you stayed with Doris, worked on a farm, then after the harvest you decided to stay over Christmas to keep your aunt company. All right? Don't forget, that's the story.' He coughed. 'Your sister Margaret will be pleased to have you back, at any rate.'

Joan nodded. The numbness had returned, doubled. She'd lost both Jack and her baby.

At home, Margaret enfolded her in a huge hug, squealing with joy. 'So good to see you, Joanie! I have so much to tell you. There's a dance, this weekend, and Father said I could take you along. Do you want to go?'

Joan smiled feebly. 'Well, I'm not sure. I think I would rather stay quietly at home. At least for a week or two. Can you help me carry my suitcase upstairs?' She wanted nothing more than to sit down, drink a cup of tea, and then get herself to bed. She sighed. It wasn't Mags's fault. She had no idea what it was like to give birth. Standing for more than a few minutes was uncomfortable, and the thought of going to a dance was intolerable. Mags had no idea either what it was to lose the love of your life, and then be forced into giving up your baby. With a jolt, Joan realised that never again would she feel she was in the same bracket as her sister. Too many experiences divided them. Mags may be the elder, by a couple of years, but Joan was the one who'd experienced so much more of the highs and lows of life. She felt as though she was eighty, not eighteen.

'Of course I will,' Mags said, picking up the case and skipping upstairs with it. Joan followed slowly, leaning heavily on the banisters. In her room, she lay down on the bed.

Mags looked at her sadly. 'Oh, Joanie. I'm so sorry. I was so looking forward to you coming home I forgot you'd be feeling sad, still. I'm sorry I was so pushy when you came in.'

Joan stood up again and hugged her sister. 'It's all right. I'd have been the same if it was the other way around. You can tell

187

me all the news, tomorrow perhaps, when I'm a bit more rested. But I don't think I'll be going to any dances in the near future.'

Mags smiled. Joan looked around. Her old room seemed so much smaller than she remembered. She sighed, took out the photo of Jack and placed it on her bedside cabinet.

* * *

The weeks dragged by. News from the front was more and more positive—the tide had indeed turned and it seemed only a matter of time before Hitler accepted the inevitable and surrendered. But even as the prospect of peace became more and more likely, Joan found herself unable to feel any sense of hope for the future. There was no future. It had died with Jack. Joan's days consisted of helping her mother around the house, doing the shopping, and taking a weekend stroll with her father, who would lecture her as they walked on the importance of learning all the skills of homemaking so that she could eventually make someone a good wife, if a man could be found who would overlook the fact she was not a virgin. Joan kept her head bowed throughout these walks, and let his words wash over her. There was only one man whose wife she could have been. Only one, and he lay buried somewhere in a French battlefield.

For the first few weeks she had watched the post eagerly, expecting to hear from whoever had adopted her baby. Surely they would write and tell her how big she was growing and how she was progressing. But no letter came, and eventually she realised that none ever would.

Mrs Atkins had called round several times since Joan's return. She'd pleaded with her to return to the WVS, but Joan had shaken her head. The thought of looking after those little children, all the while wondering what her own baby was doing, was intolerable. Mrs Atkins offered her other duties, such as sorting the donated clothing or manning the tea urn, but Joan had said no.

'Ah, well, love, when you're ready, come back to us,' Mrs Atkins had said. 'And in the meantime, if ever you need someone to talk to, someone who really understands what you've been through, you know where I am. Eh, love?'

But Mrs Atkins had kept her child, brought him up alone, and made a success of things. Joan knew she could no longer talk to her old friend, who would surely judge her for having not been strong enough to fight to keep her baby. After a few visits, during which Joan did not say much, Mrs Atkins stayed away.

Marion Simmons came once, too. But Joan found it so upsetting to be with the one other person who'd loved Jack, without even being able to mention their baby, that Father asked Mrs Simmons not to call again.

Her mother and Betty seemed not to know what to do with her. Mother sighed loudly every time she looked at Joan, and then spoke to her in an overly jolly tone as though she was a toddler who needed cheering up. Betty was more blunt. 'Why can't you just snap out of it?' she'd asked Joan one day, after finding her lying motionless on the sofa, staring at the ceiling. 'We're all very sorry for your loss, of course we are, but it was months ago! When are you going to get over it?'

Never. The only thing Joan was certain about was that she would never, ever get over losing Jack and their baby.

Even Mags wasn't able to get through. She tried, and Joan was grateful for that. Mags had sat quietly with her, just holding her hand or reading to her. She'd taken her out for walks, or to Lyons corner house for a cup of tea. She'd talked about Jack, and the few times she'd seen him, and tried to draw Joan out. She'd tried to encourage Joan to go out to dances again, and meet someone new.

'Jack wouldn't want you to spend the rest of your life alone, would he? He'd want you to be happy,' Mags had said, and Joan had agreed. Jack would always have wanted nothing but her happiness, just as Joan knew, if the situation was reversed, she would want Jack to find someone else and live a happy life. But she couldn't lift herself out of the deep chasm of gloom in which she lay paralysed. Not even for Mags. She would smile weakly, and thank Mags for spending time with her, but all the while all she wanted was to be left alone.

* * *

At the beginning of May, Joan was despairing, wondering how she could get through the anniversary of Jack's death the following month. She was sitting on her bed, fingering her pearl locket and remembering how hopeful she'd felt just a year before, when Mags burst into the room.

'Look! I was in Woolworth's, and they'd just had a delivery! I got us two pairs each!' She was flourishing packs of stockings. Two new pairs was something to rejoice in, and Joan's immediate thoughts were of how happy she'd have been a year ago to have had one new, un-darned pair, let alone two at once. She smiled at her sister.

'Thank you. But you keep them. You go out more than me— you'll need them. Or give them to Betty or Mother.'

'I've already given them some, Joanie. Oh, do keep yours. Even if you don't wear them. One day you might want to.' She hugged Joan impulsively. 'It's good to see a smile on your face, even if it's only a little one. And there's something else might make you smile—there are rumours going round that Hitler is dead! Shot himself, they're saying. Father's going to put the wireless on for the one o'clock news to see if it's true. Oh, Joanie, this war is nearly over! Isn't that something to try to be a little bit happy about?'

'Yes, Mags. That's wonderful news. And I do appreciate you giving me the stockings as well.' Mags kissed her and ran off to listen to the wireless. Joan put the stockings on her dressing table and sat back on the bed, hugging her knees to her chest. So the war was almost over. Life would return to normal. But not for her. There was no going back to normal for her.

* * *

The German surrender finally came on 8th May, and the day was declared a national holiday. There were to be street parties everywhere, and their road was no exception. Joan spent the morning helping Mother prepare jellies and sponges, sandwiches and salads, biscuits and punches. Every food coupon available was spent, and every family in the street pulled together to donate as much food and drink as possible to the party. Mags and Betty made bunting from an old sheet, dyed some red with beetroot, some blue with watered-down ink and left the rest white. They hung it between their house and the bombed-out remains of Mrs Johnson's house next door. Father pulled the kitchen table out onto the street, and all their chairs, and lined them up with those of the neighbours. Children ran round excitedly getting in everyone's way, and women bustled in and out with more and more cutlery, crockery and dishes of food.

Joan helped with everything. She lost count of the number of people who hugged her, lifted her off her feet and kissed her on the forehead, shouting in her ear that we were at peace! The boys would be coming home! The excitement was infectious—everyone was buzzing with joy and new hope for the future.

Except for her. Her smile was pasted on, her exclamations of delight at each new dish of food placed on the tables were fake, and her mind was far away in time and space from the festivities in the street. Everyone was so happy. She wished she could join in fully and feel a part of it, but she couldn't. It simply wasn't possible.

'We're starting at three o'clock,' Mother told her. 'That's half an hour away. Everyone will sit down then, Father and the other men might say a few words, and then we can tuck in. It'll be lovely, won't it?'

'Yes, it'll be wonderful,' Joan answered mechanically.

Her mother held her gaze for a moment, then patted her arm and sighed. 'Good to see you making an effort, Joan. Perhaps this will be the start of a new life for you. Put all that unpleasantness properly behind you, at last.'

Joan turned away. 'I'll just go and freshen myself up. There's nothing more to do in the kitchen, is there?'

'No, love, it's all done. Off you go, then. Three o'clock, remember.'

Joan went upstairs and lay on her bed. The sounds of the party preparations outside drifted up to her open window. She got up and closed it, then pulled the curtains across. It was easier in the dark, to go into her memories, to feel Jack with her once again. If only she could really be with him again, to see him, touch him, hear him, smell him.

She picked up the stockings Mags had given her a few days before, which were still lying where she'd left them on her dressing table. She took them out of their packets and ran them through her fingers, feeling the finely woven strength of them. One pair was tan, and the other pair grey. A thought struck her. There was, perhaps, a way in which she could be reunited with Jack again. The only way. Could she do it? She hadn't been strong enough to insist on keeping their child, but could she do this? For Jack? Yes, for *Jack* she could do anything. She went out to the landing and ran her hand along the banister, around the newel post at the turn of the stairs, and looked down. It could work. A clock struck three. Everyone else was outside; the Victory in Europe Day celebrations had begun.

She went back to her room, found some paper and a pen and scribbled a quick note. *I have gone to find Jack. I cannot live without him any longer. Joan.* She picked up the stockings, knotted all four together, and then tied them firmly around the newel post. She made a loop in the other end and slipped it over her head, pulling it tight. Choking, and before she lost her nerve, she vaulted over the banisters into the stairwell. The stockings tightened excruciatingly painfully around her neck, compressing her throat. She held her hands together behind her back to stop herself pulling at the noose, and willed herself to think of Jack. He was waiting for her. They'd be together, for all eternity, and nothing, *nothing* could ever part them again. The stockings tightened yet further, and she tried to gasp but no air could reach her lungs. She relaxed, and let the blackness wash over her, knowing that beyond it, somewhere, was Jack.

Chapter Twenty-Two

November 2014

'It's been a week now. When is that girl going to come home?' Pete pulled out a kitchen chair and sat down heavily, sloshing his mug of tea over the table.

Ali was clearing up the breakfast dishes. She sighed as she threw him the dishcloth to mop up the tea. They'd had this conversation every day since Kelly had run off from the hospital. But he had a point. The agreement had been that she could stay with Matt for a week, commuting to her nursery job by bus each day, and then they needed to review the situation. The week was up, and on her last phone call home Kelly had shown no signs of being prepared to return. 'I don't know, Pete. Well, at least it's Saturday and I have a day off. So I guess I can go and talk to her about it again. I could take her to see Gran again, and perhaps finally hear the end of the story. That might help her.'

Pete snorted. 'The end of the blinking story. Yes, about time we heard the end so Kelly can finally forget about it all and move on. It's been long enough now.'

Ali hung up the tea towel and went to sit opposite Pete. 'Yes, long enough. But as you said yourself, we have to lay this ghost to rest.'

'Now you're the one talking about ghosts!'

'It's a ghost in Kelly's mind. Whether or not we believe in ghosts, she does and that's what's fuelling this obsession and her fear of living in this house.'

'I just want her back here, so we can live together as a family. At least I've been able to get on and paint her room while she's been away. But it's done now and I'd like her here, living in it.'

Ali smiled. He'd done a good job on Kelly's room. It was cream and maroon, with some hot-pink highlights as a nod to her Barbie-obsessed past. Young and feminine, but classy. Just as Kelly had wanted. She would love it. 'She'll be back soon enough. I just hope she's happy to stay in that room and won't want to swap to the spare room.'

'She'd better not. She picked the colours, remember?'

She had. Not long after they moved in, before her obsession with the past kicked in. Ali sighed. 'I just wish we could have that girl back again. The one who picked out the colours. Our girl. We should never have moved in here. We should have sold it, like I wanted to.'

'Not that again. Ali, think about it. How were we to know this would happen?'

Ali took his outstretched hand across the table. 'We weren't. I know. But if we'd sold this place and bought somewhere smaller, we'd have a pot of savings, and I wouldn't have had to work all that overtime, and you'd have had more time to look for another job.'

Pete pulled his hand away. 'Here we go. Back to me being out of work.' He sighed. 'As I've told you many times, as soon as the renovations are complete I will work hard at finding a new job. We're nearly there. Not much more to do. Just hang on in there and soon I'll be earning again, we'll be living in a beautiful house and you'll agree it was all worth it.'

'All very well for you to say hang on in there, but there's no guarantee you'll be able to quickly find another job, is there? That's my worry. What if you can't find anything? At least if you'd been job-hunting and applying for jobs all through, you might have had a chance.' She shook her head. The thought of many more months of being the only earner, having to skimp and save to make ends meet, and still not being able to put any money aside to help Kelly and Ryan through university was hard to contemplate. The house was shaping up to be beautiful, she had to admit, but while Pete was jobless it felt like a noose around their necks. 'And we're nearly out of money. We'll be living in an unfinished mess for months.'

'Ali, it's all right. I've done the figures and we have enough to finish. Only just, but it's enough. It'll be all right. Trust me.'

She stood, picked up their mugs and put them in the dish-washer. 'Right, well, one thing at a time I suppose. I'll give Kelly a call and see if she'll come with me to Gran's this afternoon. Good job I've got a day off.'

* * *

Gran was on better form this time. She appeared to have fully recovered after her 'funny turn', as she called it, from the previous week. With Kelly sitting beside her in her room holding her hand, and Ali perched on the bed, Gran picked up the story where she'd left off.

Kelly had hung her head, tears rolling down her cheeks, as Gran recounted how Joan had killed herself on VE Day. She'd clung on to Gran's hand as though it was her lifeline, but the contact seemed to help Gran tell the most difficult parts of the story. She kept looking at Kelly, smiling gently and sympathetically at her, as though it was Kelly who'd lost her little sister in such tragic circumstances. Ali listened in silence. No wonder poor Gran had been so shocked seeing Ryan's Halloween skeleton hanging from the banisters. That must have been exactly where Joan had hanged herself.

'Father found her,' Gran said, quietly. Ali had to lean in close to hear her. 'We were all out in the street, for the VE Day celebrations.

Father went back inside for his pipe, and to see where Joan had got to. He let out the most enormous roar. She was hanging, you see, from the banisters.'

'Oh, how terrible,' said Ali. Her words sounded so inadequate. What could be worse for a parent than finding a child dead by her own hands? She glanced at Kelly, who was now sitting motionless, staring at Gran.

'I heard his shout, and ran to our front door, but Father closed it in my face. He didn't want me, or Mother or Betty, to see her like that. His face—it was ashen. He aged twenty years in a minute, that day. I hammered on the door, wanting to know what was wrong, but he shouted out that I should go back to the party, tell Mother that he was going to stay inside and rest.' Gran shook her head sadly. 'But I knew something was terribly, badly wrong. The look on his face—it was something I have never forgotten. It was an expression of the utmost horror.'

'Was she dead, when he found her?' Kelly spoke stiffly.

Gran nodded. 'Yes, he told us later. She was quite dead. Even so, he cut her down at once and tried to revive her, but there was no hope. She'd used some stockings as a rope—I'd bought them for her! I felt so guilty—I'd given her the stockings she used to hang herself with. What if I'd not given her them? Maybe she wouldn't have done it.'

'She'd have used something else,' Ali said, taking her grandmother's hand. 'Of course it's not your fault. She'd decided to kill herself and I suppose the stockings were the first thing she found.'

'Don't blame yourself, Great-gran,' said Kelly. 'I can't bear it if you do that. She'd have cut up a sheet or something if the stockings hadn't been there. Or used a scarf. She'd made up her mind to do it.'

'All these years,' whispered Gran, not taking her eyes off Kelly, 'I've beaten myself up about it, wishing I could rewind time and not give her the stockings, not even buy them. It felt like she was pointing the finger at me, in death. And here you are now, my granddaughter and great-granddaughter, finally telling me not to blame myself.'

'Of course you mustn't,' said Kelly. 'I'm sure she never meant to hurt anyone. She probably wasn't really thinking about how it would affect anyone else.'

'It ruined us,' said Gran. 'We were never really a proper family again. Father retreated into himself. He blamed himself, for being so harsh on her when Jack died and she found out she was pregnant. Mother just became even more distant—her way of blocking it all out I suppose. They both died within the next few years. Father more or less wasted away, and died of pneumonia in 1949. Mother already had cancer by the time he died, eating away at her, and she went in 1951. I met my Roy at the end of 1945, married him in 1946 and moved out. I couldn't wait to leave home.'

'It must have been so hard for all of you,' Ali said.

'Father didn't telephone the authorities until after the party was finished. He carried her body up to her room, where he laid her on her bed and covered her with an eiderdown. He had never acted as tenderly towards her as he did then, when she was dead. Finally he showed her, too late, that he loved her. When Mother, Betty and I came in, he told us she was sleeping, and bade us be quiet, for fear of waking her. I knew then, I think, that she was not merely asleep. His face—so grey and drawn. Mother fussed around him that evening, thinking he was sick. Finally, when the street party was over and the road was clear, he told us what had happened and telephoned for an ambulance.'

Gran looked tired, Ali thought. It must be so draining having to remember these terrible events from seventy years ago. A tear ran down her face, and Ali passed her a tissue. 'I'm sorry to make you go through all this, Gran. Stop if you feel too tired.'

'No, I'm all right today, and I can go on. Actually I think it's helping me, bringing it all out into the open at last. I've never spoken of this day before, you know. Only to Roy, and he was sworn to secrecy.'

'Yes, that's one thing I've been meaning to ask. Why was Joan kept such a secret?'

Gran sighed. 'Father was so ashamed. There was a stigma attached to suicide in those days, you see. People thought it was a cowardly and selfish thing to do. And especially on that day, when the rest of the country was celebrating the end of the war. All those young men, her Jack included, had fought to keep Britain free and to build a future for everyone at home. Then Joanie went and threw her future away. It seemed so very ungrateful. Even I felt that way. I tried to understand why she'd felt the need to do it, but my word, it was very hard to come to terms with it. That should have been such a joyful, happy day. But it ended up being the most terrible day of my life. Of all our lives. So Father covered it up. He told the neighbours who saw the ambulance that night that Joan had taken ill. Then he said she'd gone away again, to live in the country with Aunt Doris. Then he just stopped speaking about her, ever, to anyone. Mother followed suit, of course. And Betty. Whatever Father said was right with Betty.'

She shook her head. 'I argued with him about it. I said we should remember her, talk about her, be proud of who she had been before tragedy struck. We had some terrible fights. But he wouldn't budge an inch. I couldn't wait to leave home, get away from him. Thank goodness I met Roy. He was the only person I could talk to about Joanie. But he had never known her, of course, and although he'd listen for as long as I wanted to talk about her, it wasn't the same. Eventually I stopped even mentioning her.'

'Was this why you didn't get on with Betty?' Ali asked.

'It was certainly part of the reason. Every time I saw Betty I was reminded of our other sister. But if I tried to mention her name Betty just turned her face away and started talking of something else. She wouldn't have Joanie's name mentioned at all. Once or twice, after Father and Mother died and I'd married, I visited her in the old house, your house now, I should say, and felt as though Joanie was still there somehow. As though her presence

199

remained. I tried to tell Betty about it, but she laughed and said I was being too fanciful and, as usual, changed the subject.'

Kelly glanced meaningfully at Ali, then looked back at the old lady. 'Yes, I've always felt she was still there, too. It's why I started dressing like her, and wanting to find out what happened. Sometimes the feeling has been so strong I felt as though I was going mad.'

Ali put a hand on Kelly's shoulder. It was all making sense now. This explained Gran's reluctance for them to move into the house when Betty left it to them. Ali asked her about it.

'Yes, that was why I wasn't comfortable about your move. But then I told myself if there was a ghost, it was only my dear little sister Joanie, and she wouldn't harm anyone.'

'It's so sad, isn't it?' Kelly said. 'No wonder she couldn't rest in peace if her own family refused to mention her after her death. Not you, Great-gran. The others. That's so awful of them.'

Gran nodded. 'She lived on in my memory, but because I wasn't able to talk to people who knew her, my memories faded. Father had her remains cremated, and her ashes scattered. So there wasn't even anywhere I could go, to be with her and remember her. Until you found those photos, and Kelly here turned up wearing those old-fashioned frocks and Joan's locket, I'd almost forgotten what she looked like.'

'So,' Ali said, 'now we know the full story. We know what happened to both Joan and Jack. Is that enough now, Kelly? Do you think you can move on, and forget about them now?'

Kelly fingered the locket thoughtfully. 'Well, there's just one more thing we don't know. Where Jack's body ended up. Can't we find out? There's a website, I think, which tells you where soldiers were buried. When we get home, can't we research him? If we could find his grave, we could pay him a visit and maybe . . .'

'Maybe?'

'Maybe Joan, or Joan's ghost I mean, would come with us, and stay there with him, and leave us alone.'

Kelly muttered this last part, looking down at her hands. Ali glanced at Gran but she seemed not to have heard. She was staring into the middle distance, presumably lost in her memories of Joan.

'It's an idea,' Ali said. 'If it'll help lay her to rest, in your mind, we should certainly give it a go.'

'Give what a go, Alison, dear?' asked Gran.

Ali smiled at her. 'We're going to try to find out where Jack was buried. It'll be in France somewhere, I suppose. Then we're going to pay him a visit. You can come too, if you're well enough and if you'd like to.'

'I've never been to France,' Gran said, her eyes shining.

Chapter Twenty-Three

November 2014

It was a fine, bright day. Ali was pleased to see the sun shining—they had a long drive ahead of them. The car was full—it was a good job they had a seven-seater. Pete drove; Ali was navigating. Gran had insisted she was well enough for the trip. Kelly was there, of course, and Ryan couldn't be left alone overnight. Finally, Ali had asked Jason if he'd like to come. Jack was, of course, his grandfather. Ali had told them all they were off to visit Jack's grave.

Ali had booked rooms in a cheap hotel for that night. It was too far to go there and back in a day. She felt nervous about the day—who knew how it would go? There would be surprises all round. Only she, Pete and Jason knew exactly where they were going. Kelly had left Ali to research where Jack had ended up. She had planned to tell Gran and the kids while they were driving. And hopefully, this trip would help Kelly move on from her obsession with Joan and Jack and the war years. Ali wanted her twenty-first-century teenager back.

It had been strange introducing Jason to Gran, when they collected her from the care home early that morning. She had taken a while to fully comprehend who he was.

'My great-nephew? But Betty didn't have any children, so how can he be my great-nephew?' she'd said.

'No, but Joanie had a child, remember? She had a daughter who was adopted. And Jason is that child's son. Joanie's grandson,' Ali had explained.

Jason had stepped forward and kissed Gran's cheek. 'May I call you Aunty Margaret? You're far too young-looking for me to think of you as a great-aunt.'

'Ooh, you're a charmer, aren't you?' She'd smiled, enjoying the flattery. Pete had looked vaguely put out. Charming Gran was usually his job.

'It's lovely to meet you. I wish my mum could have known you. She would have loved you.'

'She knew Betty, didn't she?' Gran had asked.

'That's right. She lived next door to her for a few years. Did a lot of her shopping for her. She tried to talk to Betty about her sisters, but although Betty would talk about you, she wouldn't ever admit to having had another sister.'

'Your mother should have come and met me,' Gran had said. 'I wonder why she didn't.'

Jason had looked embarrassed. 'I believe Betty told her you weren't up to having visitors. I think she made it sound as though you were, well, not quite with it, any more.'

'Demented? Oh, that was just like Betty. She was probably afraid I might say something about Joan, if I knew who your mother really was. Ah well. Betty's gone now. A shame your mother's gone too, but at least you and I can get to know each other.' Gran had smiled at him, and taken hold of his arm to be helped into the car.

Well, Ali had thought, at least that reunion had gone well. But there was another one still to come.

* * *

'So, Alison, would you like to share with us exactly where we are going?' asked Gran, once the journey was underway and they were on to the motorway. 'I assume we're taking the ferry. How exciting! I've never been to France.'

Ali twisted round from her seat at the front so she could see everyone. 'Right, yes, I'll tell you all exactly where we are headed, now. As you all know, I've been researching what happened to Jack McBride. It took me a while, but eventually I found him.'

'You mean, you found where he was buried?' said Kelly. Her eyes were shining.

'That poor lad,' said Gran. 'He was only eighteen.'

'No, we're not going to visit his grave,' Ali said. This was it. Time to tell them the truth. She reached back and took Gran's hand. 'We're not going to France at all. Sorry, Gran. When I said I found him, I mean I found *him*, the man, not his grave. He didn't die in the war. He was reported missing presumed dead, but was actually taken prisoner by the Germans. He found his way home after the war ended. Poor Joan was gone by then, but Jack lived on. He's still alive now.'

'Oh my word!' gasped Gran, putting a hand to her mouth. 'Still alive, after all these years! But to think, if only Joan had known he'd survived, she wouldn't have . . . Oh my poor Joanie, my little sister, she could still have been here today, with her beloved Jack . . . Oh how different things would have been!' She gulped back a sob.

'I know. It's the most horrible tragedy. Please Gran, don't think too much on what might have been. It's too upsetting.' Ali passed her a tissue to dab at her eyes.

'Jack's alive? Wow! That's weird, like, all this time he's been like a kind of ghostly presence in my mind, same as Joan, but actually he's alive?' Kelly was shaking her head in disbelief, fingering the pearl locket, which was around her neck, as always.

'Cool,' Ryan said, craning his head from the back row of seats. 'He must be ancient.'

'He'll be younger than I am,' Gran said, with a sniff.

'Does he know we're coming?' Kelly asked.

Ali bit her lip before answering. 'Sort of. He knows we, that is, the Bradshaws, are coming. I also told him we'd bring Gran if she was well enough, which thankfully she is.'

'Of course I am. I wouldn't have missed this for anything.' Gran folded her arms and leaned back in her seat. 'Especially as it's turned out he's alive.'

'What he doesn't know about is me,' Jason said, quietly.

* * *

Jack's house was a bungalow in a housing estate on the edge of a small Midlands town. Jack had given Ali directions when she'd phoned him, but the satnav led them straight to his house with no problems. So he still managed on his own, at the age of eighty-eight, Ali thought. Well done to him. The front garden looked neatly tended, with pruned rose bushes and winter jasmine bordering a well-kept lawn.

Everyone piled out of the car, Ryan exiting via the hatch back, tugging Gran's walking frame after him. 'That thing's been poking me in the eye all journey,' he said. 'Don't they do fold-up ones or something?'

'No, they don't,' Pete replied, taking it from him and helping Gran out. 'There you are, Mrs E. Your chariot awaits.' She smiled gratefully at him, but Ali noticed her hands shaking a little more than usual as she grasped its handles.

'I'm strangely nervous,' Jason said to Ali quietly, as the party approached the front door.

She put her arm around his shoulders and gave him a squeeze. 'I'm not surprised. You're meeting your grandfather for the first time. He doesn't know you exist. It is a strange situation indeed.'

'Don't tell him immediately, will you? Let's play it by ear. I mean, if he's a bit, you know, past it, it might be better not to say anything.'

'I won't. You're in charge. You tell him if or when you feel the moment is right.' She smiled reassuringly at him. He wasn't the only one feeling nervous. Kelly looked a bit shaky as well. Only Pete seemed unaffected.

Ryan looked vaguely bored. 'Anyone going to ring the doorbell?' he asked. 'Or shall I?' Without waiting for an answer he pressed it.

Ali held her breath for what seemed like an age before she heard the sound of a security chain being removed. Gran grasped her hand as the door opened.

'You must be Alison Bradshaw?' said a tall, slim, white-haired man. 'And, I can hardly believe it, Margaret Perkins?'

'Margaret Eliot now. But yes, that's me.' Gran smiled as Jack stepped forward and clasped her in his arms. 'Steady now, you'll knock me over!'

'I'm so sorry. But to think, here you are, after all this time! Come in, come in. We have such a lot of catching up to do. Alison, it was such a wonderful surprise when you telephoned me. I still can't quite believe it.'

He ushered them all into a small but tidy sitting room. There was evidence of a female touch—floral cushion covers, ceramic dancer ornaments, a bookcase containing two whole shelves of Mills & Boon novels. Ali wondered if there was a Mrs McBride. Perhaps even now she was hiding in the kitchen, too scared to come out and be confronted by her husband's long distant past. Jason's revelation would be even more difficult in that case.

'You must be Alison's daughter?' Jack asked Kelly. He was staring at her oddly.

'Yes, my name's Kelly. I'm so pleased to meet you.' Kelly impulsively kissed him on the cheek.

Ali watched as Jack put his hand to his cheek as if in a trance, then shook his head. 'It's funny. It's so long ago but I can still bring her face to mind. You look very like her, you know. Same blonde hair and hazel eyes.'

'Doesn't she?' exclaimed Gran. 'I always thought so. My parents and Betty never let me mention her after . . . well, after what happened.' She turned to Ali. 'Does he know what happened to her? Oh my word, does he know?'

Jack put a gentle hand on Gran's shoulder. 'It's all right. I know what happened to Joan. Sit down, please, all of you, gentlemen too—I am guessing the young fellow is Alison's son and you, sir, are her husband?' He indicated Pete who nodded and shook his hand. He looked then at Jason. 'Alison's brother, perhaps?'

'Not quite. Her cousin, Jason Bergmann. Good to meet you, Mr McBride.'

'Call me Jack, please. Right then, I shall make some tea for us all and then we can tell our respective stories.'

Ali leapt up to help him make the tea. There was no Mrs McBride cowering in the kitchen, she was glad to find. But a framed photo above the small kitchen table showed a smiling Jack arm in arm with a petite grey-haired lady, golden wedding balloons floating over them. 'Your wife?' she asked.

'Yes, my lovely Vera. She died five years ago, and I still miss her every day. Could you take this tray through please? I'll follow with the teapot once it's brewed.'

Ali was glad he'd found someone else and had obviously been happy. She would hate to think he'd spent the last seventy years alone and mourning Joan. Back in the sitting room, the others had been chatting quietly. They looked up expectantly as Ali and Jack returned.

Tea poured and cake handed round, Jack gazed round at them all. 'So, then. Margaret, you and Joan and your family all thought I'd copped it, out in France?'

Gran nodded. 'Yes. That dreadful telegram came. It said "missing presumed killed" but we all took that to mean you were lost. Father said that's what it meant. Even your aunt, who came round to tell Joan, assumed the worst. And when we never heard anything more from you, even after the prisoner of war camps were liberated near the end of the war, Joan lost all hope.

I don't think she ever thought you'd survived. She told me that two days before the telegram came, she'd felt a jolt and a pain, and knew that meant you'd been shot.'

'I was shot. In my shoulder. It brought me down, but didn't kill me. I passed out, then woke up later, bleeding, with my dead friend beside me. I lay there for hours. I couldn't leave him. I kept thinking my squadron would come soon. They'd find us and get us both back home. Poor Mikey, to die in a French field like that. But it was the Germans who found us. Mikey was dead. They kicked his body. I shouted at them to stop, have some respect. They hauled me to my feet, my arm was hanging uselessly and my uniform was drenched in blood. They dragged me away, put me on a truck with a few other captured British soldiers and drove for days until we reached a prisoner of war camp. I kept thinking they'd shoot us. With all that was going on, I was amazed they didn't. But thankful, too. All I could think of was Joan.'

He paused, a faraway look in his eyes. Everyone was silent. Kelly had tears running down her face. Ali knew it must be painful for him to recount all this, after seventy years. 'Stop if this is too hard for you,' she said, quietly.

If he'd heard her, he ignored her, and continued speaking. 'I was moved several times, ending up at a camp in Germany itself. My camp wasn't liberated until right at the end of the war, and then it was another two weeks before I could get back. I wrote to Joan, and to my aunt, as soon as I could, on that glorious day when the gates of the camp were flung open. It was the ninth of May 1945.'

'The day after,' Gran whispered. 'The very next day. Oh, Joanie, why didn't you hold on? Father must have thrown away the letter. He never said anything about it. But it was too late anyway. Oh Joanie!'

'Shh, Gran,' whispered Ali, hugging her close. On the sofa opposite, Jason looked stricken, too. His mother had already been adopted by then. But perhaps Joan might have fought to keep her baby if she'd had any hope that Jack was still alive. Things could have been so different.

'When I got back to England, the first thing I did, before I even went to my aunt's, was to call at your father's house. He told me what Joan had done to herself. It, well, as you might imagine, it devastated me.' He paused, and drew a deep breath.

Gran gasped. 'I never knew you'd called!'

'I only saw your father. I suppose he kept my visit secret from the rest of the family. He looked like a broken man, not at all the disapproving ogre he'd seemed when I'd met him before. He blamed me, for not getting in contact. But I couldn't—the POW camp I was in didn't allow us to write home. Well, they let us write letters, and then they'd hang them in the lavs, to be used as toilet paper. I couldn't listen to him. I ran from there, ran, down to the beach, and along to a bench on the prom we'd called "our" bench. I sat there and, I'm not ashamed to say it, I sobbed and sobbed. I had loved her so much. Hours, I sat there. People tried to help but I shrugged them off. Eventually a policeman was called, and he got my name and address, and fetched my aunt. She hadn't known about Joan's death. The family had put it out that Joan had gone to live in the country with a relative.'

'Yes, that was the story Father concocted. And later, if anyone asked after her, he said she'd died while she was away, of pneumonia. She was cremated. I don't know what he did with her ashes.' Gran fumbled in her handbag for a tissue. 'We didn't even have a funeral service for her. He was so ashamed. You know, her suicide note said she was going to look for you.'

'I was going to ask you if there was a grave I could visit. But it seems not.' Jack shook his head sadly. 'I moved away soon after. I took a job with an engineering firm up here. Threw myself into my work to try to forget. There were many, many times when I wished I'd died in that field in France. Then I met Vera in 1953 and married her a year later. If it doesn't sound disrespectful to Joan, I'd say I found a new happiness. You never get over losing someone you love, but in time you can learn to live and love again. Vera was my saviour.' He whispered the last words.

Gran smiled at him. 'Joan would have been glad you found someone else. Did you have a family?'

'No, we weren't blessed with children, unfortunately.' He finished his cup of tea.

Ali looked at Jason and slightly raised her eyebrows. Was this the right moment for him to tell his news? Jason shuffled in his seat as though he was about to speak, but before he could, Jack spoke again.

'Well, that's my story. Your turn now, Alison, if you would. How did you find me, and what prompted you, after all these years?'

Ali told him about Betty's death, and how she'd inherited the house.

'Then on the wall in my room, under the wallpaper, we found some writing. Joan loves Jack,' Kelly cut in.

'Oh my. I can just imagine her doing that,' Jack said, with a small chuckle.

'And in the cellar there was a box. It had your letters to Joan in it, and a couple of photos. We asked Gran, and she told us about Joan. Until then, I'd had no idea she had a third sister,' Ali continued.

'Father, and then Betty, insisted we should never speak about her,' Gran said. 'I wish I'd ignored them. It's been difficult, but in many ways it has been lovely to have her memory brought back to the surface again.'

'Kelly especially was interested in finding out more about both of you,' Ali said. 'So we researched all we could. As we thought you'd died in France, I spent hours online going through the Commonwealth War Graves website, looking for you. When that didn't work I contacted your old regiment, which I knew from your letters, and they were able to tell me that you were still alive. I found you in the end by using Google. You popped up on a website for a hospice, on a page thanking people for helping at their summer fundraising event. There was enough detail about you to be sure it was you. Then I just looked you up in the phone book for this area.'

'Vera died in that hospice. They were wonderful to her in her last weeks. I was glad to be able to give something back. To think you found me on the Internet! Well, well, well. Modern times, eh?'

'I love the Internet,' Ali said with a smile. 'I must admit, I was terrified when I rang you. What if you didn't want anything to do with Joan's family, after so many years?'

Jack reached over and patted her hand. 'I was astounded, but delighted, when you telephoned and said who you were. I've felt quite alone since Vera died. I had no brothers or sisters, neither did she, and of course we had no children. So although you and I are unrelated, because you are related to my dear Joan it feels as though you are almost my family. And may I say I am very, very pleased to meet you all.' He beamed round at the party.

This was the moment, surely? Ali looked at Jason. He nodded at her, and cleared his throat.

'Jack, um, there's something else we need to tell you,' he began. He'd been quiet up till then. Jack looked at him with surprise. Everyone else held their breath. 'The thing is, I don't think you were aware, but when you left to go to war, Joan was, well, she was pregnant.'

Jack gasped, and clapped his hand over his mouth. 'Oh my word. It was just the once, only the once, and we were engaged after all . . .'

'Her father forced her to give up the baby for adoption. It was a girl. Her name was Constance.'

'I have a daughter?'

'I'm so sorry; Constance died a couple of years ago. But she married, and had a son.' Jason's face was beetroot red by now. How hard it must be, thought Ali, finding the right words to break the news.

'A son?'

'Your grandson, Jack. That's me. Constance was my mother. Which means you, sir, are my grandfather.'

'Oh my word,' said Jack quietly. He stared down at his clasped hands for a moment, as if to let everything sink in. Ali held her breath. The room was totally still, the atmosphere tense, as though everyone else was also holding their breath. Just the rhythmic ticking of a clock on the mantelpiece broke the silence.

When Jack looked up he was grinning broadly. 'Jason Bergmann. Well I never. My grandson! Come here, lad, and give your old granddad a hug!'

The two men stood and embraced, holding on to each other tightly as if to make up for the lost years. Ali let out the breath she'd been holding and found she had tears streaming down her face. She glanced around and realised she was not the only one. Even Pete was sniffing and gulping. Ryan, too cool to cry, started clapping and cheering, and soon everyone joined in.

'This is splendid,' said Jack, when at last Jason let go of him and he was able to sit down again. 'Now I have a grandson, a nearly-sister-in-law—you would have been, of course, if Joan and I had the chance to marry,' he said, looking at Gran, 'a nearly-great-niece, her husband and her two lovely children. And only this morning I had no one. I am rich indeed. Kelly, my dear, I cannot get over how much you look like Joan.'

'Great-uncle Jack, do you recognise this?' Kelly went to kneel at his side, and pulled the pearl locket out from under her jumper. Jack leaned in close to inspect it, and gasped once again.

'Yes, I most certainly do. It was my mother's. I gave it to Joan when we became engaged. There was no time or money to buy a ring. How did you come by it?'

'It was in the box, in the cellar. I've worn it ever since we found it. You know you say I look like her, well, it's funny, and they don't believe me, but I always felt as though she was still there, in our house. Right from when we first moved in.' Kelly reached to the back of her neck and unclasped the locket. She handed it to Jack. 'I think you should have this back.'

Jack turned it over and over in his hand. 'Oh, no, my dear. You keep it. It looks so pretty on you.'

'No,' Kelly said, firmly. 'You must have it. It's like we're giving Joan back to you. I believe when we go back home I won't feel her presence any more.'

'Kelly, all this talk of a presence, it's not—' began Ali. She hoped Kelly wouldn't spoil the reunion with her fanciful ideas.

'Mum, I tried to talk to you about it. I know you think it's rubbish, but some people are more sensitive to the spirit world than others. Maybe I'm one. Anyway, it's been doing my head in. That's why I wanted to stay at Matt's.' She turned back to Jack. 'I really hope you'll keep the locket. I think she'll then stay here with you.'

He smiled, and kissed her on the forehead. 'It'll be lovely to have her back with me. Of course I'll keep it.'

Kelly hugged him, then went back to her seat on the sofa. Ali watched her. She seemed noticeably more relaxed now. Maybe there was something in what she'd said. Who knew?

'Well, I think that's probably enough surprises for one day,' Ali said. 'Jack, may I help clear up? We're staying in a hotel nearby for tonight. Perhaps we can take you out for lunch tomorrow before we head home?'

'Sunday lunch with my whole family. I should like that very much indeed,' Jack replied, grinning broadly.

Chapter Twenty-Four

December 2014

Ali had just finished putting the finishing touches on the Christmas tree. The house had such a lovely big hallway they'd decided to go for a huge nine-foot tree, and had placed it in the stairwell. The top of the tree reached the newel post on the half landing, where Ryan had hung his skeleton at Halloween. This was a much better use of the space, she thought. She took a step back to admire her work. In the oven, Christmas-shaped cookies were baking. In the study, Pete was filling in a job application. Upstairs, Ryan was playing online games, having borrowed Ali's laptop. Little did he know he was getting his own for Christmas. And Kelly, bless her, was in her room doing homework, getting it out of the way before Matt came round.

She was so glad Kelly had gone back to college. As soon as they'd got home after the trip to meet Jack, Kelly had announced, much to Pete and Ali's relief, that she was giving up the nursery job and returning to college. The nursery had only wanted a week's notice, as it had been understood the job was on a trial basis only. She'd stopped wearing the 1940s clothes too. And Matt was back in her life. Things were back to normal.

The letterbox clattered and Ali went to collect the post. One envelope caught her eye. Thick cream paper, with a handwritten address in a careful, old-fashioned script. She went through to the kitchen and sat at the table to open it. It was from Jack.

Dear Alison,

It was so wonderful to meet you and your family, and my grandson, Jason. I am so grateful to you for tracking me down. You have made an old man very happy, and I am very much looking forward to seeing you all again in the New Year.

I met with my solicitor last week. Thinking I had no relatives, I had intended leaving my estate to a selection of charities. I have now drawn up a new will, and I would like you to be aware that while the charities will still get a substantial legacy each, the bulk of the money will be shared between your family and Jason. I hope it will help you in the future.

I would also like, if you will allow me, to put aside some money now to help Kelly and Ryan through university. You said it was your dream for them to go, and I understand how expensive it is. Rather than have them left with a large loan to pay off at the end, I'd consider it an honour to be able to help. Consider it an advance on what you will receive when my time is up.

I will telephone you soon to arrange transfers into their savings accounts. And to arrange when I might come down to stay with you all!

With much love,
Jack

Ali read the letter with an open mouth. 'Pete, Pete, come and look at this!' she called. He was barely in the kitchen when the doorbell rang. Ali thrust the letter at him, and went to answer the door. It was Jason.

215

'Did you get a letter from Jack?' he asked. His face was flushed and he was grinning broadly. 'Nice tree, by the way.'

'I did. About his will?'

'Yes. What a marvellous, kind man he is!'

'Pete's reading it now. Come in, I'll make you coffee.'

Pete looked up from the letter as Jason entered. 'Jason, mate, about this will—I can't deny it'd be welcome money, but it should be all yours. You're his grandson. We can't take any of this.'

Ali watched as Jason sat down beside Pete and looked straight at him. 'The money is Jack's, and he can do what he wants with it. He's made it clear what he wants, and I think he's doing exactly the right thing.'

'But, but . . .'

Jason raised a hand. 'No arguments. I'm as surprised as you are to be mentioned in his new will. In any case, I hope it will be many years before the will is executed.'

'Of course,' said Ali. 'Lovely Jack. Lovely, lovely Jack.' She put a cup of coffee and a plate of still-warm cookies in front of Jason.

'Mmm, thank you. Actually, there was another reason I came round.' Jason pulled a sheet of paper out of his pocket. 'I printed this off from my company's website. We're recruiting. That job description made me think of you.' He handed it to Pete, gulped his coffee and pocketed another cookie, with a wink at Ali. 'I'll be off, then. Thanks for the coffee.'

She showed him out, then went back to Pete. He was gazing in awe at Jason's sheet of paper. 'Bloody hell, Ali, I am *made* for this job! I've got exactly the experience and knowledge they are looking for. I'm going to apply for it right now. He's a good neighbour. And a good friend.'

Ali smiled. 'And a fabulous cousin.'

* * *

The doorbell rang again. Kelly came clattering down the stairs. Matt had just texted to say he was on his way. She reached the door before her mum and gave him a huge kiss.

'Yay, you're here!' she said.

'Want some fresh air?' Matt asked, wrapping his arms around her.

'Ice cream!' she replied, grabbing her jacket and scarf.

'In December?'

'All year round. Mum, we're off out, back for tea, OK?'

'Sure,' came the reply.

They went to the end of the road, down the zigzag path that led to the prom, and walked along hand in hand, buying ice creams from the first kiosk that was open. The sun was shining, the sky was a dazzling blue, and if it wasn't for the fact the temperature was barely above zero you could almost imagine it was a summer's day. Kelly let go of Matt's hand and instead put her arm around his waist, pulling him close. He smiled, and twisted round to kiss her. He tasted of vanilla ice cream. She was glad to be back with him. Whether they had the kind of love that lasted, like Joan and Jack's, remained to be seen, but for the moment she was happy to be part of a couple again.

She thought back over the events of the last few months, all that had happened since they moved into Betty's house. It was hard to believe that she was the same girl now, the one who'd dressed in forties clothing, given up college for a job at the nursery, pushed lovely Matt away with her obsession about the past. Thank goodness that was all over now. As soon as she'd handed over the gold-and-pearl locket to Jack, she'd felt as though a weight was lifted from her. And returning home, she realised she could no longer feel Joan's presence. She'd gone. Despite now knowing that someone had died in their house, it felt a happier place—more like a home.

She'd given the bundle of letters back to Jack as well. Only the two photos, the one of the three schoolgirls and the other one of Jack in uniform, remained. Kelly had tucked them away in a drawer.

'Shall we sit down for a bit?' Matt asked, pointing to a bench under an old Victorian shelter. Kelly looked to where he was pointing. For a brief moment, she thought she saw a young girl in an old-fashioned dress and coat sitting there, her hands clasped in her lap and a gentle smile on her face as though she was waiting patiently for her sweetheart. The girl smiled and nodded at her, and then the vision faded.

'Sure, let's sit,' she said. 'I've always liked this bench.'

If you loved *The Pearl Locket* turn the page for an exclusive extract from Kathleen McGurl's haunting novel *The Emerald Comb*.

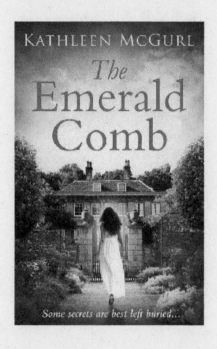

Prologue

Kingsley House
North Kingsley
Hants
November 1876

To my dearest son, Barty St Clair
This is my confession. I am the only soul still living who knows
the truth. It will pain me to write this story, but write it I
must, before I depart this life. I have not long to live, and I fear
death – heaven will not be my final resting place. Dear Barty,
when you have read this in its entirety you will understand
why I know I am destined for that other, fiery place, to burn
with guilt and shame for all eternity. ·

You must read this alone, sitting in the worn, red armchair
by the fireside in the drawing room of Kingsley House. Or
perhaps you will sit in my study, at my old walnut desk.
Where ever you choose, have a glass of whiskey to hand to
fortify yourself. You will need it.

Read this only after I am dead, after I am buried. Read
this and understand why you must <u>never sell Kingsley House</u>.

You must live in it until the end of your days, guarding its secrets, as I have.

Tell no one the contents of this confession. Not even your brother, William. Especially not your brother, William. It would grieve him, he who worshipped his mother and believed she could do no wrong, even more than it will grieve you. You will understand this when you have reached the end of my story.

Destroy this document when you have read it. You must carry the shameful secret within you, as I have done, but at least you will not also carry guilt.

There, I have written an introduction, but I must rest before I begin my story. Bear with me, my dearest son, while I recoup the strength I need to write this sorry tale.

Your ever loving, repentant father,
Bartholomew St Clair

Chapter One

Hampshire, November 2012

The weather matched my mood. A dark, low sky with a constant drizzle falling meant I needed both headlights and wipers on as I drove up the M3. Whenever I'd pictured myself making this trip I'd imagined myself singing along to the car radio beneath blue skies and sunshine. The reality, thanks to a row with my husband, Simon, couldn't have been more different. All I'd asked of him was to look after our kids for a single Saturday afternoon, while I went to take some photos of Kingsley House, where my ancestors had once lived. Not much to ask, was it? I'd planned it for weeks but of course he hadn't listened, and had made his own plans to go to rugby training. Then when it was time for me to leave, he'd made such a fuss. I'd ended up grabbing my bag and storming out, leaving him no choice but to stay and be a parent for once, while the kids watched, wide-eyed. Perhaps that's unfair of me. He's a wonderful parent, and we have a strong marriage. Most of the time.

It was a half-hour drive from our home in Southampton to North Kingsley, a tiny village north of Winchester. Just enough time to calm myself down. Funny thing was, if I'd wanted to do something girly like go shopping or get my nails done, Simon would have happily minded the kids. But because I was indulging my hobby, my passion for genealogy, he made things difficult. I loved researching the past, finding out where my family came from. Simon's adopted. He's never even bothered to trace his biological parents. God, if I was adopted, I'd have done that long ago. I can't understand why you wouldn't want to know your ancestry. It's what makes you who you are.

The rain had eased off; I'd calmed down and was buzzing with excitement when I finally drove up the narrow lane from the village and got my first glimpse of Kingsley House. Wet leaves lay clumped together on its mossy gravel driveway. Paint peeled from the windowsills, and the brickwork was in need of repointing. An overgrown creeper grew up one wall almost obscuring a window, and broken iron guttering hung crookedly, spoiling the house's Georgian symmetry.

Kingsley House was definitely in need of some serious renovation. I fell instantly and overwhelmingly in love with it. It felt like home.

Gathering my courage, I approached the front door. It was dark green and panelled, with a leaded fanlight set into the brickwork above. There was no bell-push or knocker, so I rapped with my knuckles, wondering if it would be heard inside. Was there even anyone at home to hear it? There were no cars outside, and no lights shone from any window despite the deepening afternoon gloom. Maybe the house was uninhabited, left to rot until some developer got his hands on it. Or perhaps the owners were away. I'd checked the house out on Google Street View before coming, and had the idea it was occupied.

I knocked again, and waited a couple of minutes. Still no response. But now that I was here, I thought I might as well get a good look at the place. After all, my ancestors had lived here for a hundred years. That gave me some sort of claim to the house, didn't it? The windows either side of the front door had curtains drawn across. No chance of a peek inside from the front, then.

To the left of the house there was a gate in the fence. One hinge was broken so that the gate hung lopsided and partially open. I only needed to push it a tiny bit more to squeeze through. Beyond, a paved path led past a rotting wooden shed to a patio area at the back of the house. I tiptoed round. A huge beech tree dominated the garden, its auburn autumn leaves adding a splash of colour to the dull grey day.

French windows overlooked the patio, and the room beyond was in darkness. Cupping my hands around my eyes I pressed my nose to the glass. It was a formal dining room, with ornately moulded cornices and a fine-looking marble fireplace. Had my great-great-great-grandfather Bartholomew and his wife dined in this very room, back in the early Victorian era? It sent shivers down my spine as I imagined their history playing out right here, in this faded old house.

'You there! What do you think you're up to?'

I jumped away from the window and turned to see a gaunt old man in a floppy cardigan approaching from the other side of the building, waving his walking stick at me. Behind him was a neatly dressed elderly lady. She was holding tightly on to his arm, more to steady him than for her own benefit. The owners were not on holiday, then. I silently cursed myself. Today was really not going according to plan. First the row with Simon and now being caught trespassing.

The man waved his stick again. 'I said, what do you think you're up to, snooping around the back of our house?'

'I'm . . . er . . . I was just . . .' I stuttered.

'Just wondering if the place was empty and had anything worth stealing, I'll bet,' said the lady.

'No, not at all, I was only . . .'

'Vera, call the police,' said the old man. His voice was cracked with age. His wife hesitated, as if unsure about letting go of his arm to go to the phone.

I held out my hands. 'No, please don't do that, let me explain.'

'Yes, I think you had better explain yourself, young lady,' said Vera. 'Harold dear, sit yourself down before you topple over.' She pulled a shabby metal garden chair across the patio and gently pushed him into it.

He held his stick in front of him like a shotgun. 'Don't you come any closer.'

God, the embarrassment. I felt myself redden from the chest up. They looked genuinely scared of me.

'I'm sorry. I did knock at the door but I guess you didn't hear.'

'There's a perfectly serviceable bell, if you'd only pulled on the bell-rope,' said Vera.

Bell-rope? Presumably part of an original bell system. I shrugged. 'I'm sorry, I didn't notice the rope.'

Vera shook her immaculate grey perm and folded her arms. 'In any case, you had no answer, so why did you come around to the back?'

I gaped like a goldfish for a moment as I searched for the right words. I'd imagined meeting the current inhabitants of my ancestors' house so many times, but I had never once thought it would happen like this. We really had got off on the wrong footing. I could see my chances of getting a look inside vanishing like smoke on the wind.

'The thing is, I was interested in the house because' – I broke off for a moment as they both glared at me, then the words all came out in a rush – 'my ancestors used to live here. I've researched my family tree, you see, and found my four-greats grandfather William St Clair built this house, then his son Bartholomew inherited it and lived here after he got married, then *his* son, another Bartholomew but known as Barty lived here right up until—'

'1923!' To my utter astonishment both the old people chorused the date.

'You're a St Clair then, are you?' said Vera, looking less fierce but still a little suspicious.

226

'I was Catherine St Clair before I got married. Plain old Katie Smith now.'

I put out my hand and thankfully she took a tentative step forward and shook it. The atmosphere instantly felt less frosty.

'Vera Delamere. And this is my husband, Harold.'

I shook his gnarled and liver-spotted hand too, while he stayed sitting in his chair. 'I'm so sorry to have frightened you. I shouldn't have come around the back. I was just so desperate for a glimpse inside. And I wasn't even sure if the house was occupied at all . . .' Oops, was I implying it looked derelict? I felt myself blushing again. I thought quickly, and changed the subject. 'You know about the St Clairs?'

'Not all of them, but we've heard of Barty St Clair,' said Harold. 'When we moved here in 1959 a lot of people hereabouts remembered him still. He was quite a character, by all accounts.'

'Really? What do you know about him? He was my great-great-great-uncle, I think.' I counted off the 'greats' on my fingers.

Vera sat down beside Harold and gestured to me to take a seat as well. 'I remember old Mrs Hodgkins from the Post Office telling me about him. Apparently he wouldn't ever let anyone in the house or garden. He wasn't a recluse – he'd go out and about in the village every day and was a regular in the pub every night. But he had this great big house and let not a soul over the threshold – no cook or cleaner, no gardener, no tradesmen. Mrs Hodgkins thought he must have had something to hide.'

'Ooh, intriguing!' I said. 'Perhaps he had a mad wife in the attic or something like that.'

Vera laughed. I smiled. Thank goodness we'd broken the ice now. 'Well, by the time we moved in there was no evidence of any secrets. Mind you, that was many years after Barty St Clair's day. It was a probate sale when we bought it. It had been empty for a few years and was in dire need of modernising.' She sighed, and gazed at the peeling paint on the patio doors. 'And now it's in dire need of modernising again, but we don't have the energy to do it.'

She stood up, suddenly. 'Why are we sitting out here in the damp? Come on. Let's go inside. I'll make us all a cup of tea, and then give you a tour, Katie.'

Harold chuckled. 'Then you'll see for certain we have nothing worth stealing, young lady.'

I grinned as I watched Vera help him to his feet, then followed them around to the kitchen door on the side of the house. I felt a tingle of excitement. Whatever secrets the house still held, I longed to discover them.

Chapter Two

Hampshire, November 1876

Kingsley House, November 1876

My dear Barty
I have rested for a day or so, filled my ink-well, replenished my paper store and summoned the courage I need to begin my confession. And begin it I must, for the date of my death grows ever nearer.

Barty, I shall write this confession as though it were a story, about some other man. I will write 'he did this', and 'he said that', rather than 'I did', and 'I said'. At times I will even write as if in the heads of other characters, as though I know their thoughts and am privy to their memories of those times. It is from conversations since then, and from my own conjectures, that I am able to do this, and I believe it is the best way to tell what will undoubtedly become a long and complex tale. It is only by distancing myself in this way, and telling the tale as though it were a novel, that I will be able to tell the full truth. And you deserve the full truth, my true, best-loved son.

We shall begin on a cold, snowy evening nearly forty years ago, when I first set eyes upon the woman who was to become my wife.

Brighton, January 1838

Bartholomew St Clair leaned against a classical pillar in the ballroom of the Assembly Rooms, watching the dancers whirl around. There was a good turnout for this New Year's ball. He ran his fingers around the inside of his collar. The room was warm, despite the freezing temperatures outside. He could feel his face flushing red with the heat, or maybe that was due to the volume of whiskey and port he'd consumed since dinner.

He scanned the room – the dancing couples twirling past him, the groups of young ladies with their chaperones at the sides of the room, the parties of men more interested in the drink than the dancing. He was looking for one person in particular. If his sources were correct, the young Holland heiress would be at this ball – her first since she came out of mourning. It could be worth his while obtaining an introduction to her. Rumour had it she was very pretty, but more than that, rich enough to get him out of debt. A couple of bad investments had left him in a precarious position, which only a swift injection of capital would resolve.

He watched as a pretty young girl in a black silk gown spun past him, on the arm of a portly man in military uniform. Her white-blonde hair was in striking contrast to her dress, piled high on top, with soft ringlets framing her face. She was smiling, but something about the way she held herself, as distant from her dancing partner as she could, told Bartholomew she was not enjoying herself very much. He recalled that the Holland girl was currently residing with her uncle, an army captain. This could be her.

The dance ended, and now the band struck up a Viennese waltz. Bartholomew kept his eyes fixed on the girl as she curtsied to her partner, shook her head slightly and made her way across the room towards the entrance hall. He straightened his collar, smoothed his stubbornly curly hair and pushed through the crowds, to intercept her near the door.

'You look hot,' he said. 'May I get you some refreshments?'

She blushed slightly, and smiled. 'I confess I am a little warm. Perhaps some wine would revive me.'

He took a glass from a tray held by a passing waiter, and gave it to her with a small bow. 'I am sorry, I have not even introduced myself. Bartholomew St Clair, at your service.'

She held out her hand. 'Georgia Holland. I am pleased to meet you.'

So it was her. She was even prettier viewed close-up, in a girlish, unformed kind of way, than she was at a distance. He raised her hand to his lips and kissed it. Her skin was soft and smooth. 'Would you like to sit down to rest? Your dancing appears to have exhausted you.'

'It has, rather,' she replied, as he led her towards some empty chairs at the side of the room. 'I am unused to dancing so much. This is my first ball since . . .' She bit her lip.

'Since . . . a bereavement?' he asked, gently. Sadness somehow suited her.

'My father,' Georgia whispered. She looked even prettier with tears threatening to fall. 'He died a year ago. I have only just begun to rejoin Society.'

'My condolences, Miss Holland. Are you all right? Would you like me to fetch someone for you?'

She shook her head. 'I am quite well, thank you. You are very kind.' She took a sip of her wine, then placed it on a small table beside her chair. She stood, and held out her hand. 'It has been a pleasure meeting you, Mr St Clair. But I think I must take my leave now. My uncle is here somewhere. Perhaps he will call a cab to take me home.'

Bartholomew jumped to his feet. 'I shall find your uncle for you. Though I could fetch you a cab myself.' And accompany you home in it, he hoped, though it would not be the normal course of behaviour.

'My uncle is my guardian,' she said. 'I live with him. So I must at least inform him that I wish to leave.' She scanned the room.

'Ah, there he is.' She indicated the portly man in a captain's uniform with whom he'd first seen her dancing.

So that was the person he needed to impress. From the way she'd held herself when dancing with him, it seemed there was no love lost between them, on her side at least. Interesting. Bartholomew took her arm, and led her through the crowds towards the captain, who was talking with a group of people in a corner of the room. She seemed tiny at his side – her slightness contrasting with his fine, strongly built figure.

'Uncle, this is Mr St Clair. He has very kindly been looking after me, when I felt a little unwell after our last dance.'

Bartholomew bowed, and shook the captain's plump, sweaty hand. 'Pleased to meet you, sir.'

'Charles Holland. Obliged to you for taking care of the girl.'

'Excuse me, sir,' said Bartholomew. He took a step forward and spoke quietly. 'Your niece wishes to return home. With your permission, I shall call a cab for her.'

Holland turned to regard him carefully. 'Very well,' he said. 'You wish to continue taking care of my niece. You may do so. She has money, as you are no doubt already aware.'

'Sir, I assure you, your niece's fortune is not of interest . . .'

Holland waved his hand dismissively. 'Of course it is, man. It's time she married and became someone else's responsibility. You look as likely a suitor as anyone else, and perhaps a better match than some of the young pups who've been sniffing around. You may take her home.' He nodded curtly and turned back to his companions.

Bartholomew opened his mouth to say something more, but thought better of it. What rudeness! But if Charles Holland didn't

232

much care who courted his niece or how, at least it made things easier. He glanced at her. She was standing, hands clasped and eyes down, a few feet away. Probably too far to have heard the exchange between himself and her uncle. He took her arm and led her towards the cloakroom and the exit.

Outside, a thin covering of an inch or two of snow lay on everything, muting sound and reflecting the hazy moonlight so that the world appeared shimmering and silver. Georgia shivered and pulled her cloak more tightly around her.

'Come, there should be a cab stand along Ship Street,' Bartholomew said, steadying her as she descended the steps to the street. He grimaced as he noticed her shoes – fine silk dancing slippers, no use at all for walking in the snow.

'It's a beautiful night,' she said. 'I should like to see the beach, covered in snow. It always seems so wrong, somehow, to have the sea lapping at snow. Can we walk a little, just as far as the promenade, perhaps?'

'But your shoes! You will get a chill in your feet, I fear.'

'Nonsense. They will get a little cold but the snow is not deep. And the night air has quite revived me. I feel alive, Mr St Clair! Out of that stuffy ballroom, I feel I want to run and skip and – oh!'

He clutched her arm as she slipped in the snow. 'Be careful! Hold on to me, or you will do yourself more damage than cold feet.'

She tucked her arm through his and held on. Bartholomew enjoyed the warmth of her hand on his arm, the closeness of her hip to his. Her breath made delicate patterns in the cold night air, and he imagined the feel of it against his face, his lips . . . Yes, she would do nicely. He smiled, and led her across King's Road onto the promenade. It was deserted, and the snow lay pristine – white and untouched, apart from a single line of dog paw prints. On the beach, the partially covered pebbles looked like piles of frosted almonds.

Georgia sighed. 'So pretty.'

'Indeed,' said Bartholomew, watching her as she made neat footprints in the snow, then lifted her foot to see the effect. She had tiny, narrow feet, and the slippers had a small triangular-shaped heel.

'See my footprints? We could walk a little way, and then you could pick me up and carry me, so when others come this way it will look as though I had simply vanished.' She giggled, and pushed back the hood of her cloak to gaze up at him.

Her eyes glinted mischievously, and even in the subdued moonlight he could see they were a rich green. He was seized by the urge to take her in his arms and kiss her.

'Let's do it!' he said, taking her hand to walk a dozen more steps along the prom. Then he scooped her up, his pulse racing at the feel of her arms about his neck, her slight figure resting easily in his arms. Her hood fell back and tendrils of her golden hair fell across his shoulder. For a moment he stood there, holding her, gazing into her eyes and wondering whether she would respond to a kiss.

'Well, come on then, Mr St Clair – you must walk now, and make your footprints look no different to before. You must not stagger under my weight, or it will be obvious what has happened. Gee up, Mr St Clair!' She gently kicked her legs, as though she was riding him side-saddle.

'Yes, ma'am!' he laughed, and walked on along the prom. After a little way she twisted to try to see the footprints he'd left, and he, feeling he was losing his grip on her, put her down. She instantly walked on a few more steps and turned back to see the effect.

'Look, I appeared from nowhere!'

'Like an angel from heaven,' he said. 'Come, I must escort you home. It is late, and the snow is beginning to fall again.'

Georgia tilted her head back and let a few large flakes land on her face. 'It's so refreshing. Thank you, Mr St Clair. Since meeting you I have had a lovely evening. We can walk to my uncle's house, if you like – he lives in Brunswick Terrace.'

Bartholomew noted she had not said 'we live' – clearly she did not feel as though her uncle's house was her home.

'On a fine evening, Miss Holland, I could think of nothing better than to take your arm and stroll along the promenade as far as Brunswick. But I shall have to postpone that pleasure for another day. Your feet will freeze, even more than they already have. Look, we are in luck, here is an empty cab.'

He waved at the cabman who brought his horse to a skidding stop beside them. They climbed aboard and Georgia gave the address. She shivered and pressed her arm tightly against his. Minutes later the cab halted outside the grand terrace, its whitewashed walls gleaming in the wintry moonlight.

Bartholomew paid the cabman and asked him to wait. He helped Georgia down from the cab and led her up the entrance steps of her uncle's house. The door opened as they approached, and a maid ushered them inside, into a grand hallway where the remains of a fire smouldered in the grate.

'Oh, Miss Georgia, I am so glad you are back. Mr Holland were back a half-hour ago and he said you had left the ball before him. I were fretting about you.' She bustled around, taking Georgia's cloak and exclaiming over the state of her shoes.

'Agnes, I am perfectly all right. Kind Mr St Clair has been looking after me. We decided to walk part of the way home.'

The maid glanced accusingly at Bartholomew. She was a striking-looking woman, blonde like her mistress but with more mature features, as though she had grown into her looks. She was an inch or two taller, and looked, he thought, as Georgia might in a few years' time, when she'd outgrown her childish playfulness. Beautiful, rather than pretty.

'Sir, forgive me for speaking out of turn but my mistress were not wearing the right sort of shoe for a walk in the snow. See, the silk is ruined and her poor feet are froze. Sit you down here, Miss Georgia, and I will fetch a bowl of warm water to wash them.' With another stern look at Bartholomew, she hurried along the hallway towards the kitchen stairs.

'Agnes has been with me since I was fourteen. She does fuss, rather.' Georgia sat on an uncomfortable-looking carved-back chair and rubbed at her feet. 'But a warm foot-bath sounds just what I need. Perhaps, Mr St Clair, you would help me rub some life back into my toes?' She looked up at him, a half-smile flirting with the corners of her mouth.

But Bartholomew was still gazing in the direction the maid had taken. For all Miss Holland's coquettish ways, she was young and immature. Bartholomew was no stranger to women – he'd been near to proposing once to a merchant's daughter in Bath, but she had accepted a better offer from a baronet's son. He'd had a brief affair with the bored wife of a naval captain, until she tired also of him. And of course, there had been plenty of women of the night, who waited outside the Assembly Rooms to accompany lone men to their lodgings.

None of these women, however, had ever had quite the effect on him that the maid, Agnes, had. A thrill had run through him the moment his eyes met hers, leaving him hot with desire, his palms tingling, his heart racing. She was returning now, with the basin of water. She glared again at Bartholomew.

'Sir, you are still here? You may think me bold to suggest it, but I think you ought to leave, afore the snow becomes too deep for cabs. I can ask the footman to fetch you a brandy if you need fortification before venturing out.'

He felt his blood thrill again at the forthrightness of the woman. A lady's maid, who thought nothing of speaking to guests in her employer's house, as though they were her wayward sons.

'A brandy would be excellent, yes.' He nodded at her, and she pulled on the bell-cord. A moment later a footman arrived, and Agnes sent him for the brandy. He was back a minute later, closely followed by Charles Holland, who had exchanged his captain's jacket for a woollen dressing gown.

'Is that my niece back home at last? What do you think you are doing, keeping my staff up and waiting for you on such a night?' He stopped in his tracks when he noticed Bartholomew.

'Ah, I see. Sir, I thank you for bringing her home. Please, call on her again tomorrow morning. You will be most welcome.' He nodded curtly and left.

Georgia smiled up at him. 'You will come back tomorrow, won't you? As my uncle said, you will be made most welcome.'

Bartholomew started. He'd almost forgotten about Georgia. The maid, Agnes, had filled his mind completely. But maids don't have money, he reminded himself. And it was money he needed most. He dragged his gaze away from Agnes and returned Georgia's smile.

'Miss Georgia, you are forgetting yourself,' scolded Agnes. 'Come, dry your feet. I will help you upstairs. Sir, please ring the bell should you require anything more.'

Bartholomew gulped back the brandy brought by the footman, relishing the fiery warmth it brought to his belly. He watched as the two women crossed the black-and-white tiled hallway and made their way up the stairs. Each of them gave him one backwards glance – Miss Holland's smile was cheeky and inviting; the maid's glare was challenging, but with a half-smile and a raised eyebrow as though she had guessed the effect she'd had on him.

Without a doubt he would return tomorrow. And the day after, and the day after that. He left his empty glass on a side table and let himself out of the house. Thankfully the cab was still there, though the cabman grumbled about how long he'd had to wait in the dreadful weather. Bartholomew gave the address of his lodgings in Kemptown and sat back, huddled in his cloak, planning his ideal future which involved both of the women he'd met that night.

Chapter Three

Hampshire, November 2012

I followed Vera Delamere through a tired 1970s kitchen into a large wood-panelled hallway, and then through to a cosy sitting room. She flicked on the lights, and crouched at the fireplace which was already laid with a mixture of logs and coal. As she struck a match, Harold shuffled in and sat down beside the fire, leaning his stick against the side of the mantelpiece.

'Good-oh, we could do with a bit of warmth in here,' he said, and she turned to smile fondly at him. They'd obviously been together for a very long time. I hoped Simon and I would be like them, one day. If we managed to resolve our differences and stay together long enough.

I looked around the room. A large built-in shelving unit occupied one wall. It was made of dark wood, and was clearly very old. It was beautiful.

'That was here when we moved in,' Mrs Delamere said, nodding at the shelves. 'Riddled with woodworm, unfortunately, though we have had it treated.'

'It's gorgeous. I wonder if it was here when my ancestors lived here?'

'I'll go and make the tea,' said Vera. 'Sit down, Katie, do. By the fire, there. It'll get going in a moment.'

I sat opposite Harold in a well-worn fireside chair. 'This is a lovely cosy room.'

Harold nodded. 'We think this was originally a study. There's a much bigger sitting room across the hall, but it's too hard to heat it. When there's only Vera and me, this room's just right for us. So, you're a St Clair, are you? I thought old Barty hadn't had any children. Certainly no one to leave the house to.'

'You're right, he didn't. I'm descended from his younger brother, William.'

'Ah, that would explain it,' said Harold, nodding with satisfaction.

Vera bustled in with the tea tray. She gave it to Harold to balance on his lap for a moment as she tugged at a shelf in the old unit. It folded out, creating a desk, and she put the tea tray on it.

We chatted comfortably about the history of the house and my research while we drank the tea, then Vera offered me a tour of the house.

Harold had fallen asleep in his chair, his head nodding forward onto his chest. Vera gently took his tea cup out of his hand and put it on a side table. I followed her back into the huge hallway. 'Are you sure you don't mind showing me around? I must admit I'm dying to see the house.'

'Oh, it's quite all right. Lovely to have a visitor, if truth be told. Well, here's the living room. Drawing room, I suppose I should call it.'

She ushered me into a large, cold room, with a window to the front of the house. It had a grand fireplace which looked original, brown floral seventies carpet and cream woodchip wallpaper. Family photographs showing a younger Vera and Harold with two cheeky-looking boys jostled for position on the mantelpiece, and heavy crushed-velvet curtains hung at the window.

'We don't come in here much, except in the summer when it's the coolest room in the house,' Vera said.

She led the way back through the hallway and into the dining room I'd peered into from outside. I crossed to the window and looked out. The garden was surprisingly small for such a large old house, and I commented on this.

'It would have had much more land originally,' Vera explained. 'Most of it was sold off before we moved in. There would have been stables and other outbuildings – we think those stood where Stables Close is now. But what's left is a lovely garden. It catches the evening sun. And we're very fond of that tree.' She pointed to a huge beech which stood against a crumbling garden wall.

'I bet your children enjoyed climbing that,' I said.

'Oh, they did, they did! Tim would be sitting up there where the main trunk forks, and Mike would push past him and go up higher. I couldn't watch, but Harold always thought it was better for boys to climb trees than artificial climbing frames in sterile playgrounds.'

I laughed. 'My dad always says the same thing. My sister and I were both tomboys and spent half our childhoods up trees.'

'Good for you! I think it's essential for children to play outside. Shall we continue with the tour?'

She took me down a dark corridor to the kitchen with its walk-in pantry and a rather damp utility room which might once have been called a scullery. Then upstairs, where four large bedrooms and a bathroom occupied the first floor, and another two smaller attic bedrooms filled the second floor. I loved every inch of it. I suspected none of it had seen a lick of paint or a roll of new wallpaper since the sixties or seventies but the house oozed charm and character. I tried to imagine my ancestors here: Barty and his brother William, my great-great-grandfather, running up and down the stairs as boys; their father Bartholomew writing letters in the study downstairs; their mother serenely embroidering a sampler by the fireside in the drawing room. There would have been servants here too, living in those attic bedrooms.

We finished the tour and went back downstairs. Harold was still dozing beside the fire in the old study. 'Thank you so much, Mrs Delamere,' I said. 'I have really enjoyed imagining my ancestors living here. It's a wonderful house.'

'It is, yes.' She shook her head. 'Sadly it's too much for Harold and me nowadays. We shall soon have to think about moving out and into somewhere smaller. But I hate the thought of developers carving it up into flats, and I'm certain that's what would happen. We've been approached by a couple of developers already.'

'Mmm, yes, I can see you'd want it to stay as it is.'

'Oh, I wouldn't mind the idea of it being done up inside. Lord knows it needs it – tastes have changed and I know it's very dated. But I'd want to think of it remaining as a single family home. Ah, well.' She caught hold of my hands and leaned in to kiss my cheek. 'Katie, it's been so lovely to meet you. I hope you'll come again – I'd love to hear more about how you researched your ancestors, and how you knew they lived here.'

'Well, it was all via the census records,' I said, as I slipped on my coat. 'They're available on the Internet now, which makes it all pretty easy.'

Vera smiled. 'I'm afraid we don't even own a computer.'

As I left the house I sensed someone's eyes on me, and turned to look back. Vera was standing at the study window, watching me go with a wistful expression on her thin face. I waved, and she smiled and waved back. I crossed the street and took a few photos of the house for my records, then headed back home to Southampton. As I drove back down the motorway I wondered what kind of mood Simon would be in. Hopefully he'd have got over himself by now. I was buzzing with excitement about having seen inside my ancestors' home and wanted to be able to share it with him.

* * *

241

Simon was in the kitchen, stirring a pot of bolognese sauce for the kids' tea. I put my arms around him from behind, stretched up and kissed the back of his neck.

'Mind out! You nearly made me knock the pan over.' He shrugged himself out of my hug.

'Sorry. I'll take over if you like.' I gave the pot a stir then waltzed off around the kitchen. Our four-year-old, Thomas, came in pushing a small yellow digger along the floor and making engine noises. He giggled when he saw me dancing. I scooped him up and danced with him.

'Hey, not while I'm cooking!' said Simon, brandishing his wooden spoon. 'There's no space in here for mucking about. I take it from your happy dance that you found what you were looking for?'

'Yes, I found the house!'

'What house was this?'

'Oh, Simon, I told you this morning!' I put Thomas down. He retrieved his digger and resumed excavations in the hallway. 'It was the house where the St Clairs lived, for over a hundred years. My great-great-grandfather William St Clair would have been born there, and his father Bartholomew before him.'

'Ah, yes. You've been rummaging around in the pointless past again while I look after the future, a.k.a. our children. So you got a photo of this house?'

'More than that – I went inside! The owners are a lovely elderly couple called Harold and Vera Delamere and they remember how the older folk in the village told them stories of Barty St Clair when they moved in. Apparently he was a bit strange. Very sociable but wouldn't let anyone in the house. Maybe he was hiding something – ooh, maybe there're some skeletons in my ancestors' closets!'

'Good stuff. I don't get this obsession with your ancestors, but whatever floats your boat, I suppose.' He grinned, and patted my shoulder. His way of apologising for the morning's row. I smiled back, accepting the apology.

'Kids! Dinner's ready!' Simon called. He plonked three plates of spag bol on the table, then left the kitchen. Looked like supervising the kids' dinner time was going to be my job, then. Fair enough. I'd had my time off. I helped Thomas climb up onto a chair, and ruffled Lewis and Lauren's hair as they sat at the table.

'Hey, mind the gel!' Lewis ducked away from my hand. Only ten but already spending hours in front of the mirror before school each day.

'What do you want to put gel in your hair for, you're not a girl.' His twin sister Lauren flicked his ear. 'With those spikes you'll puncture the ball when you next play rugby with Dad.'

'You don't head the ball in rugby, *derrr*,' retorted Lewis. 'Don't you know *anything*?'

'More than you, stupid.' Lauren swished her blonde mane over her shoulder and stuck out a bolognese-encrusted tongue in his direction.

'That's enough, you two,' I said. 'Eat up and if you can't speak nicely to each other don't speak at all.'

They glared across the table at each other but otherwise got on with it. Little Thomas, as usual, was keeping his head down and out of trouble. He caught my eye and flashed me a winning smile. Apart from the strand of spaghetti that was slithering down his chin it was one of those expressions you just wish you'd caught on camera.

I made myself a cup of tea while the children finished their dinners. Once they were finished and the kitchen was clean, I sat down at the table sipping my cup of tea, and drifted off into a pleasant fantasy in which the Delameres sold up and somehow Simon and I could afford to buy the house, move in and discover all its secrets.

Dear Reader,

We hope you enjoyed reading this book. If you did, we'd be so appreciative if you left a review. It really helps us and the author to bring more books like this to you.

Here at HQ Digital we are dedicated to publishing fiction that will keep you turning the pages into the early hours. Don't want to miss a thing? To find out more about our books, promotions, discover exclusive content and enter competitions you can keep in touch in the following ways:

JOIN OUR COMMUNITY:

Sign up to our new email newsletter: hyperurl.co/hqnewsletter

Read our new blog www.hqstories.co.uk

🐦 : https://twitter.com/HQDigitalUK

📘 : www.facebook.com/HQStories

BUDDING WRITER?

We're also looking for authors to join the HQ Digital family!
Please submit your manuscript to:

HQDigital@harpercollins.co.uk

Thanks for reading, from the HQ Digital team

If you enjoyed *The Pearl Locket*, then why not try another gripping historical novel from HQ Digital?

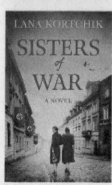